ELEMENTAL POWER

Also by Rachel Morgan

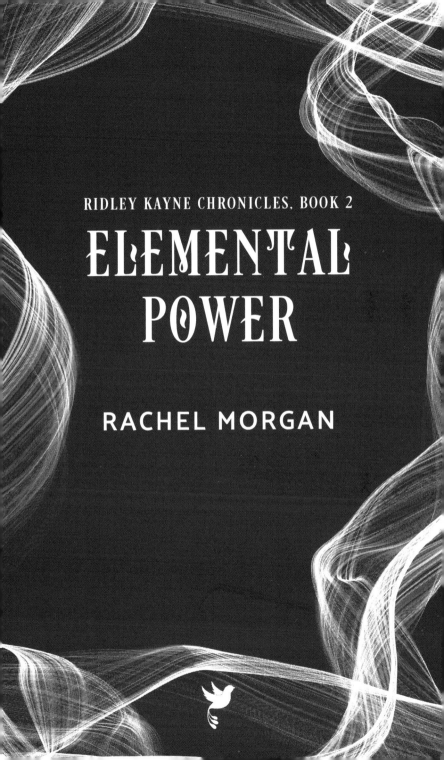

RIDLEY KAYNE CHRONICLES, BOOK 2

ELEMENTAL POWER

RACHEL MORGAN

PROLOGUE

ELEVEN AND A HALF YEARS AGO

LUMINA CITY GLITTERED with the bright morning light of spring, but the interior of Kayne's Antiques was as creaky, dark and mysterious as always. Filled with towering piles of fascinating objects and the smell of very old things, it always felt to Ridley like stepping into another world.

Ridley's grandfather was at the counter near the back of the store, finishing up with a customer, while Ridley and her best friend Lilah peered at a rusty typewriter sitting on the store's front table. They both knew the rule: no touching. But for curious six-year-olds, this was an immense challenge. Lilah's hand reached toward the typewriter, and Ridley stifled a gasp as her finger aimed for one of the faded typewriter keys.

"Delilah Davenport," her mother scolded. Lilah jumped, snatched her hand back, and looked over her shoulder at her mother. "Hands behind your back please," Mrs. Davenport said.

"Sorry, Mom." Lilah tucked the offending hand out of

sight, her eyes wide as she grinned at Ridley.

"You too, Riddles," Ridley's father added, and she realized her hands had somehow moved to her sides. She couldn't remember how that had happened, but she quickly clasped them together at the small of her back as she giggled at Lilah.

"All I'm saying," Mrs. Davenport continued, speaking to Ridley's father in a low voice, "is that maybe you could convince him to move in with you and Claudia and Ridley. You have plenty of space, don't you? And this place ..." Ridley followed Mrs. Davenport's gaze as it rose toward the ceiling and the cobwebs gathered in the corners. "I can't believe anyone would live up there. It must be so cramped, and the stairs are only going to become more difficult for him as he gets older. You mentioned he hasn't been well recently. I'm sure you'd all be happier if he was living with you in Aura Tower."

Dad laughed as he finally finished unlocking the cabinet he and Mrs. Davenport were standing in front of. "My father wouldn't be happy in Aura Tower, I can assure you that. He likes it here. It's been his home for ... well, at least half my life."

"Don't you worry about Ridley's safety though?" Mrs. Davenport pressed. "When you bring her here to visit, I mean. It isn't exactly the safest neighborhood."

It isn't? Ridley thought. She'd noticed, of course, that this area wasn't pretty like the part of the city she lived in, but she didn't know it was *dangerous* here.

"It isn't the worst either," Dad said, and Ridley relaxed. She was certain her father knew more about these sorts of things than Mrs. Davenport. "Anyway," Dad continued, "since you didn't see anything in my workshop that appealed to you, here's the piece I thought you might like." He removed a cushion from the cabinet and lifted a tiara. Ridley stared in wonder as he held it up for Mrs. Davenport to see. "The central stone is an emerald, and these other smaller stones—" he pointed along the sides "—are where I can add the magic effects you asked about."

"I see. So they'll appear to twinkle?"

"They won't just appear so; they *will* twinkle," Dad told her. "And the other option ..." He returned the tiara to the cabinet and reached for something else as Ridley realized that Lilah had wandered toward the back of the store where Grandpa was tidying his oversized desk.

"Mr. Kayne, can I write with the feather pen again?" she asked. Ridley, not wanting to miss out, hurried after her.

"Yes, come on over here," Grandpa answered with a smile. "It's called a quill, remember?"

"Lilah, please don't get ink on your dress," Mrs. Davenport called across the store.

"I won't, Mom," Lilah said as Grandpa helped her up onto his desk chair. He nudged magic toward a bottle of ink that stood on the corner of the desk beside several mugs of pens. After curling his fingers in the air, the bottle slid forward.

"Can I go next?" Ridley asked, wrapping one arm around Grandpa's waist.

"You most certainly can." Grandpa paused to give Ridley a quick sideways hug and a kiss on top of her head, then placed a blank piece of paper in front of Lilah. Next, he handed her the quill and opened the ink bottle. As she dipped the quill nib into the ink, Ridley's eyes traveled over the contents of the desk, coming to rest on a closed cardboard folder. Several pages stuck out the bottom, just far enough for Ridley to see a few lines of foreign, handwritten words.

"What's this?" she asked, carefully touching one corner.

"Oh, just copies of something very, very old." Grandpa picked up the folder and slipped it into a drawer. "Myths and legends from different parts of the world that I'm attempting to translate."

"Like fairy tales?"

"Yes, a little bit like that." His eyes—a light, bright gray behind his glasses—smiled at her. "Stories so old that most people don't even know they ever existed."

"Wow." Ridley ran her finger along the edge of the desk. "That sounds really old."

"Why isn't this working?" Lilah complained. "It's not writing nicely."

"Here, just change the angle a bit," Grandpa said, gently adjusting Lilah's grip on the quill.

Ridley bobbed up and down, eager for her turn with the special pen. Her attention landed on a yellow notepad that had been hiding beneath the folder Grandpa removed. She reached out and pulled it closer, trying to read his handwriting and understanding only a few of the words. "El ... em ..." She stood on tiptoe and leaned over the notepad as she tried to spell out one of the longer words. "What's that last part?"

she asked, pointing to the second half of the word 'elementals.'

"Oh, nothing exciting," Grandpa said, swiftly lifting the notepad from the desk and dropping it into another drawer, which he closed firmly before leaning against it and tousling Ridley's hair.

"Grand-pa," she moaned. "Let me try again."

"Okay, let's try a different word," Grandpa said, reaching for a blank notepad and quickly pulling a wisp of magic from the air. He flicked it toward one of the mugs, where it wrapped around a pen.

"Actually, Dad, we need to get going," Ridley's father said as the pen reached Grandpa's hand.

"Yeah, I can't get this quill thing to work anyway," Lilah said, placing the quill flat on the page and climbing out of Grandpa's chair. "We don't have to fetch Archer now, do we?" she asked her mother.

"We do. He should be ready now."

"Ugh, it's so much better when he's not around," Lilah moaned.

"I know," Ridley agreed. Then she hugged her grandfather quickly and said, "Bye, Grandpa. See you soon."

"Lilah, please don't say things like that about your brother," Mrs. Davenport told Lilah as she and Ridley reached the front of the store. "One day you'll miss him when the two of you are apart."

"Whatever," Lilah muttered with a dramatic roll of her dark eyes.

"Thank you so much for your time, Mr. Kayne," Mrs. Davenport said to Grandpa. "Maverick will let you know which of the pieces I've decided on." She gave Grandpa a brief wave before ushering Lilah out of the door.

"Thanks again, Dad," Ridley's father said. "See you on the weekend for dinner?"

"See you then," Grandpa said with a smile.

Outside, Ridley ran up to Lilah and linked arms with her. She couldn't wait to get back to Aura Tower for Erin Lopez's birthday party that afternoon. There would be games and cake and presents, and she would finally get to wear the new shoes Dad had conjured for her. Every time she tapped her heels together, the rainbow painted over the front of each shoe would detach itself, spin around her ankle, and then reattach itself to the shoe. Even Lilah didn't have shoes like that, and Lilah had pretty much everything.

"Who's that?" Lilah asked as the driver of the Davenports' car opened the rear door for them. Ridley looked to where Lilah was pointing. Across the street, a boy with straight black hair and a wide smile, similar in age to Ridley and Lilah, waved madly.

"Hi, Shen," Ridley called, waving back.

Lilah crossed her arms and pouted. "Is he your friend?"

"Um, not really. I just know him. Sometimes he's in the store when we go to visit Grandpa. He lives across the road."

"Oh." Lilah's expression relaxed into a smile. "Good."

They all climbed into the spacious vehicle, and Mrs. Davenport told the driver to take them back to the Opal Quarter.

As they sped away, the details of that morning's visit—including the mysterious word written on Grandpa's notepad—vanished from Ridley's memory.

CHAPTER 1

RIDLEY KAYNE STOOD IN the living room of the cramped apartment that should have felt like home, but now seemed a bizarre mix of familiar and foreign. It wasn't the piece of plastic concealing the jagged hole in the window, or the wooden crate that had replaced the broken coffee table, or even the dark, wet patch on the floor where Ridley and her father had wiped away blood less than an hour ago. It was the secrets Ridley now knew lurked in every shadowed corner of this apartment.

It was also the person sitting on the couch across the room.

"Grandpa?" she whispered, her eyes trained on the elderly man. Goosebumps crawled across her arms and up the back of her neck. The letter with the tree drawing on it—the letter that had finally told Ridley exactly what she was—slipped from her fingers. The man on the couch seemed thinner than she remembered, and his hair was completely gray. But it was, without a doubt, Jonas Kayne.

With some difficulty, he pushed himself to his feet. "Ridley. Little Riddles. You're so grown-up."

She shook her head and reached back to grip the doorframe. Her knees decided she might handle this situation better on the floor, so they slowly gave in. "This isn't real," she said, her own voice reaching her ears as if from a great distance as she knelt in the doorway.

"Ridley," her father said, rising hastily from the armchair. "I know this must be a huge shock for you, but—"

"What the hell is going on?" she demanded in a hoarse whisper. "First *that*—" she gestured shakily to the letter on the floor "—and then ... *this*?" She looked up and met Grandpa's eyes. "I went to your funeral. I know I was little, but I definitely remember a funeral. You *died*!"

"Ridley." Dad moved closer and reached for her arm.

"No, don't touch me." She shrank away from his touch. "You've been lying to me about *everything*. It was bad enough when I thought it was just all the stuff in that letter, but you lied about Grandpa as well?" She managed to climb to her feet, tucking her blond hair—still damp from her recent shower—behind her ear. "*What is going on?* Did I accidentally step into an alternate reality tonight? One of my best friends is a murderer, I'm some weird version of human called an elemental, and my grandfather isn't dead?"

Dad and Grandpa exchanged a glance, and for several moments, the only sound in the apartment was the music playing quietly in the background. Ridley grabbed the remote from the makeshift crate-coffee table, pointed it at the vintage sound system, and turned it off. Then she tossed the remote back onto the crate. "Explain."

"Why don't you sit?" Dad suggested.

"I don't want to sit. I want answers."

"No hug for your grandfather?" Grandpa asked, giving her a sheepish smile. His gray eyes twinkled behind his glasses. "I know you're upset and confused, but it's so good to see you, Ridley. I've missed you all these years."

Ridley folded her arms over her pajama top and didn't move an inch toward Grandpa. "Are you like me?" she asked. "Are you also an elemental? And don't you dare lie."

Grandpa shook his head. "I'm not an elemental. No one else in our family is." He lowered himself to the couch. "You may not want to sit, but I'm an old man. I can't stand for long these days."

"It wasn't all a lie," Dad said, his piercing blue eyes staring into Ridley's. Like her, he remained standing. "Grandpa did get sick. He was in the hospital for a legitimate reason. But ..." Dad looked at Grandpa. "He didn't actually die."

"Yeah, no kidding," Ridley muttered. "Why the hell would you *pretend* to be dead?"

"Because there are things I know," Grandpa said. "Certain conjurations. Old, dangerous ones that most historians believe were forgotten centuries ago."

Ridley blinked and shook her head. "Conjurations? This is about conjurations? What conjurations?"

"We don't need to go into that. The point is, the wrong people found out. They wanted me to pass on my knowledge.

I refused. They began to threaten my family. The stress of it all is what landed me in hospital. And while I was there ..." He let out a long sigh. "I decided it would be better if I never left. Not officially, anyway. Your parents ..." Grandpa's eyes moved to Dad, but Dad refused to look at him now. "Well, after many arguments, they agreed to help me. We didn't exactly part on good terms though. We haven't been in contact much since I left the city and went into hiding. Especially after the Cataclysm. Staying in touch became even harder then."

"So ... then ..." Ridley shook her head, still trying to accept the fact that this wasn't a dream. "Why are you back now?"

"I became aware late last night of a threat to all the elementals living in Lumina City. Naturally, I was concerned for your safety. I contacted your father, and he told me not to worry. That he would try to find out what was going on. But I'd already decided to come. I left early this morning and traveled the entire day. Only got here about twenty minutes ago." He looked at Dad. "First time I've seen my son in more than a decade, and the first thing he said was that I shouldn't have come. That he'd already taken care of the problem."

"Can we please not do this now?" Dad said to Grandpa in clipped tones. "Ridley doesn't need to witness the dysfunctional side of our family."

"I really don't care how dysfunctional this family is," Ridley said, "as long as no one's lying to me anymore."

"On that note," Grandpa said. "Your father—"

"Don't," Dad interrupted.

"Don't what?" Ridley asked.

"Don't get involved," Dad said to Grandpa. "*I* will explain things to Ridley."

"Really? You haven't exactly done much—" Ridley stopped at the sound of a creak on the stairs leading up to their apartment from the store below. Her head whipped toward the doorway at the top of the stairs. Grandpa pushed himself to his feet again. "Are you expecting someone?" he whispered.

"Calm down," Dad told him. "It's probably just—"

"Mrs. Lin?" Ridley said as the petite woman from across the street appeared at the top of the stairs. Ridley had known her for years, but all of a sudden it felt as if she were looking at a stranger. This wasn't just Shen's mother. She was the woman who knew as many secrets as Shen did. She knew what Ridley was. And just like Dad and Shen, Mrs. Lin had never said a word to Ridley.

"I only saw the message a few minutes ago," Mrs. Lin said, a smile deepening the wrinkles around her eyes as she looked at Grandpa. "It's so good to see you again, Jonas," she added as she crossed the room. She wrapped her arms around Grandpa, and he returned the embrace.

"You too, Mei. It's been far too long."

Ridley's mouth fell open. Then she shook her head. "Why am I surprised that you know about this secret?" she said, throwing her hands up. "Of course you know my grandfather isn't dead. Just like you know about every other secret Dad's been keeping for years."

"Ridley, I didn't see you over ..." Mrs. Lin trailed off as a frown wrinkled her brow. "Other secrets?"

"Don't pretend you don't know what I'm talking about," Ridley said. "I only found out minutes ago, but Shen already knew. He wasn't surprised at all when he saw me using my own magic earlier tonight. He told me his family knows too." Shen had said his family understood what was at stake. That they'd looked out for Ridley just as he had. His words made no sense at the time, but he hadn't stopped to explain any further before shooting the mayor's son, jumping off the side of a building, and making a dramatic escape on a scanner drone. But Ridley now understood what he meant. "I'm an *elemental*," she said slowly and clearly to Mrs. Lin. "You want to tell me you don't know about that?"

"Ah," Mrs. Lin said, her gaze falling on Dad. "Those secrets. I wasn't aware those were out in the open now."

"She received a letter," Dad said, pointing to where the folded page lay on the floor.

"I see." Mrs. Lin nodded. "Well, perhaps I should make us all some tea?" she suggested.

"No," Ridley answered before Dad or Grandpa could say anything. "No tea." She bent quickly and retrieved the letter. "Your whole family gets to know the truth about what I am, so don't you think it's time I get to know?"

"Not my *whole* family," Mrs. Lin corrected as she lowered herself to sit beside Grandpa. "The younger two don't know yet. But Bo and I know, and we told Shen soon after the Cataclysm when the two of you became friends. My parents, my grandparents ..." She settled on the couch. "I come from a long line of people who have always known about elementals and have committed themselves to protecting them. We know about the myths that are so old barely anyone remembers them. The myths that were never myths."

"What myths?"

"The old stories that speak of a time when some people were born with magic in their blood. They didn't have to pull it from the elements. They still learned to manipulate it with conjurations, but the elements—in their raw form—would respond to a person's will without the need for any conjuration. According to the stories, these people lived more in harmony with nature. Those who had to work harder to pull magic from the world were jealous of those who had easier access to power, and so they tried to get rid of them. The stories say that none of these people survived, which we know, of course—" she gestured to Ridley "—isn't true. Elementals did survive, and they've been living in hiding for centuries. Barely anyone knows about them. Even those who live in secret beneath our city, practicing magic illegally, have no idea of the existence of elementals."

"But how has it remained a secret?" Ridley asked. "If my parents hadn't told me to keep it to myself, I'm sure I would have told people."

"Those who don't know they should be hiding don't last long, I'm afraid," said Mrs. Lin. "Did your letter mention the Shadow Society?" Ridley nodded as she looked down at the page in her hand, then placed it on the crate. "Well, there you go," Mrs. Lin continued. "That's what happens. The Shadow Society gets rid of them, and any stories floating around become rumors that are forgotten."

Ridley looked at her father. "And how long have you known about all this? A few years? My whole life?"

Dad's eyes rose slowly to meet hers. "Longer than that."

"Why didn't you ever tell me?" she cried. "I can understand you keeping this secret from the rest of the world, but from *me*?"

Dad opened his mouth, but no sound came out.

"We all keep secrets, Ridley," Mrs. Lin said quietly. "Surely you have your own?"

Ridley met the older woman's gaze as the memory of every theft she'd ever committed slammed into her. Of course she'd never told Dad what she spent her free time doing. He wouldn't approve. But sometimes it was the only way to make a difference, and Ridley refused to feel ashamed for what she'd done. "Yes," she said, pulling herself a little straighter even as her cheeks flushed. "I do have secrets. But they're nothing compared to this. They're nothing compared to telling me my grandfather is *dead* when he isn't. Or compared to keeping important information from me about how I'm ... I don't know, a different *species*!"

"I don't think that's technically correct," Mrs. Lin murmured.

"Ridley." Dad looked at her with pleading eyes. "You have to know that I've only ever wanted to protect you. Surely you understand that?"

"Yes, I understand that, Dad. I do. But protection doesn't have to equal lying to me."

"It would have made no difference to the way you lived your life if I'd told you the truth. You still would have had to keep your magic a secret."

"Of course it would have made a difference! I would have grown up knowing I wasn't a complete freak. I would have known I wasn't alone." She swung away from him, her hands clenching into fists at her sides as she swallowed against the emotion tightening her throat. "I can't believe you kept this from me. This is a fundamental part of *who I am*, and you decided I didn't need to know about it."

"Riddles ..."

"No, seriously." Her voice grew higher in pitch and took on a wobbly quality, but she fought the tears back. "Maybe it made sense when I was little, but *now*? Dad, I'll be eighteen soon. I'm not a child anymore." She faced him again. "Were you *ever* planning to tell me the truth?"

Instead of answering, Dad stepped closer and wrapped his arms around Ridley. She stood there, her back rigid, her arms pinned to her sides, pressing her lips tightly together as she refused to cry. "I'm so sorry," Dad said. "I didn't really have a plan. I just wanted to keep you away from all of this for as long as possible. It's dangerous. Extremely dangerous."

"I know," Ridley murmured against his shoulder. "It's life-and-death kind of dangerous. But knowing there are others like me wouldn't have changed that."

"True, but you might have wanted to go looking for them, and I couldn't allow that. It isn't safe to be anywhere near them. That's why we left."

"We left?" Ridley pulled away and looked at Dad. "Left where? Who? The elementals?"

Dad inhaled deeply, exchanged a glance with both Mrs. Lin and Grandpa, then returned his gaze to Ridley. "There are groups of elementals living in hiding all over the world. You and your mother and I lived with some of them. Further north. But our community was discovered. Many were killed, the group scattered, and the three of us were fortunate to get away. But we decided then to keep our distance."

"We—what? We used to live with—" Ridley shut her eyes and pressed her fingers to her temples. How many more secrets did she have to unearth before she could finally get a clear picture of her own past? "How old was I?" she asked, opening her eyes. "Because I don't remember any of that."

Dad shook his head. "You wouldn't. You were less than a year old. We came to Lumina City after that and lived here with Grandpa for a little while."

"And he also knew about the elementals back then?"

"Yes," Grandpa answered. "I've known for a long time. I unearthed enough secrets in the early days of my research—before I was married or had your dad—that I decided to go in search of the truth."

"And the Lins ..." Ridley looked across as Mrs. Lin. "You've also always known."

"Yes," she answered. "We're in contact with some of the elemental communities living out in the wastelands. We pass information to them in secret and keep tabs on any elementals we know of living in our area."

"Like me."

"Yes."

"Okaaaaay." Ridley exhaled, pushing her hands through her hair and turning away from Dad. "This is ... just ... my brain doesn't even know what to do with all this. Grandpa's alive. I'm an elemental. I'm not alone. And there's this ... this *Shadow* Society. Shadow? Really? They couldn't come up with anything better than that?"

"We can't be certain how the name came about," Mrs. Lin said, leaning forward and resting her elbows on her knees, "but we think it's because they were trying to extinguish magic, and magic has always manifested in a glowing form, illuminated by its own light. Light can't exist where there is darkness, hence—"

"Hence the word 'shadow.' Right. It's just ... you know." Ridley threw her hands up. "It's a stupid name. Like some conspiracy theory no one would ever believe. I mean ... there's *actually* something called the Shadow Society that hunts people and kills them? *How is that real?*"

"It's very real," Dad said.

"I know," Ridley answered with a sigh. "I'm not questioning that." She folded her arms again and slumped against the wall. "I'm questioning their lack of creativity in choosing a name for themselves."

"Unfortunately, creativity is something they have plenty of when it comes to concocting ways in which to kill elementals so it looks like an accident."

"Like Serena Adams," Ridley said quietly. Thinking of

the elemental girl her letter had mentioned reminded her of everything Shen had revealed earlier that evening. Her gaze rose slowly from the floor and landed on Mrs. Lin. "Do you know about Shen?" she asked—and there was that infuriating wobble in her voice again. "Do you know about everything he's done?"

Mrs. Lin's eyes slipped away from Ridley's. "I didn't until yesterday. He only told us about it after he was released from jail. Not for one moment did I believe he could have killed a man until he told us himself."

"What?" Grandpa asked. "Shen was responsible after all?" Deep furrows formed across his brow. "That's ... goodness. I wouldn't have believed it either."

"I know." Mrs. Lin shook her head. "He was almost consumed with guilt over killing an elemental."

"Wait," Ridley said. "That man—the guy who died in our alley—was an elemental?"

"Yes. Shen never would have killed him intentionally. He was trying to get rid of a Shadow Society member instead. Archer Davenport."

"Archer Davenport?" Dad repeated. "That can't be right."

"It isn't," Ridley said. "Shen was wrong about Archer. Archer's been trying to keep the elementals' secret since the moment he returned to Lumina City."

Mrs. Lin frowned. "Shen was certain Archer was also part of it. After Serena's death, he started following Lawrence Madson around, trying to get as close as he could, and he saw a video call between Lawrence and Archer that convinced him Archer was also involved."

"Hang on," Dad said. "Lawrence Madson killed Serena Adams? I remember you telling me it wasn't accidental, but you didn't say any more than that."

"Yes. Shen saw Serena's death. From a distance, at least. He saw Lawrence Madson and two other people with her on top of that building. He was too far away to do anything. During the weeks that followed, he got as close to Lawrence as he could. He listened in on conversations. Discovered for sure that he was a member of the Shadow Society. He and Archer are the only ones we know for sure are part of the society. It seems Shen took it upon himself to get rid of them both."

"He must have been pretty determined," Ridley said, "considering the number of attempts he made."

"Number of attempts?" Mrs. Lin frowned. "What else don't I know about?"

"Did you hear about the shooting at Wallace Academy? That was Shen. He was trying to kill Archer. He also blew up a car, but Archer wasn't in it. And tonight, he showed up at Sapphire 84 and tried again. He—" Ridley broke off, finding it difficult to say these particular words about the guy who'd been one of her best friends for years. "He shot Lawrence Madson," she finished quietly.

Mrs. Lin swallowed. "Yes. Your father told me that last part in his message to me earlier tonight. Shen was ... was determined to avenge Serena's death. And while he seemed certain Archer was involved with the Shadow Society as well, I suppose it's possible he was wrong. The elementals we're in contact with outside Lumina City generally inform us who can be trusted within the city, and they haven't mentioned Archer Davenport. But I'm sure there are trusted people we don't know about."

"Right. Exactly," Ridley said, but doubt had begun to grow at the back of her mind. Had Archer somehow been fooling her this entire time? She shook her head and cleared her throat. "Do you know where Shen is now? He escaped from one of the Brex Tower balconies earlier this evening. On a scanner drone he seemed to know would be flying by at the exact moment he jumped."

"No, I have no idea what Shen was planning. We haven't seen or heard from him since about lunch time today. I suspect he's ..." Mrs. Lin sighed. "I think he's left the city. I think he's trying to outrun his guilt. He doesn't know how to live with himself having killed an elemental, one of the people we've spent our lives trying to protect. Bo is busy contacting everyone we know who might have helped him to see if we can find out where he is."

"I might know a few people you can try reaching out to," Grandpa said.

"Oh, yes, we should compare names," Mrs. Lin replied. "If you don't mind coming across to our place for a little bit." She looked at Dad. "I know the two of you have a complicated history, and you probably have a lot of things to talk through. And Ridley will want to spend some time with her grandfather before he leaves, so we'll be quick."

"Wait, when are you leaving?" Ridley asked. "You only

just got back."

"I'll be here tonight and tomorrow night," Grandpa said. "Then I need to get far away from here. Those people who threatened us years ago are all still alive. I can't afford for anyone to find out I didn't actually die."

"But how will anyone find out as long as you stay hidden inside this apartment?"

"It isn't that simple, Ridley. I require assistance to get safely out of the city. I've already made plans with certain people."

"Oh, well if you've made *plans*, then I guess that settles it," Ridley said. "No one ever heard of plans being changed."

Grandpa chuckled as he pushed himself to the edge of the couch and stood. "Sarcasm. I seem to remember your father being full of sarcastic comments when he was your age."

Dad let out a quiet groan and rubbed his hands over his face.

"Well, let's do this quickly," Mrs. Lin said as she stood. "Maverick, I won't keep your father long."

"Not a problem," Dad said with a sigh.

"See you a little later," Grandpa said to Ridley as he crossed the room with Mrs. Lin. "Or tomorrow, if you're asleep when I get back." He looked at his watch. "It's rather late for a school night."

Ridley rolled her eyes. "Yeah, that's my biggest concern right now. Going to bed late on a school night."

Grandpa's eyes twinkled as he smiled at her. "More sarcasm. I love it."

Ridley crossed her arms and glared, which, she realized in

retrospect, Grandpa probably loved even more than the sarcasm. "I'll let you out," Dad muttered, following Mrs. Lin and Grandpa.

As the three of them headed down the stairs, Ridley crossed the room and sank onto the couch in the spot her grandfather had just vacated. "Grandpa is alive," she murmured, staring across the room at nothing in particular. "I'm an elemental. And Grandpa is alive." She pressed her fingers against her temples and squeezed her eyes shut. "I'm an elemental, and Grandpa is alive," she repeated, as if she were trying to rewire her brain, her memories, to incorporate this information that should have been there all along.

"You okay?" Dad asked. Ridley opened her eyes and saw him standing at the top of the stairs.

She shrugged. "I guess."

"But you're still mad at me."

"I ..." She shook her head. "I don't know. Maybe a little. Does it make sense to say that I understand why you didn't tell me any of this, but I still wish that you had?"

"Yes." He walked around the crate and sat beside her. "Do you mind if I read the letter?"

She shook her head, and Dad leaned forward to pick it up. "I had no idea about Shen and Serena," she said, tucking the tangles of her hair that had fallen forward behind her ears. "He must have been devastated after her death, but I don't remember noticing anything different. He never said a word."

Dad lowered the letter and looked at her. "It was a busy time for you at school. You didn't see much of Shen during the weeks following Serena's death. I think he'd managed to pull himself together by the time you were hanging out again."

"Okay. I still feel bad though. I should have been there for him, but I didn't even know what he was going through." Ridley tilted her head back, then jerked it upright again as another thought occurred to her. "Wait, what about Meera?" she asked, referring to her other best friend. "Does she know any of this?"

"No," Dad murmured, his attention still on the letter. "Meera knows nothing."

Ridley nodded. This one thing, at least, made sense. Unless Meera was the world's best actress, there was no way she could possibly be involved in anything secretive and magical. "So ..." She said eventually, when she figured enough time had passed for Dad to have read the letter at least three times. "Apparently we need to leave the city and go into the wastelands."

"Not anymore," Dad said. "This letter was written before we managed to get the flash drive back and destroy it. You're safe, Ridley. We don't have to go anywhere."

Ridley shifted to face her father. "Are you sure? Whoever wrote this said the society will eventually find out who I am."

Dad sighed and rubbed one hand over his thinning hair. "It says the society knows how many elementals are in Lumina City, but I don't see how that puts you in any more danger than you were in before. Whoever wrote this wants you to know that the society won't stop looking, but they've never stopped looking. You just weren't aware of it before."

"But, Dad—"

"Trust me, Ridley. The best way to fly under the radar is to continue with life as normal. You can go back to school tomorrow and—"

"There were other letters, Dad," she interrupted. "Mine wasn't the only one. There are other elementals in Lumina City who need to know the truth."

Dad paused, his eyes searching Ridley's face as he frowned. "There are other letters just like yours?"

"Yes. They were all inside the envelope that man—the one who died in the alley—was carrying."

Dad pressed his lips together, then said, "You don't need to do anything with those letters. Just forget about them. If you're not in danger, then neither are those other elementals. We don't have to get involved with any of them."

Ridley pulled her head back. "Are you kidding? Even if they're not in immediate danger, they still need to know what's in the letters. What if they're like me and they don't even know there are others like them? Don't you think they deserve to know?

"Ridley, this is not our responsibility," Dad said firmly. "We can't go looking for these people. It'll only put you in more danger."

"Dad, I put myself in danger all the time. I've been putting myself in danger for years, and I'm still fine."

"You've been—what?" Dad shook his head. "What are you talking about?"

Ridley sighed. She figured it was time to come clean about all the stealing. She couldn't very well demand that her father keep no more secrets from her while she still kept some of her own. "Sooooo, there's this unofficial extra-curricular activity that I'm quite good at," she said carefully.

Dad folded his arms. "I'm listening."

"You really don't need to freak out about it."

"Ridley, just tell me what you've been doing."

"It's actually a *good* thing, okay?"

"Now I'm getting worried. Can you please just spit it out?"

Ridley bit her lip, trying to decide how best to 'spit out' that she was a thief. But before she could say another word, a loud knock sounded from the door downstairs. Both Ridley and her father looked toward the stairway. "Grandpa?" Ridley whispered. "I didn't think he'd be back so quickly."

"Neither did I," Dad said, pushing himself up from the couch. "And why would he knock? Mei has a key. She'd let him back in."

"You think it's someone else?"

Dad left the letter on the crate and crossed the room. "Wait here."

Ridley stood. Her heart thumped a little faster than usual as she edged toward the doorway and watched Dad descend the stairs. He reached the bottom—the room behind the antique store—and disappeared from sight. She heard him unlock the door. Then a quiet voice reached her ears. A male voice. Not Grandpa, though. Someone younger. He walked forward into Ridley's line of vision and looked up, sending a jolt through her chest.

Archer Davenport.

CHAPTER 2

RIDLEY TURNED AWAY FROM the stairs and inhaled deeply as white-hot anger flashed through her once more. She shut her eyes and tried to beat it down with every step Archer climbed toward the apartment. But he was yet another person who had known exactly what she was and chosen to keep her in the dark, and this knowledge filled her with an odd mixture of embarrassment and hurt that she could only hide with anger.

"Hey," he said as he reached the top of the stairs. *Hey.* As if it were just an average evening. As if he showed up at her home late at night all the time.

Ridley whipped around to face him. "Why are you here?"

He hesitated for only a second before answering. "I came to see you."

"In the middle of the night?"

Archer walked forward, his dark eyes never leaving Ridley's face. He must have been home since they'd parted earlier this evening. The blood was gone from his face, and he'd changed his clothes. "I figured you would have read your letter by now."

Ridley pressed her lips together to hide her intake of breath. Archer wasn't supposed to know the envelope of letters had survived the flames on the Brex Tower balcony. She crossed her arms, tilted her chin upward, and tried to look as superior as one could look while wearing pajamas. "And why do you think that?"

"Because the more I thought about it, the more I realized you would never have let that envelope burn. You wanted answers, and you knew some of them were probably inside that envelope. I figured you must have lied when you said—"

"I lied? *I lied?*" Ridley's arms tightened around her middle as she shouted, "You lied to *me*, Archer!"

"That's why I'm here. I wanted to explain—"

"I asked you if Serena was like me, and you looked me in the eyes and flat-out lied to me."

Archer swallowed. He appeared far less sure of himself than he usually did, but he managed to hold Ridley's gaze as he said, "I told you there's no one else like you. I meant it."

"You know I didn't mean it that way!"

He nodded. "Yes. I know. But I chose to interpret it that way so I wouldn't have to lie to you."

"You didn't *have* to lie to me! You have no idea what it's been like, thinking I've always been alone. That no one else could ever understand what a freak I am. You had the answer—the truth about *who I am*—and you decided not to give it to me. Did you think it was funny? Were you laughing inside about how completely clueless I was?"

"No, of course I wasn't laughing." Archer glanced over his shoulder to where Dad was now leaning in the doorway, watching this unpleasant exchange with concern etched onto his face. "I wanted to tell you," Archer said, turning back to Ridley. "I thought you should know the truth. But—"

"Right, there's always a 'but,' isn't there."

"I made a promise, okay?" Archer said. "I promised not to tell you."

"Oh, wonderful. That's right. You promised this mysterious person who wants to keep me safe," Ridley scoffed. "Someone who probably doesn't even exist. Just a convenient excuse for you to use whenever you don't feel like telling me—"

"It was me," Dad said. He uncrossed his arms and walked forward. "I made him promise."

Ridley's gaze swung toward her father. Her mouth formed a silent 'O' as the rest of her response to Archer died on her tongue. "You?" she asked. Her eyes moved back and forth between the two men in front of her. "Wait, you guys know each other? As in ... more than just the handful of times you met when Lilah and I were friends?"

"He helped me recently," Archer said. "I owed him big time. He made me swear not to get you involved in any of this."

"A promise you weren't very good at keeping," Dad reminded him.

"I tried." Archer turned toward Dad again. "Believe me, I did. And I never once mentioned the elementals. But she wanted answers, and there was nothing you or I could do to keep her from getting them." His eyes met Ridley's. "Which is why you didn't let that envelope burn. You took it while we were all fighting on the balcony, didn't you?"

Ridley ignored Archer's question and focused on her father. "What help?" she asked, barely able to keep her voice from shaking. "What help did you give him?"

"He needed somewhere to hide."

"It was the last time I returned to the city," Archer added. "A few months ago. I had hidden the flash drive, and people were after me. They didn't know exactly who they were chasing, thank goodness, but they knew it was someone with information on the elementals. I needed to hide somewhere. There was an accident near Jasmine Heights, and the roads were all blocked off that way. I couldn't get back down to the bunker. I was running, and I was desperate. I knew by then that your father was someone I could trust, that he knew about the elementals. So I came here."

"Where was I?" Ridley asked.

"You were here," Dad said. "But it was late. I think you were already asleep."

Ridley shook her head and turned away from them. The confusing mix of emotions rising inside her was almost overwhelming. But there was no way in hell she was about to cry in front of Archer, so she blinked back her tears. "So the two of you—and the Lins—get to run around and have secret meetings and pass information back and forth about *me* and other people just like me, all while letting me remain totally, stupidly unaware."

"Riddles, there's nothing stupid about—"

"Of course there is!" She swung back around to face them. "I had no clue any of this was going on. And some of it was happening *inside my own home*. While I was here!" She sucked in a breath and blurted out, "I'm a thief."

Dad hesitated, his mouth half open, before saying, "Excuse me?"

Ridley couldn't say why she picked that exact moment to finally reveal her own secret—perhaps it was because, selfishly, she didn't want to be the only confused person in the room—but if she could have taken the words back, she would have. Explaining her illegal activities while in such a confused and angry state was not ideal. Neither was having Archer present while she did it. "I steal," she said, pushing her shoulders back and trying to sound as calm as possible. "I steal from disgustingly wealthy people like Archer. Then I sell the things I steal. And then I give the money to people who need it."

"I ... you ..." Dad screwed his face up. "You *what*?"

"And I use my magic to help me. I've been doing this for years. Ever since Shen got so sick and almost died because his parents couldn't afford the treatment."

"I ... I don't even know what to say right now."

"Good. You don't need to say anything. It's Archer's turn."

Archer raised his eyebrows. "My turn?"

"Dad explained his secrets before you got here, I've explained mine, so now it's your turn. Are you part of the Shadow Society?"

Archer's mouth dropped open. "Am I—Why would you think that?"

"Shen's mother just told us why Shen was so convinced you were part of the Shadow Society. She said Shen saw a video call between you and Lawrence that convinced him you're one of them."

"Yes, he probably did," Archer said without missing a beat. "If he's been following Lawrence around, then I wouldn't be surprised if he witnessed multiple calls between us. I've been trying to infiltrate the group for months, but they don't exactly trust people who haven't been part of their society for generations."

Ridley narrowed her eyes at him. "When you were talking with Lawrence at his house that night I was hiding there, you mentioned a meeting. You said something about taking that envelope of letters to the next meeting. What was that?"

"The next meeting of the society. I've been trying to get him to invite me, but you can probably tell we're not—we *weren't*—the best of friends, so it hasn't exactly worked out."

Ridley's gaze flicked to her father before moving back to Archer. "How are we supposed to know if this story you're telling is true?"

"Ridley, I—" Archer pushed his hand through his hair. "I don't know what else to say. I've been trying to keep you safe—trying to keep everyone like you safe—for months now. Since before I returned to the city. You've seen what's happened in the past few days. I almost got myself killed trying to get that flash drive back."

"So you could give it to the society?" Ridley asked.

Dad shook his head. "He destroyed it as soon as we got away from Brex Tower, remember?"

"Exactly," Archer said. "Ridley, just think. Why would I have gone to so much trouble to get it back from Lawrence if we were both part of the society and he already had it?"

"Okay, okay." She placed her hands on her hips and looked into his eyes. "So ... you're not one of them? That's the truth?"

Without blinking, he said, "That is the absolute truth."

Ridley pursed her lips, then said, "Okay. Sorry. It's just that you've lied about other things, so it was possible you might have been lying about this too."

"Okay, I get that. But since I'm not, does that mean we're good now?" Archer asked, his eyebrows raised in question.

Ridley sighed and rubbed both hands over her face. Her heightened emotions had kept her going, but as they receded, exhaustion crept in to take their place. "Here's the thing I was trying to explain to my dad," she said as she lowered her hands. "Even if I can understand why you lied, it still hurts that you did. So no. We're not good. Because part of me is still mad at you."

Archer opened his mouth, but it seemed he had no plan for what to say next, because no sound came out.

"While we're on the subject of lying," Dad said. "Can we go back to the part where you've been *stealing from people*?"

Ridley groaned, took a few steps back, and dropped onto the couch. "I knew you wouldn't understand."

"What were you *thinking*?" Dad demanded. "Aside from

how dangerous that is, it's just downright wrong! I thought I raised you better than that."

"You did," Ridley said, "but my best friend was about to die, and that rich woman who was so rude to you didn't need all that cash in her purse. So I chose to do the wrong thing for the right reason. And after I'd done it once, it was easier to do it again. And yes, I know I've been breaking the law, but I'm not sorry I helped people."

"Ridley ... that's ... just ..." Dad lowered himself onto the couch beside her as he struggled to put whatever he was thinking into words. His eyes traveled across her face, confused, as if he didn't understand what he was seeing there.

"What?" she asked. "Are you looking at me and thinking you don't even know me? 'Cause that's kind of how I've been feeling since the moment you showed up at Brex Tower in a masquerade mask and fought off Lawrence's bodyguards. You're shocked by the things I've done, but I'm just as shocked by the things you've done. Dad, you've ... you've *killed* people."

His eyelids slid shut for a moment as he exhaled. "Ridley, that was—"

"Different? Please don't say that was *different*."

He looked at her. "Your life was at stake."

"Well, guess what? Most of the times I've stolen, it's because someone's life was at stake. So don't tell me that your kind of wrong and my kind of wrong are different."

Dad's expression softened slightly. "Okay. You're right. We've both done terrible things that, apparently, neither of us regret. And we've both kept secrets. A lot has been revealed tonight. We'll probably be able to talk about everything more rationally in the morning."

"You mean like how we're going to contact the other elementals and get out of Lumina City?"

"No. We've been over that already."

"We haven't. You told me your opinion and didn't give me a chance to give mine."

"Because I'm still your father, and that means I get the final say."

"Uh, maybe I should go now," Archer said.

"I don't understand," Ridley said to her father, sitting straighter and pushing herself to the edge of the couch. "You keep talking about protecting me. That's what you've spent my whole life doing, right? But now when a real threat shows up, you don't want to do anything about it?"

"Ridley, the threat has been taken care of. We destroyed the flash drive. And any other threat that letter is referring to—" he pointed to the crate "—is the same threat you've been living with your whole life. You just didn't know about it before. Yes, there are people who discovered what you are within the past few days, but none of them are alive now to tell the tale. The society doesn't know any more than they did before. But if we suddenly disappear? *That's* suspicious. They'll catch us before we get too far into the wastelands, or they'll track us from a distance and only make their move once we eventually find the elementals hiding out there. And neither of those paths is an option, okay? You need to go back to school and act as if nothing has changed, and *that* is what will keep you alive."

"Act as if nothing has changed," Ridley repeated. She let out a humorless laugh. "Do you know how hard that's going to be?"

"Yes. I do. Fortunately, I also know that you're entirely capable of mastering difficult things, so this shouldn't be a problem for you."

"Uh, so sorry to interrupt you guys again," Archer said, "but are you aware there's a magic-mutated cat inside your home?"

"What?" Dad said immediately. He looked around, then jerked back against the cushions as the cat in question rubbed itself against his shins. "Where'd that come from?"

"The wastelands, I'm guessing," Ridley said, leaning forward and reaching her hand toward the four-eared cat with eyes that glowed magic blue. Entirely black aside from one white paw, the cat was slim but without the mangy look of a street cat. Perhaps magic kept it looking healthy, Ridley thought. "I've seen it here twice in the past few days," she said. "It doesn't seem to want to leave." The cat sniffed her knuckles, then rubbed its head against her hand.

"Don't get attached," Dad said, but even as the words left his mouth, he extended one hand and ran it along the length of the cat's back. "I mean, you know I don't have anything against pets, but we'll only wind up in trouble for not handing over a magic-mutated animal. We don't need that kind of attention."

"Yeah," Ridley said quietly as the cat purred.

"Where are the other letters?" Dad asked, sitting back.

Ridley pushed herself to her feet and walked to her bedroom. After taking a quick look at the other letters to confirm they were the same as hers, she folded them all and slid them back into the envelope. "They're all in here," she said as she returned to the living room. She held the envelope out toward Dad and noted that the cat had curled up on the cushion next to him.

"Thanks," Dad said as he rose from the couch and took it. "I'll be keeping these. Just in case you find yourself tempted to go looking for these people."

"Oh, darn," Ridley deadpanned. "If only I hadn't memorized all the names already.'

"This isn't a joke, Ridley. I don't want you looking for them. The society might be tracking one or two of them already, and you certainly don't need to get caught up in that. You'll get yourself killed."

Ridley swallowed. "Yeah. Okay."

"Okay? Seriously?" Dad looked like he didn't believe her.

"Yes, seriously. I could have been killed earlier tonight. I don't want that to happen again."

Dad's shoulders lowered as he relaxed. "Good. I'm glad you're finally being sensible about this."

"But maybe you should ask Mrs. Lin if she recognizes those names," Ridley added. "If she or Mr. Lin know who those people are, maybe they can pass on the letters. Unless they think it's too dangerous, of course."

Dad nodded. "I'll talk to her about it."

"Thanks." She looked at Archer and found him watching her with a doubtful expression. "What, you don't believe me?" she asked. "You think I'm still planning to go looking for them?"

"Well—"

"I am actually telling the truth, Archer, whether you want to believe me or not. And anyway, I think it's probably time for you to leave."

"Yes, it is very late," Dad said. Ridley remembered Grandpa's comment about it being a school night, and the realization that her grandfather was alive—*alive!*—jolted through her once more. She almost told Archer before remembering it was still supposed to be a huge secret. Then again, Archer seemed to know so much about her life that she wouldn't be surprised if he knew about Grandpa too. But Dad didn't say a word about him, so Ridley remained quiet.

"Thanks for letting me come by so late, Mr. Kayne," Archer said. "I know it was unexpected. It's just that ..." He looked at Ridley. "Once I figured out you probably knew about everything, I didn't want to wait any longer to explain my side of things. I knew the longer I waited, the angrier you'd be when you did eventually see me again."

She nodded. "Yeah. Probably."

"Try not to be so mad at me?" he suggested with a small smile.

"Uh huh," she said noncommittally as she gestured toward the stairs. "Dad can let you out. I'm sure you two have a few more secrets to whisper about."

Dad let out a weary sigh. "Ridley."

"Sorry. That was a joke. Sort of." She turned toward her bedroom, and when the cat leaped off the couch and followed her, she didn't shoo it away.

CHAPTER 3

THE WALLACE ACADEMY uniform for girls consisted of a blue and gray pleated plaid skirt, matching tie, white shirt, dark gray blazer and socks, and black shoes. Ridley gave herself an unimpressed once-over in the mirror stuck to the inside of her wardrobe door before leaning down to pull her wrinkled socks up to her knees. For a few fleeting moments last night, she'd thought she would never have to put this uniform on again. But Dad was so insistent about continuing with life as normal that missing school was out of the question. And he was probably right. He'd been hiding from the Shadow Society a lot longer than Ridley had. He knew what would keep her safe.

After making a face at herself in the mirror, Ridley swung the wardrobe door shut and grabbed the strap of her school bag. Her white-blond hair was pulled up in a ponytail that was probably on the too-messy side of Wallace Academy hair regulations, but after accidentally ignoring Dad's repeated knocks on her door one too many times this morning, she didn't have time to fix her hair. She didn't even have time for breakfast, she realized as she rushed out of her bedroom while pulling her bag onto her shoulder.

"Take an apple," Dad said, grabbing her arm as she reached the living room and pulling her to a stop.

"Fresh fruit?" she asked, looking at the shiny red apple he pressed into her hand.

"Special treat for the first day of school," he said. "Remember to act normal, and if something does happen to go wrong—"

"Get the hell out of there and contact you ASAP?" Ridley asked.

"Yes. And I know I've always told you not to use magic, but if the society does somehow track you down one day—which I think is highly unlikely, given that you've remained hidden this long and essentially nothing has changed—then you do whatever you have to do to get away from them. Become one of the elements, use magic to fight back, whatever. I don't care, just make sure you get away."

Ridley nodded. "I will."

"But if I honestly thought you were in imminent danger, I would do exactly what that letter says. I'd get you out of the city. So if I'm telling you to go to school instead—"

"It's because you think I'll be fine," Ridley finished. "I know. I understand. Oh, and, uh ..." Her smile slipped as she looked around. "Did Grandpa come back last night?" A small part of her expected Dad to look at her like she was crazy. *Grandpa?* he would ask. *You mean the grandfather who died years ago? Why would he have come back last night?*

But Dad said, "Yes. I gave him the bed in my room. Couldn't let the old man sleep on the couch out here."

Ridley breathed in deeply as the truth sank in yet again: *Grandpa is alive.* She cleared her throat and said, "How selfless of you."

"Yes, well ..." Dad trailed off, and Ridley had a feeling there was a lot he wasn't saying. "Anyway, I think he must still be asleep. You can spend some time with him after school."

"Okay. It's just ..." She hesitated, then shook her head. "I still can't believe he's here."

Dad nodded. "Are you still mad at me?"

"I don't know. Not really." She looked away from him, her eyes landing on the pile of blankets neatly folded on the armchair with the magic-mutated cat curled on top of them. "It just feels so weird. Oh, and what about Shen? Do you know if the Lins have heard from him?"

"No news yet," Dad said.

"And did they recognize any of those elementals? The names on the letters, I mean?"

"No. And Mei reminded me again that they didn't know the man who was carrying the letters. The one Shen accidentally—well, you know." Apparently Dad didn't feel comfortable using the words 'Shen' and 'murdered' in the same sentence either. "Mei said he must have been from one of the elemental communities they don't know about."

"Okay. So that means none of those people will know the truth."

"Ridley, it's not your—"

"I know, I know. I said I wouldn't get involved."

A knock on the door downstairs interrupted her before she could say anything else. "Ridley, come on!" Meera's muffled voice floated up the stairs. "We're gonna be late!"

"Okay, I gotta go." Clutching the apple in one hand, Ridley hurried downstairs. She crossed the antique store's back room, dropping the apple into her school bag and pulling her keys from a side pocket as she went.

"Finally," Meera said as Ridley swung the door open. She pushed her long black hair—far neater than Ridley's—over her shoulder and adjusted her oversized glasses. "I cannot wait for you to get a new commscreen today. I sent you a ton of messages yesterday hoping you'd at least look at your commpad, but I guess you had more important things to do." The hurt in Meera's voice was unmistakable.

Yeah, important things like trying to stay alive, Ridley thought. "Meera, I'm so sorry," she said as she stepped outside and pulled the door shut. "I had to help my dad. I was busy all day, and most of the evening as well, and I didn't even think to look at my commpad." None of those statements were lies, exactly, which Ridley was pleased to note. Perhaps she could navigate her way through this web of vague half-truths and never have to outright lie to her remaining best friend. "I'm really sorry," she added again, wrapping her arms around Meera.

After a brief hug, Meera stepped back and said, "Well, anyway, happy first day of senior year."

"Wow. Yeah. Senior year." Ridley tried to inject some

enthusiasm into her voice. But Grandpa was alive, and Shen and Dad had killed people, and Ridley was one of a top secret group of magical humans. Starting senior year was nowhere near the top of the list of items jostling for the number one spot in her thoughts.

Fortunately, Meera didn't seem to notice. "And look," she said, pointing up. "The sun's actually out today."

Ridley squinted between the buildings at the almost cloud-free sky. On a bright day like today, it was impossible to make out the arxium panels that hovered above the tallest buildings, shielding the city from the wild atmospheric magic. The gaps between the panels provided more than enough space for today's sunlight to beam through. Hopefully no stray magic found its way down along with the light. "Wow, this is what sunlight feels like?" she said. "I'd almost forgotten."

Meera shoved her playfully. "Don't be silly. And come on, we need to run or we're going to miss the bus." They took off together, more speed-walking than running. "Anyway, I'm taking this as a good sign," Meera added. "Our senior year has to be a good one if it starts off with a sunny day, right?"

"I really hope so." Ridley's bag bumped back and forth against her side. "Some might say the year started off with a shooting, but let's go with a sunny day instead. Way more positive."

"Ugh, the shooting. Don't remind me. My parents almost wouldn't let me leave the house today. But that net-mail yesterday from Principal Colson said there's security surrounding the entire school now, so that helped. And my parents firmly agree with him on the whole academics come first thing, so that made it easier for them to let me out."

"That's good." Ridley figured the school shooting probably hadn't even entered her father's mind that morning. It certainly hadn't entered hers.

"But still, they haven't caught the shooter," Meera continued breathlessly as they rounded another corner. "So even though there's increased security, I don't think I'll feel completely safe until we know who did it or why."

"Uh, yeah." Ridley put her hand down to keep her bag from bumping around too much—but mainly because she felt the need to do *something* instead of replying to Meera's comments. She didn't want to accidentally tell Meera that it was their best friend who'd done it.

"Oh, hey, do you know why Shen hasn't been replying to my messages either?" Meera asked, and for a second, Ridley wondered if she'd spoken his name out loud after all. "What do you mean?" she asked, stalling as her mind raced to figure out what to say.

"You guys were both super quiet the whole of yesterday," Meera panted as they ran across a street and around an upturned garbage bin spewing its contents onto the sidewalk. "First *you* bailed on me, then I was supposed to hang out with Shen, but then he canceled too. Have you heard from him?"

"No, sorry." At least that was a question Ridley could answer honestly.

"Oh, right, no commscreen." Meera slowed beside Ridley as they reached the bus stop. "I keep forgetting."

At the intersection further up the street, the bus rumbled around the corner. "Just in time," Ridley said. They joined the queue of people shuffling forward, and soon they were climbing the stairs into the bus. Ridley dropped onto the first available empty seat and slid across to make room for Meera. After sitting, Meera pulled her bag onto her lap and removed her commscreen. She frowned at the slim rectangular device, then gave it a shake. "I think my commscreen's being glitchy too," she told Ridley, tapping at the screen a few times on various apps that didn't seem to want to open. "Maybe it's about to die like yours did. They just don't make these things the way they used to."

"You sound like my dad," Ridley said with a chuckle. "Good thing we're both getting a new one today." As scholarship students at Wallace Academy, the first day of a new school year meant receiving new versions of all the tech items most filthy rich Wallace Academy students took for granted.

"Yeah, thank goodness." Meera lowered the device with a sigh. "I just wonder if maybe Shen's been replying but his messages haven't come through."

"Mmm, yeah, maybe that's it," Ridley said with a small nod. She swallowed and turned her head to face the window as the bus pulled away from the curb. Her gaze moved blindly across the flashing advertisements on the billboard screen across the road as her mind drifted. She didn't want to think about Shen, but she couldn't help wondering what he was doing at this very moment. Had he somehow made it out of the city? Was he traveling through the wastelands now, just as her letter had told her she should do?

"Hey, is everything okay?" Meera asked, nudging Ridley's arm. "You're being weirdly quiet this morning."

"Um, yes." Ridley faced Meera with a smile. "Sorry. I zoned out there for a moment. I'm just tired after getting to bed so late."

"Okay." Meera shifted in the seat until she was fully facing Ridley. "So anyway, I was thinking of … like … maybe …"

Ridley raised an eyebrow. "Maybe what?"

"Maybe, um …" Meera's shoulders rose until they were almost by her ears. A pink tinge appeared in her cheeks. "Telling Shen how I feel about him," she said quickly, a wide and somewhat terrified smile stretching her lips.

"Oh," Ridley said.

Meera's face fell instantly. "Oh? Seriously? I thought you'd tell me to go for it."

"Yes, of course, sorry." Ridley smiled and forced out a laugh. "You just took me by surprise. I thought you'd deliberate over this decision for *weeks*, at least."

"So you think I should do it?"

"I—well—it is quite a big step, you know. Taking your friendship to the next level." Desperate for an excuse to avoid Meera's gaze, Ridley opened the flap of her school bag and rummaged inside until she found the apple. "I mean, what if he doesn't feel the same way?" She rubbed the apple against her skirt. "Do you think things will be really awkward afterwards, or will you guys just go back to normal around each other?"

Meera hesitated. Then, in a voice so quiet Ridley could barely hear her, she asked, "You don't think he feels the same way?"

"Well, I just … I really don't know." *And I hate myself so much for lying right now*, Ridley added silently as she took the largest bite she could manage out of her apple.

"Yeah, maybe I should wait a bit," Meera said, staring past Ridley out of the bus window. "See if I can figure out how he feels."

Ridley nodded as she chewed the apple and made a grand effort at pushing down the emotion rising in her chest. She'd successfully managed to keep the secret of her magic and her stealing from Meera for years, telling herself that those parts of her life had nothing to do with Meera. But this? Lying about the guy who was their closest friend? Ridley didn't know how she was supposed to keep it up. But telling the truth wasn't an option either. Revealing anything about Shen would only lead to more questions.

"Oh my gosh. Oh my *freaking gosh*. Did you see this?" Meera shoved her commscreen in front of Ridley's face. "The mayor's son. He's dead."

A shiver raced through Ridley as the words on Meera's screen blurred and the scene from the night before flashed through her mind. Shen with a gun, swinging it back and forth between Lawrence and Archer, trying to decide who to get rid of first. The crack of the weapon, and then Lawrence sliding to the balcony floor.

" … no leads yet, apparently," Meera was saying as she

scrolled through the news article. "It was on a private balcony at that fancy restaurant in Brex Tower, so no one saw what actually happened."

Ridley cleared her throat. "That's insane."

"People heard a gunshot ... Lawrence's bodyguards ran onto the balcony ... and then ... *what*? Something about a guy in a masquerade mask?" Meera's eyes scanned the article. "But that was only after the gunshot. And he was nowhere to be seen once the waiters managed to get onto the balcony." She looked up. "This is just so freaking weird. What the heck do rich people get themselves involved in?"

"That's a good question," Ridley said. "One we probably don't want to know the answer to."

"Yeah, you're right." Meera tapped her commscreen a few more times before adding, "Wow, okay, finally."

"What?"

"I just got a message from Shen."

Shock jolted through Ridley's body. "You did?"

"Well, via his mom." Meera handed her commscreen to Ridley to show her the message.

Mrs. L: Morning :) Shen asked me to pass on this message: Hey, I'll be out the city for a while. Emergency family situation my parents needed me to deal with. Don't know when I'll be back.

"I wonder why he didn't just message me himself," Meera said as Ridley handed the commscreen back to her.

"Yeah, I wonder," Ridley answered, though she was almost certain she knew the answer: That message wasn't from Shen. Ridley was willing to bet Mrs. Lin had written it, and that she still had no idea where her son was.

"What family does he have outside Lumina City?" Meera asked. "I mean, he has family on another *continent*, right? But that can't be who he's talking about. The Lins can't afford to send Shen on the TransAt."

Ridley shrugged. "He must have some family in another city not too far from here. I think I remember him mentioning a cousin or something." She bit into the apple again before any more lies could escape her lips.

Meera narrowed her eyes and tilted her head to the side. "If you knew something, you'd tell me, right?" Ridley inhaled a piece of apple and started choking. "Jeez, sorry." Meera laughed and smacked Ridley on the back. "I wasn't accusing you of anything. I just mean that you've known him longer than I have, so maybe you're aware of some history or something that he never got around to telling me."

"No—I—I don't," Ridley said between coughs. She straightened, took a deep breath, and wiped her watering eyes. "I don't know anything. Do you, um, want the rest of this?" She held the apple toward Meera.

"After you've spluttered all over it?" Meera rolled her eyes. "No thanks." She groaned and tipped her head back against the seat. "Well, even if we don't know all the details, at least we know Shen's okay. It's the *not knowing* that's worse."

The truth of Meera's statement struck Ridley squarely in

the chest. Not knowing *was* worse. If she had the option of rewinding her life by a day or two and never discovering the things she now knew about herself, she would never choose that path. Ignorance was worse. Having that perpetual question at the back of her mind—*Is there anyone else out there like me?*—was worse. How could she seriously have considered keeping that information from the other elementals living in Lumina City?

She couldn't. She had to find them and tell them the truth. She knew Dad was worried about her safety, but she didn't have to be reckless about this. She could pass on the letters in the same discreet manner in which she'd conducted her thefts for years. Some might even say her stealing had prepared her for this new mission.

Ridley settled back against the seat, the tumultuous ocean of her thoughts calmer now that she had new purpose.

CHAPTER 4

RIDLEY HURRIED HOME after school, her thoughts split between which elemental to track down first and what to say to Grandpa when she walked into the apartment. What if things were totally awkward with him? What if she couldn't remember all the questions she wanted to ask? And when it came to looking up the names of the elementals, what if she found there were multiple people with the same name living in Lumina City? Surely that was possible, even in a post-Cataclysm world with a decimated population.

But all thoughts fled Ridley's mind as she walked into her kitchen and stopped at the sight of Archer sitting at the table. "Um, hi?" She looked around for Grandpa, but he was nowhere in sight. "Well," she said, facing Archer again. "This is creepy, you just sitting here all alone in my apartment. Almost as creepy as that time I found out you have hidden cameras in your bedroom."

Archer stood. "Those are for security."

"Right, like you really need the extra security in your *bedroom*."

"I'm just not sure who I can trust anymore, that's all. If someone in my family starts to think I'm involved with the elementals and goes looking through my stuff, I want to know about it."

Ridley tucked her thumb beneath the strap of her bag. "So you're paranoid enough to hide cameras in your room, but you don't bother securing your computer with a password?"

"Not necessary," he said. "I don't store anything important on that computer. Fortunately for you," he added with a pointed look, which she assumed was meant to be a not-so-subtle reminder of the video she'd posted from his account.

"Okay, whatever." She folded her arms across her chest. "How did you get into my kitchen?"

"Your dad let me in."

Ridley groaned. "Can we go back to a time when my dad didn't like you? Things were less weird then."

"Oh, I'm still not sure he *likes* me," Archer said. "But we happen to agree on a few key issues, so the rest doesn't really matter."

"And these key issues are what, exactly?"

He shrugged. "You know, the important stuff. Magic, the Shadow Society, keeping you safe."

"Wonderful," Ridley muttered.

Archer grinned. "Why don't you tell me what you're planning to get up to this evening?"

"Uh, how about I don't?" She lowered her arms to her sides as she turned away. "My plans have nothing to do with you." She left the kitchen and headed along the passage to her bedroom. Archer followed.

"Okay, why don't I guess then." He leaned against the doorframe. "You're going to go and find those other elementals on your own."

Ridley's heart jumped into her throat, but she refused to let him see he'd guessed the truth. She dumped her bag on the bed and returned her gaze to his smirking face. He was so damn sure of himself, it was infuriating. "You know what I realized last night after you left?" she said. "I was trying to fall asleep and I suddenly remembered everything we spoke about when we were locked underground together. That whole conversation where you pretended to guess things like me not being able to have arxium under my skin. You pretended to *guess*, you pretended to be *surprised*, when you actually knew everything already."

Some of Archer's confidence disappeared. "I know. I'm sorry. But what else was I supposed to—"

"And you let me believe that the information on the flash drive was about Lumina City's underworld of magic users."

"Look, I explained this last night. I had to let you believe that because I couldn't tell you about the elementals. Your dad didn't—"

"Yes, right, okay. You and my dad are all buddy-buddy, and you'll do whatever he says."

After a moment of quiet, Archer said, "It's really not like that."

Ridley sighed. Of course she knew it wasn't like that. She was just being petty because for some reason, it bothered her that Dad and Archer had a shared history she knew nothing about.

"So," he said, that smirk creeping back onto his face. "You were thinking about me in bed last night."

She gave him a withering look. "Yes, and that was the point at which I fell asleep. Because the thought of you is even more boring than counting sheep."

"Admit it," he said. "You're planning a secret mission to go elemental hunting tonight."

She opened her mouth to deny it, but the words died on her tongue. What would be the point in lying? He'd already guessed the truth. "Last night, when I told my dad I wouldn't go looking for them, I was telling the truth. But I've ..." She tugged absently at her tie, flipping the end back and forth. "I've changed my mind. I was thinking of how I'd never choose to go back to not knowing what I am. Knowing the truth is so much better than feeling confused and alone. If I can spare anyone else that lost, confused feeling, then I will."

Archer watched her in silence for a moment, then looked away. Instead of answering, his eyes traveled around the small bedroom. Ridley crossed her arms and tried not to feel self-conscious. It was weird that she knew exactly what every room inside the Davenports' home looked like, but this was the first time Archer had seen inside her bedroom. After the first few months of living here, she'd come to appreciate this tiny space. She'd made it her own with dozens of photos pegged to strings across the wall in front of her desk, twinkle lights wound around the head and foot of her metal bed frame, and every one of her mom's blue scarves draped over the top of her wardrobe. The space was distinctly hers, and she hated the way it suddenly felt not quite good enough because Archer was no doubt comparing it to his palatial home.

"What if other people aren't like you?" he said, looking at her again. "What if they'd prefer not to know?"

"Look, it's none of your business," Ridley said, turning her back to him and opening her bag, "so you don't need to worry about it."

"It's dangerous," Archer said. "You don't know if the society may already be tracking one or more of these people. You don't want to get caught in the way of that kind of thing."

Ridley paused in the process of removing all her new devices from her bag and looked back at him. "You're saying you don't want me trying to save someone the Shadow Society is planning to kill? You realize how hypocritical that sounds, right? You know, after the big fuss you made about us getting the flash drive back so that innocent people didn't have to die?"

"What I'm saying," Archer continued as he pushed away from the doorframe and stepped into the room, "is that you could give me the names, and *I'll* go looking for these people. You can get on with your life, just like your dad wants you to."

"No."

"Ridley—"

"No," she repeated. "Do you think these people are going to trust you? Archer Davenport? The guy whose father was so vocal about banning magic after the Cataclysm?"

He sighed. "Okay fine. Maybe I can't talk you out of doing this, but you can't do it alone. You need my help. You don't know what these elementals look like, so if there are multiple people with the same name, you might end up giving the letter to the wrong person. I, at least, saw the files on the flash drive before we destroyed it, so I'll recognize the faces when we look up these names."

"But …" Ridley lifted her new laptop from the bed and moved it to the desk as she frowned. "Why do you need me to give you the names then? Surely you know them already?"

"Look, my memory's not *that* great, and I didn't spend a long time examining the information. I just scanned through the files specifically for Lumina City because I was interested to see how many elementals are living here. I'm better with faces than names, so that's the part I remember."

"Okay, so how about I give you the names, you look them up and confirm who these people are, and then *I* will go talk to them and hand over the letters."

"Or I could go with you," Archer countered, "and make sure you stay safe while doing this."

"I don't need you to make sure I'm safe." She placed the new commpad in the top drawer of her desk on top of the old one. "I've been sneaking around for years on my own."

"Does your father know you've changed your mind about wanting to find these other elementals?"

"Will you leave if I say yes?"

"Uh—"

"Yes, he knows everything. I've told him my whole plan."

Archer raised an eyebrow. "Ridley Kayne, you're a terrible liar."

She rolled her eyes. "Yeah, well, maybe compared to the *expert* standing in front of me—"

"Ah, here you are," Dad said, peering into the room and smiling at Ridley. "I was just checking to see if Archer waited for you or if he'd left."

"Nope, still here," Archer said, raising his hand in a small wave.

"But he'll be leaving soon," Ridley added quickly. "Because there's that person you wanted me to talk to, right?" She gave her father a meaningful look he would hopefully understand. "That, um, important customer. I thought he was going to be here when I got home. Is he … out somewhere?"

"Oh, right," Dad said. "He had to go deal with something. He'll be back soon. But you can, uh …" He glanced at Archer, then back at Ridley. "Well, it's a family secret. Obviously. But for someone who already knows most of our other family secrets …" Dad shrugged. "You can tell Archer if you want. That's all I'm saying. Aaaaanyway." He rocked forward on the balls of his feet and clapped his hands together. "How was your first day back? Everything … normal?"

"Yes. Totally normal. I lied to my best friend, and apparently so did Mrs. Lin, so Meera doesn't think anything *too* weird is going on with Shen."

Dad's smile faded. "Ridley," he said softly.

"I know, I get it," she said, already wishing she'd kept her flippant comment to herself. "This is the way it has to be.

I understand."

"You do?" Dad's eyebrows rose toward his receding hairline. "So you really are happy to move on with life as normal?"

Ridley's eyes darted immediately to Archer, expecting him to announce that she'd changed her mind about searching for the other elementals. But he gave her a small smile and kept his lips firmly sealed. "Yes," she finally said. "I'm carrying on with life as normal." Which was *sort of* the truth, she tried to convince herself. It wouldn't take long to deliver a few letters, and other than that, her life would be as normal as it had been since the Cataclysm.

"Okay," Dad said. "Great. Anyway, I need to get back to the store. Just in case there's a hoard of rabid customers waiting outside and getting ready to tear down my 'Back in 10 Minutes' sign."

"That's the spirit," Ridley said.

As Dad's footsteps disappeared along the passage, Archer asked, "What was all that about an important customer and family secrets?"

Ridley ignored the question, letting her eyes travel over him for a moment as she tried to figure him out. "Why didn't you tell him what I'm planning?"

Archer lifted one shoulder, then moved closer to the desk and leaned against it. "What would that have accomplished? You'd just go off on your own without telling either of us. I'd rather show you that you can trust me so you'll let me accompany you."

"Does it matter if I don't need your company?"

He tipped his head to the side. "I promise I'm not trying to make your life difficult. It's just ... what if you're on your own and something happens to you? What would that do to your dad? It'll be easier to get out of a sticky situation if there are two of us. You know, like that time you passed out in the mayor's lounge and I had to go ring the doorbell and pretend I was paying a visit so Lawrence wouldn't find you."

Ridley pursed her lips, not wanting to admit that Archer might have a valid point. "That's something else you knew about and didn't tell me. You knew I must have breathed in something with arxium particles in it, and that's what made me pass out."

"Yes." Archer nodded. "I didn't realize Lawrence had it in a handy little spray canister—though I probably should have—but I knew about the air freshener inside his home. Not something that's on the market, obviously, but Lawrence mentioned it to me on a previous visit when I was fishing for information. His father's completely paranoid about elementals breaking into their home and using magic on them. And even though I couldn't tell you about it, I *did* try to warn you that something similar might happen if you went after Lawrence to get your father back."

Ridley frowned and chose not to answer, mainly because Archer was right.

"Look, I know you're still mad at me for keeping things from you," he continued. "It's like you said last night: even though you understand why I couldn't tell you everything, that doesn't automatically stop you from being angry about it. But before you found out I'd kept all this information from you, when you realized Lawrence had taken your father, you came to me for help. Remember? You asked for my help, and I helped you. So ... I guess I'm hoping you'll focus on that and let me help you again."

"Fine," Ridley said. "We can do this together."

Archer paused. "Okay, you made that decision way too quickly. Are you just saying that to keep me happy while planning to go off on your own?"

"Apparently I'm not a good liar, so why don't you tell me?"

His eyes searched hers for several moments. "I don't think you're lying."

"Thank you." She lowered herself to the edge of the bed and sighed. "I guess I see the value in what you're saying. I do need you to verify that I'm handing letters over to the correct people. And it's probably a good idea not to do this alone in case something goes wrong."

"Great." Archer straightened, pushed away from the desk, and held one hand out. "So we're doing this together?"

Reluctantly, she placed her hand in his and gave it a firm shake. "We're doing this together."

"Okay." He lowered his hand and asked, "Did you write the names down, or are they in your head?"

"I wrote them all down during first period." Ridley picked up her new commscreen and tapped a few times. She didn't have much on it yet—she still needed to link all her social accounts, her bank card, bus pass, and anything else she used her commscreen for—but she had used the notes section several times today. She located the note with the elementals' names and handed the device to Archer.

"I thought there were more," he said as he frowned at the five names.

"I guess we elementals really are that rare."

"No, I'm pretty sure I saw more people when I looked through the files on that flash drive. But maybe the others already know what they are. Or maybe they've already left the city. It's been a few months since I looked at that information." Archer removed his own commscreen from his pocket, tapped hers a few times, then added, "Okay, I've sent the note to myself." He returned the device.

"Thanks. I'll make copies of my letter tonight, seeing as Dad confiscated the others."

"Okay. Were the others the same?"

"Yes, I took a quick look at them all before giving the envelope to Dad last night. I know I probably shouldn't have, since they weren't addressed to me, but the way mine was written, typed with a blank line for someone to fill my name in at the top ... I kind of guessed they'd all be the same."

Archer nodded. "Well, I guess I should probably get going then." He pushed his hands into his pockets. "You've probably got homework or something. I assume you need to maintain that straight-A image if you want everyone to believe nothing's changed in your life."

"Right," Ridley said with a nod. "Homework." But so many other thoughts had occupied her mind throughout the day that she honestly couldn't remember whether any teacher had assigned homework for the first day back.

"So, that other thing your father mentioned," Archer said. "The important customer, the family secret ... I know I have no right to ask, given all the secrets I've kept, but ..."

"But you're asking anyway."

"Well, yeah. Can you blame me for being curious?"

She crossed her arms and decided to just say it. "My grandfather is alive."

Archer's expression remained blank. Then he blinked. "What?"

"Yeah. He showed up last night."

"The grandfather who used to own this place?"

"That's the one. He never actually died. People were threatening us because of him—because of certain things he knows—and so he pretended he was dead. Apparently my dad didn't think I needed to know about this gigantic family secret until Grandpa arrived last night. I don't think he ever would have told me if Grandpa hadn't come back."

"That's ... wow." Archer ran one hand through his hair. "He's *alive*? That's crazy."

"Yeah. Anyway, I have one night to get to know him, and then he's disappearing again."

Archer raised both eyebrows. "No pressure."

"None at all."

"I'd better not waste any more of your time then." He turned toward the door. "I'll let you know what I find out about the people on the list." He glanced back at her over his shoulder. "Have a good evening with your grandfather."

"Thanks." He walked out, and Ridley placed her face in her hands. After letting out a quiet groan, she flopped back onto her bed. "Carry on with life as normal," she murmured. "So ... not ... possible."

CHAPTER 5

RIDLEY HAD ALMOST FINISHED preparing dinner when Grandpa returned home that evening. She was still in her school uniform, though she'd removed her socks and shoes at some point. Slow footsteps on the stairs told her it was Grandpa rather than Dad who was ascending, and by the time he'd moved through the living room and reached the kitchen, her insides were once again a churning mix of nerves and annoyance.

"So," she said, turning to face him with a soup ladle in one hand. "You told me you need to leave Lumina City because it's too dangerous for you to stay, even inside this apartment, but apparently it's not too dangerous for you to go out in the bright light of day?"

With an amused curve of his lips, Grandpa said, "It was the bright light of day that convinced me to go out. I didn't want to miss the rare opportunity to spend some time in the sun."

Ridley pointed the ladle at him. "That, I'm pretty sure, is not true."

"It is true, although it's only part of the truth." Grandpa eased himself onto a chair at the kitchen table, then reached down to rub his left knee. "There was someone I needed to see. And I was very careful, don't worry. I even wore a disguise. A hat and a fake mustache. Horrible bushy thing. Quite itchy."

"I have no idea now if you're making this up."

He laughed. "Check the filing cupboards in the back room downstairs. You'll find my dress-up kit hiding there. It probably wasn't even necessary, considering no one's actively looking for me anymore. But it's always good to be careful."

"If no one's actively looking for you, and it's so easy to get around without anyone recognizing you, then why not stay longer?"

Grandpa let out a heavy sigh and moved to rubbing his other knee. "I wish I could, but I can't. I'm sorry, Ridley."

She nodded, saying nothing, then turned back to stir the contents of the pot on the stove. She told herself not to be upset that Grandpa had other things to do that were more important than getting to know his granddaughter. He had a life somewhere else that he needed to get back to. A life that didn't include her.

"It isn't that I don't want to spend time with you," he said. Apparently he could read her body language as clearly as if she'd spoken her thoughts out loud. "I would love to stay longer. But there are things I need to get back to."

She nodded again and placed the ladle on a plate beside the stove. *It's fine*, she told herself. *This is fine. Don't ruin the one evening you have with him.* But it seemed her brain wouldn't listen to her, and as she faced Grandpa again, she asked, "Do you think about us? Do you miss us?"

"Every day," he answered immediately. He rose from the chair. "I wonder every day what life would be like for our family if I'd never had to leave. I think about *you* every day. I wonder about the kind of person you've grown into, your hobbies, your friends, all the things you're good at."

Ridley's legs seemed to move without her permission, and then her arms were around Grandpa, and he was hugging her tightly, and she felt like a little girl again. "I'm so, so sorry I had to leave," he murmured. "You understand why, don't you?"

"I do," she whispered, because speaking any louder would probably make her voice crack beneath the emotion she was trying to hold back. She cleared her throat and stepped out of the embrace. "Is, um, is Dad coming up soon?"

"He closed the store early and left at about the same time I got back. Said he needed to go visit an old friend who might know something about Shen."

Ridley crossed the kitchen to turn the stove off before turning to Grandpa again. "So he's avoiding you."

Grandpa's gaze slid away from Ridley, but he said nothing as he sat.

"He hasn't seen you in, what, almost twelve years?" Ridley continued as she leaned against the counter. "And he decides he has to go and see this friend of his *tonight* instead of some other night?"

"Yes, well." Grandpa sighed. "It's complicated."

"I had no idea you and Dad had such a dysfunctional relationship."

"We didn't. Things were mostly fine until the whole ..." He waved his hands as if trying to come up with the right words.

"The whole faking-your-death-and-disappearing thing?" Ridley supplied.

"Yes. That. We disagreed. And once we started arguing about *that*, all the other issues began to resurface. Things we probably should have spoken about years before."

"Things?"

"Oh, you know. Just family stuff. People are people. We make mistakes, hurt each other, hold on to grudges, don't communicate properly. All these things fester over time if you don't deal with them. You think nothing's wrong until one thing upsets the balance, and then everything implodes."

"Wow. You make it sound like some dramatic soap opera."

Grandpa chuckled. "It's really not that bad. Just people being people."

"Okay. If you say so. But I still think Dad should be here tonight."

"So do I, but it's his choice." Grandpa leaned his elbows on the table. "Are you still angry with him because of all the secrets?"

Ridley let out a long breath and reached back to twist the end of her ponytail around her finger. "Only a little. I under-stand why he kept everything from me, so that helps. I still wish he *hadn't*, but we can't go back and change that, so ..." She trailed off, shrugging and lowering her hand.

"That's good," Grandpa said. "Life is far too short to hold on to anger."

"See?" Ridley said. "Dad should be here. You should be telling *him* that, not me, because clearly he's still mad at you."

"Yes. We have spoken about this, but, as I said, it's complicated. Anyway." He nodded to the pot on the stove and asked, "What are you making?"

"Oh, uh ..." Ridley glanced at the mushy contents of the pot. "A *super* spectacular gastronomic creation." When Grandpa did nothing but peer at Ridley over the top of his glasses, she sighed. "It's just three-bean and barley soup. Nothing fancy."

Grandpa nodded, a sad smile finding its way onto his lips. "A world away from the types of meals your parents used to enjoy making in their state-of-the-art kitchen in Aura Tower."

"I know, but you can't get half the food Mom and Dad used to cook before the Cataclysm. We all survive on whatever's available now. Well, unless you have buttloads of money to spend on rare ingredients." Her mind flashed briefly to the fancy restaurants in the Opal Quarter where people like the Davenports were frequent patrons. "Uh, are you ready to eat now?"

"Yes, definitely. I had to walk a lot further than I'd anticipated today. Somehow this city seems bigger than I remember."

"Probably just your old-man legs," Ridley teased as she reached into a cupboard below the counter for two bowls.

"Probably." Grandpa chuckled. He pushed his chair back and stood again. "Can I get you a drink? I think the glasses are—yes, right where they've always been," he said as he opened a cupboard above the sink.

"Yes, thanks, I'll just have water," Ridley said. She ladled soup into the two bowls and carried them to the table. "I wanted to ask you something last night," she said as she sat. "Who was it that came after you because of the conjurations you know? Not the Shadow Society, right? Because if so, then the rest of our family would have been on their radar ever since, and Dad would have made us leave Lumina City years ago to start over somewhere else."

"No, these weren't Shadow Society members." Grandpa placed a glass of water next to Ridley's spoon before moving back to his seat. "Or if they were, I didn't know about it. Our interactions weren't related to elementals in any way. They were people from a government department, acting in a more official—albeit top-secret—capacity. Their research was in weapons development. Melding magic and technology. They wanted to use my knowledge, and I refused."

"And you didn't think they would try to go after Dad once you were gone? Try to find out if you'd passed on your knowledge?"

"They tried that before I was gone, actually. It's part of what made me realize how serious they were about their threats. They took both your parents, interrogated them, and satisfied themselves that neither knew anything about the relevant conjurations."

"Wow, seriously?"

"That was the start of our ..." Grandpa sighed and picked up his spoon. "Well, the erosion of our relationship, I suppose. Your dad was furious that I'd brought this on us. That it led to your mother being snatched off the street in broad daylight while shopping and taken to a secret government facility for questioning. That it led the authorities so close to *you*, even though they had no idea what you were. So they turned their attention back to me. When the real threats began—the threats to harm you and your parents if I didn't cooperate— that's when I knew we had to resort to drastic measures. I know it seems extreme, but it worked. No one ever came back to bother your family once I was gone."

"Holy crap, that's completely crazy." Ridley's spoon was in her hand, frozen over her soup. She'd forgotten about her food entirely while Grandpa spoke. "I had no idea any of that was happening."

"Good. Your parents didn't want you to know. You were so young, you would have been terrified."

"Thank goodness it wasn't the Shadow Society," she said. "It might have been the end for our family if they'd been the ones who wanted to know those conjurations."

"Probably." Grandpa leaned over his bowl and started eating, but Ridley's next questions were already on the tip of her tongue.

"So what do you know about them? The Shadow Society? Do you know any of the people in it?"

"I don't know any of the members—although I think we

can now safely assume the mayor's family is involved, given everything you discovered over the past few days—but I do know a little about their structure. The society has chapters all around the world. Probably at least one in every remaining city. Each chapter has its own chairperson, and then there's a director who oversees the society as a whole."

"So they really are everywhere." Ridley tapped her spoon lightly against the edge of her bowl. "I wonder if the mayor is the chairperson for the chapter here in Lumina City." She was about to expand on her theory when her commscreen, sitting on the other side of the table, buzzed. It was rude to look, but she glanced at it out of habit anyway. The screen displayed a message from Archer.

Archer: Free tomorrow night? We can start with MH.

MH, Ridley repeated in her head as she mentally went through the list of names. Malachi Hollings. That was the only one that fit. She reached for the device and turned it over. "Sorry about that," she said to Grandpa.

"That's okay. I assume you have many other questions," he added, "but perhaps we should eat first. Your food's going to end up ice-cold otherwise. Then we can talk while we wash dishes. I'm guessing you don't use magic for that?"

Ridley's eyebrows jumped. "You know Dad would have a heart attack, right? He didn't know I've been using magic *at all* until yesterday, and he was not happy to discover that."

Grandpa chuckled. "I can imagine."

Ridley ate quickly, managing to keep most of her questions to herself until she and Grandpa were done. As she began clearing the table and the rest of the kitchen, piling dirty dishes beside the sink, Grandpa told her how, long ago before he was married, his work as a historian had led him to discover a very old text that mentioned elementals. It had been studied before by others, but he'd interpreted the text in a different way. He thought there might be some truth to the story, and so he went searching for elementals—and eventually found a group of them living in a secluded farm area.

"I learned so much from them," Grandpa told her as he picked up a dishcloth and began drying the dishes as Ridley washed them. "It's truly fascinating, the way things used to be. The way people used to live so in harmony with nature. They didn't need to pull magic because it existed within them, but if they ever did pull it, it was easy. An instinct, rather than something that had to be learned. They lived so in tune with the elements, traveling on the wind or in water, moving through mountains as earth, or creating fire in an instant by simply becoming it."

"That sounds both amazing and scary," Ridley murmured, her hands going still in the hot, soapy water as she imagined what that kind of life must have been like.

"It is amazing," Grandpa said. "You're capable of incredible things, Ridley. Have you experimented?"

"Well, sort of." She picked up the pot and lowered it into the water. "I can become the air. I've traveled on the wind. I even spun into a mini tornado recently. Like, very mini. But it's scary if I get too high and the natural currents in the air happen to be too strong. I end up out of control."

"Out of control?" Ridley sensed Grandpa staring at her, and she turned her head to meet his eyes. "This isn't about control," he said. "That's the beauty of being an elemental. You shouldn't ever be working *against* the elements. You're working *with* them. Your magic, nature's magic, the two work together. And you may feel small compared to the vastness of what's around you, but the magic within your body is so much stronger—so much more *concentrated*—than you think it is. If you just let go of it instead of trying to control it, you'll see how powerful you can truly be. Hurricane winds. Infernos that cleanse lands. Floods that bring new life."

Ridley turned fully to face Grandpa, the dishes forgotten for now. "Okay, firstly, infernos and floods sound really destructive and I'm not interested in that kind of thing. And secondly, what do you mean I need to *let go*? I already let go. I'm not consciously holding anything back when I use magic. My skin turns blue and magic rises away from my body and then ... I use it."

"But if you're trying to control what happens, then you're not fully letting go."

"Um ... I don't know." Ridley leaned her hip against the side of the sink. "It sure feels to me like I'm letting go when I use it. Maybe I'm just not the type of elemental who can start hurricanes and move mountains."

Grandpa's piercing eyes smiled at her from behind his glasses. "All elementals are that kind of elemental."

"So it's not like some have more power than others?"

"Well, yes, some definitely do have more power, but—"

"Okay, so I'm obviously on the other end of the scale then."

Grandpa shook his head. "I don't think so."

"Besides," she added, "I get really tired and headachy—like migraine headachy—after using my magic too much. That wouldn't be the case if I had all this power you're talking about."

"Headaches. Ah, okay. You're definitely trying too hard to exert control instead of giving yourself over to the elements."

"But I'm not!"

He smiled in a knowing way that only frustrated Ridley more. "I imagine this is tough for you to hear, being a straight-A student and all that. You're not used to the feeling of being slow to learn something."

If Ridley were a few years younger, she might have petulantly moaned, "You don't know me!" Instead, because she was a tiny bit more mature than that, she took a calming breath and turned back to the dishes. "Okay. Maybe you're right. Next time, I'll try to do this letting-go thing properly."

"Don't try. Just—"

"Don't *try*? Seriously?" Her hands tightened around the pot.

"Don't do anything," Grandpa said gently. "Just ... let go and fall into it."

"Fall into it? Really? I'm going to end up flat on my face."

"Not if you trust the magic around you."

"Yeah, okay," Ridley said with a sigh. "I'll ... *not* try next time." She fished around in the water for the sponge and began scrubbing the inside of the pot. "So ... tell me something else. How does one end up born as an elemental? Clearly it isn't something that's passed on genetically. Or maybe it is genetic, but it isn't always passed on. Because neither Mom or Dad were elementals." She moved the pot to the rinse water. "It's a weird coincidence, don't you think? That you discovered elementals, then one day my parents decided to go live with them, and then when they had me, I turned out to *be* one. Or did they only go and live with the elementals *after* I was born because they realized I was one of them?" She looked at Grandpa as she handed him the pot.

"You were born amongst the elementals," he told her, focusing on the pot as he made sure to dry every inch of it. "*After* your mom and dad decided to live with them. They had friends in that community—because your dad grew up knowing about elementals, and we visited fairly regularly—and in the end they decided they wanted to live there."

"Okay. So it is just a weird coincidence that I ended up being—Oh, wait." She paused as an idea clicked in her brain. "Maybe that's how the ability is passed on. Maybe it's something to do with being around others who have magic within them. Could that be possible?"

"I, uh, I'm not sure about that." Grandpa picked up a stack of dry dishes and carried them across the kitchen. "It could be possible." He opened cupboards and drawers and began putting items away. "People have studied this, of course. There is definitely a genetic component. For most elementals I've met, it's something that runs in their family." He pushed a drawer shut and returned to her side. "But I have met a few who didn't know of any of their ancestors having magic, so perhaps it is influenced by environmental factors, like being exposed to the specific kind of magic that exists within other people." He pointed at the sink and added, "Are you going to wash those last few things?"

"Oh, right, yes." She reached for the sponge again. "Sorry, I keep getting distracted. There's so much to ask you about."

They continued chatting late into the evening. Grandpa told Ridley the story of how he'd ended up buying the antique store, and how he continued to hunt down any ancient texts he could locate that had to do with elementals. He also told her where he'd traveled to after pulling off his fake death—pretty much everywhere on the continent—before finally settling in a small seaside town. The town itself had no arxium protection, but Grandpa and several others managed to get to a bunker someone had built beneath their house, and so they survived the Cataclysm that way. They'd all left the town after that, but while the others had set off for one of the surviving cities, Grandpa had made his way to a small elemental community he knew of.

When Grandpa felt he'd answered enough questions, he asked Ridley about her friends and hobbies and the plans she had for her future—which were probably supposed to be the same as they'd always been, if she was going to follow Dad's instructions and continue with life as normal: Graduate with flying colors, snag an internship at The Rosman Foundation, and finally get to help people in a meaningful way that didn't involve stealing. But, somehow, she couldn't see that happening anymore. When she tried to imagine her future, all she got was a hazy half-formed picture that might have been the wastelands and might have contained elementals.

Dad would not be happy if he knew.

When it was far too late for a school night—which Grandpa kept telling Ridley, and she kept ignoring—Ridley finally agreed to go to bed. "Can we stay in contact after you're gone?" she asked before heading to her room.

"We can try, but it isn't easy." He removed his glasses and rubbed the bridge of his nose. "The networks are great within the cities, but out there in the wastelands, there's no functional infrastructure. I have to get near a city, or at the very least, near one of the inter-city train lines." He replaced his glasses and gave her a lopsided smile. "If it's an emergency and you need my help, you'd probably be better off sending a huge fireball into the air."

Ridley waited for him to start laughing, but he didn't. "Is that a joke?"

"Actually, no. People used to do it. Take a huge chunk of rock, make it burn, hurl it through the air at a magical speed."

"Sure, yeah," Ridley said with an exaggerated shrug. "Sounds so easy."

"Apparently it is."

"Well, not for this elemental right here."

"You'll figure things out," Grandpa told her with a reassuring smile. "Just remember: It isn't about control; it's about letting go."

CHAPTER 6

THE FOLLOWING NIGHT, after arriving in an area roughly halfway between her home and the opulent center of Lumina City, Ridley looked around and spotted Archer waiting for her in front of Rosiello's Pizza. Though it was almost 10 pm on a Tuesday night, this part of town was still bustling with activity. The sidewalks were crowded with tables, chairs and menu stands in front of each restaurant, and strings of colorful lights zigzagged from one end of the street to the other. Chatter, laughter and the occasional shout formed a continuous low-level hum in Ridley's ears, while the smell of cooking food wafted through the air. Like most other nights, heavy clouds blotted out the sky, but fortunately, it wasn't raining.

"So all we're doing is handing over a letter," Archer said as she reached him. "We don't need to hang around and wind up in any sort of trouble."

Ridley pushed her hands into her jacket pockets and tipped her head to the side. "Are you afraid of trouble, Archer? That doesn't seem like you."

"I have no problem with trouble. I'm well acquainted with

it, in fact. It's *you* I'm worried about."

"Look, we can't just give him the letter and leave." Ridley paused as a man with a takeout box walked out of Rosiello's and hurried past them. A chilly breeze curled around her neck, and she raised her shoulders against the cold, pushing her hands deeper into her pockets. When there was once again no one within earshot, she continued, "We at least need to explain a little bit."

"What exactly are you planning to explain? Doesn't the letter say enough?"

"No. The letter mentions stolen information that the society will soon have. That's not the case anymore. So we need to explain that it isn't as urgent to get out of the city as the letter suggests. That we elementals are in no more or less danger now than we were before."

Archer's eyes followed something behind Ridley, and she glanced over her shoulder at two women engrossed in their commscreens as they crossed the street. "I doubt Luc would have agreed," Archer said, "even if he knew the flash drive had been destroyed."

Ridley's gaze shot back to him. "Luc?"

Archer paused for a moment, confusion crossing his face. "The man who died outside your home. Sorry, I forgot I didn't tell you his name."

"So you *did* know him."

"Yes, I did. I couldn't tell you before, and then ... well, I guess that bit didn't come up the other night."

"I'm assuming there's a lot that didn't come up the other

night. Like everything you've been doing since the moment you left Lumina City at the beginning of last summer."

Archer nodded. "Pretty much."

She opened her mouth to ask for more details, but her brain was backpedaling. "Wait, so you … you knew him. And then he died right in front of you." She let the memory of that night sink into her, imagining it from Archer's point of view for the first time. "Wow, that's—I'm so sorry. I can't imagine what that must have been like."

"Yeah." Archer nodded, his eyes focusing somewhere behind her. "We weren't close, but I knew him. So it was a shock."

A breeze caught a few strands of Ridley's blond hair and blew them across her face. She tucked the flyaway hair behind her ear and returned her hand to her pocket. "Did you know he was in Lumina City?"

"No. That was part of the shock. Lilah and I left your store, and after we ordered food, I wandered outside while she waited for it. I happened to walk past the alley by your back door, and that was when I saw him. He barely had time to explain what he was doing here before Lawrence … and then the knife …"

He didn't need to finish; Ridley knew what had happened. And since it was her best friend who'd thrown the knife, she felt a weird sense of indirect responsibility. After a quiet moment, she said, "I'm so sorry."

Archer glanced over his shoulder into the window of Rosiello's Pizza. "Anyway, this is where Malachi Hollings works."

Ridley blinked at the abrupt subject change but decided to go with it. "Uh, yes. Right." She looked through the window into the busy pizzeria. It was tiny compared to some of the other restaurants around here, and the few tables inside were all occupied. "You said you couldn't find a home address for him?"

"Correct." Archer moved a few steps to the side and leaned his shoulder against the pole of a street light. "I found a public profile on the social feeds, which is where he mentioned working at Rosiello's. And that's where I saw a photo of him, which I recognized from the information on the flash drive. We can try to catch him when he leaves here at the end of his shift. Maybe follow him into the next street over where it's quieter and talk to him there."

"And until then? We're just going to lurk outside?"

"Lurk? I don't know about you, but I was planning to stand here like a normal person."

Ridley rolled her eyes. "You know what I mean. It's weird if we hang out here for hours. People will notice."

"It won't be hours. This place closes in about twenty minutes. He'll be done soon after that." Archer pushed away from the street light with a sigh. "But yeah, maybe it would be better to get a drink next door and watch from there."

They moved further along the sidewalk to the restaurant beside Rosiello's Pizza. Ridley took a seat at the only empty table outside while Archer headed through the doors, aiming for the bar. He returned a few minutes later with a glass in each hand. "Sorry, the menu's limited here." He slid a glass across the table before sitting opposite her. "It's a non-alco-holic sangria."

"Thanks." Ridley pulled the glass closer, managing to re-frain from making a comment about how every menu must seem limited compared to what was on offer at places like De-Luxe or Sapphire 84. "Did you look up the other names on the list I gave you?"

"Yes. There were only two I couldn't find any informa-tion on. I'll go and see Christa and ask her if she knows them. It's possible they're living beneath the city and never reported themselves as survivors after the Cataclysm."

Ridley frowned. Christa, the woman who was in charge of the enormous bunker housing Lumina City's illegal mag-ic users, had seemed friendly enough when Ridley met her, but Ridley still wasn't sure the woman could be trusted. "Are you going to tell Christa why you're looking for these people? Does she know about—" Ridley paused, glancing around at the crowded tables. "Does she know people like me exist?"

"She ..." Archer rubbed the back of his neck. "It's compli-cated. She does know about them, and she knows I've been living with a group of them. But when I was first put in con-tact with her—the first time I returned to the city—I was told not to reveal any more information than necessary. Possibly for her safety and the elementals' safety. So no, I'm not plan-ning to tell her that they're your kind of people."

"Okay." Ridley nodded, then took a sip of her sangria. It was overly sweet and had an artificial quality to it, but she managed to keep from making a face as she lowered the glass. She wiped her hand—wet from the condensation—on her jeans as her eyes scanned the tables behind Archer. She couldn't help noticing the number of people who were looking this way. Because of Archer, no doubt. He'd been on the news multiple times recently because of the murder outside her building. And there was also the simple fact that he was a Davenport. His family had the kind of celebrity status people were awarded purely for being rich and beautiful.

Wonderful, she thought to herself. "The other reason you should have let me do this on my own," she said quietly, "is because of all the people who stare at you whenever you're out. You're ridiculously conspicuous just because of who you are."

"Don't worry about it," he told her. "We'll make sure we're far away from prying eyes before we talk to Malachi."

"We'd better." She took another sip of the sangria, mainly because it was sitting in front of her and there wasn't much else to do. "So ... can I ask about your time away? I mean, how did you first get involved with my kind of people? Did you go looking for them? How did you even know they existed in the first place?"

Archer stared into his glass for several moments before speaking in a voice so low that Ridley had to lean forward to hear him. "I found them by accident. I was doing this hiking trail in the French Prealps. A completely illegal activity out in the wastelands for thrill seekers. We wore these weird arxium suits—like hazmat-type things—to protect us from the magic. Anyway, we were on La Tournette, which used to be fairly easy to hike, but obviously it changed with all the upheaval during the Cataclysm. So there were no paths or anything. There was a storm, and I ended up separated from the group, and I just sort of … stumbled across them."

"Like in caves or something?" Ridley asked.

"Partly. Not like a campsite though. They've got some permanent dwellings set up there. No arxium protection at all since most of the people living there are your kind of people, so the wild magic leaves them alone."

"Really? But the wild magic here wasn't exactly gentle when it tossed me around a few days ago on the other side of the wall."

Archer smiled. "That *was* gentle, Ridley. You were fine when it let you go. Once it realized you're made of magic."

"Once it *realized*," Ridley repeated softly, her mind expanding at the implication of that statement. Was magic really as *intelligent* as Archer made it sound? Or was it just one kind of magic detecting another kind of magic and leaving it be?

"Anyway, they didn't know what to do with me at first," Archer continued. "They obviously didn't trust me, so they wouldn't let me leave. I guess I was technically a prisoner, but …" He shrugged, staring again at his drink instead of looking at Ridley. "I didn't really mind. I was kind of … lost? Not *literally* lost. You know what I mean. I was trying to figure myself out, and way out there in the wastelands of another country seemed like a good spot to do it. It was a good place to find … I don't know … purpose." It seemed his cheeks flushed a little as he said that, which didn't surprise Ridley. This was probably uncharted territory for him, revealing something so personal about himself. "Anyway." He sighed and ran a hand through his hair. "It's a long story, but the short version is that I slowly became part of their community."

"And what did your family think this whole time? They never publicly said anything about you being missing, but they must have had someone looking for you."

"I was allowed to contact them, actually. People traveled to the nearest city every few days to send messages. They obviously didn't reveal any important information in the messages they sent on my behalf, but they said enough to let my family know I was fine. I've never been one to explain the exact details of my activities, so I guess my parents assumed I was doing what I've always done—my own thing. Partying away my trust fund. Though I guess they didn't look too closely or they would have seen I wasn't spending any money."

"And *that* would have made them suspicious, I'm sure," Ridley said.

Archer grinned, raised his glass, and said, "Exactly." He took a swig of his amber-colored drink before returning it to the table.

"So you learned all about these people?" Ridley prompted, her voice still low. "Their history, and the Shadow Society, and how their magic works?"

"Yes. They weren't all ele—um, people like you. There were other regular people like me who happened to be connected to them in some way and were part of the community. There were obviously no scanner drones out there, and everyone lived the way we used to live. So after a while, I had my—

uh ..." He faltered, glanced about, then surreptitiously rubbed his finger along the two small scars just below and behind his left ear. The spot where his arxium amulets were implanted.

Ridley raised her eyebrows. *Removed?* she mouthed, assuming he meant his AI2. That was the one that prevented people from pulling magic from the environment.

Archer nodded. "But I had it put back a little while before I returned. I figured it was the safer option."

"Good thing you did," Ridley said, "considering you were arrested shortly after you got back."

"Yes. Though the first time I returned, I didn't have it. That was quite a risk."

"Why'd you come back that time? Was it only because of the flash drive? And was that when you traveled through the wastelands?"

"Yes. And even though I have no magic of my own, I was fine. I did get tossed around a bit here and there, but as long as I remained calm and didn't try to fight back I was always okay in the end. It was a challenge, of course, basically acting like a rag doll and letting magic hurl me through the air, but it worked."

"It's not about control," Ridley murmured as Grandpa's words came back to her.

"What's that?" Archer asked, leaning closer.

"Um, my grandfather told me some things last night. Things that sounded kind of unbelievable. He said I'm trying too hard to control what happens when I'm using magic, and that if I just let go completely, I'll be capable of way more. Like hurricanes, floods, traveling right through solid mountains. Sounds crazy, right?"

Archer shook his head, a frown forming. "No."

"It's ... not?" Ridley asked, a chill racing along her arms. They were speaking barely above a whisper, but their faces were so close by now that she could still hear him.

"I'm sorry, Ridley, I just assumed you knew these things. I've seen you become air, and I saw the way that underground river responded instantly to you. And then you explained to me—when you thought I didn't know any of this—that you can become the elements. So I just assumed you'd already figured out the extent to which your magic can influence the environment around you."

"Nope. I spend most of my time *hiding* that part of me, not trying to test how powerful I can be. And besides, there are the headaches. They can reach migraine level if I use too much. So I'm pretty sure I'm not capable of the kind of stuff Grandpa was talking about."

"Oh yeah, the headaches. I thought it was weird when you told me about that. But I couldn't say anything because at that point, you didn't know about elementals, and I wasn't supposed to tell you."

"Grandpa says it's because I'm trying too hard to control the magic."

"Maybe. All I know is that you're definitely capable of more. If you let go properly, you'll see."

"What does that *mean*? I kept telling Grandpa that I *do* let go."

Archer inched his elbows forward a little further on the table. Anyone watching might have thought he was about to kiss her. Ridley had no problem with anyone thinking that as long as no one knew what they were really talking about. "So, you know how you get those patches of blue that glow just beneath your skin?" Archer asked. "They kind of pulse, fading in and out?"

"Yes?"

"Your whole body will do that when you're letting go properly."

A beat of quiet passed between them. "My whole body?"

"Yes."

"You've seen this?"

He nodded. "I have."

She continued watching him, unsure of what to say next, and Archer did nothing except stare right back. She couldn't help noticing that, up close, his eyes weren't just a flat dark color. Countless rich brown tones bled into one another. Depthless, warm, inviting. It was easy to see how so many girls had fallen under the spell of those eyes.

A burst of particularly raucous laughter from the table next to theirs cut through the moment, and Ridley leaned back. "Well, uh, that definitely gives me something to think about. At least I know it wasn't just Grandpa totally overestimating my abilities. Anyway, uh ..." She picked up her glass and took a quick sip. "You were telling me about the time you returned with the flash drive."

"Yes. Right." Archer relaxed against his chair. "Sensitive

information about all the communities around the world needed to be passed to someone in Lumina City, and I offered to bring it. I was the only one there at the time who had any knowledge of this city, so it made sense."

"And they trusted you by then?"

"Oh, yeah. Definitely. I'd had plenty of time to prove myself by then."

"And when you returned this time? Were you bringing information again?"

Archer traced a pattern in the condensation on the side of his glass. "No, this time it was because of my family. My father demanded I return home. Our agreement was that I could do whatever I wanted for a year, and I'd already pushed it a few months beyond that, so it was time."

"So now what?" Ridley asked. "Time to grow up and learn the family business and forget everything you discovered in the mountains on the other side of the world?"

"According to my father, yes. I'm being groomed to take over Davenport Industries one day." Archer gave her a grim smile. "Thrilling stuff, arxium mining."

"And according to you?"

He sat forward again, and his voice was low once more when he said, "I'm biding my time. Waiting for a chance to get out of the city again. For good this time. I need to do it properly. I need to make sure my family will never find me."

His words left Ridley feeling oddly cold. She couldn't imagine running away from her father like that. "Do you really mean that?" she asked. "Won't you miss them terribly?"

Archer sighed. "My parents ..." He shook his head. "We have a complicated relationship that borders on toxic. Lilah, on the other hand ... I know you two have your differences, so you may not agree with me on this, but she isn't that bad. I missed her a lot while I was away, and if I leave for good ..." He paused, lifted his drink, and downed what remained of it. "That's the only thing that might change my mind. Leaving my sister behind. When I think of family, I think of her. But I can't tell her the truth. You know I can't. She believes everything my parents have ever told her about magic. She would never understand me giving up everything to live with people who are born with it. She'd probably turn me in before letting me do something like that."

Ridley shook her head, remembering the text message conversation she'd had with Lilah after the other girl had tracked down the footage of the murder in Ridley's alley. "No she wouldn't," Ridley said. "She'd do anything to protect you."

A frown line creased Archer's brow. "You think?"

"Yes. As you would do for her."

"Well, okay. Perhaps she wouldn't hand me over to the cops, but she'd never understand. Telling her is not an option."

Ridley nodded, turning her glass in small circles. She wondered how much time had passed since they'd sat down. "So," Archer said before she could pull out her commscreen to look at the time. "Are you still mad at me?"

The question caught her off guard, and she had to think about it before answering. *Life's too short to hold on to anger*, Grandpa had said the night before. "No," she answered eventually, looking directly into his eyes so he'd know she was being truthful. "You, me, my dad, Grandpa ... we've all kept secrets. I might want to get all self-righteous and tell myself that the secrets you kept were way bigger and that you should have told me the truth. But ... I don't know. I can't really be self-righteous considering the things I've done, can I? And now that the shock of discovering everything has passed, it just seems like too much effort to stay mad at you."

With a straight face, Archer said, "That's so mature of you, Ridley."

She rolled her eyes and muttered, "Shut up."

Archer laughed. "I take it you've forgiven your father as well then?"

"Yes." She pushed her glass forward and rested her elbows on the table. "We spoke a lot earlier this evening after Grandpa left. I told him about everything from the past few days. Stealing the figurine, running and hiding after the shooting at Wallace, the fact that I know about the city's—" she lowered her voice and whispered, "—magical underworld."

"Ah, yes. Your dad knows Christa, doesn't he?"

"Yes, though he said he's had no contact with her since just after the Cataclysm. He doesn't want to have anything to do with that bunker or anyone who lives down there."

"Naturally," Archer said with a nod. "He wants to keep you safe, so obviously he doesn't want to get involved with them in any way."

"Yeah. And we spoke about all my thefts from the past

few years, and how he strongly feels that I should never, ever, *ever* steal from someone again."

"Looks like I have something else in common with your dad."

"Yeah. I'm still figuring out my position on that one. Maybe it's a good thing Ezra's been ignoring me since we showed up underground. If I don't have anyone to sell stolen items on my behalf, then maybe—"

"Ohmygoodness, *Archer*! Hello!" A girl in a white mini dress dropped into the chair beside Archer, interrupting Ridley mid-sentence. "Where have you *been*?" she exclaimed as she flipped her sleek black hair over her shoulder. "You totally disappeared from all the social feeds for like a *year*, and then we saw you on the news because of that murder, and none of us even knew you were back."

"Aaaaah, it's Archer!" a second girl squealed as she slid into the empty chair next to Ridley. Her outfit was almost as skimpy as her friend's, and she ran her hands up and down her arms as the chilly breeze gusted along the sidewalk. "Okay, you have to tell us *everything*. I saw Lilah at Voletti's on the weekend, but she was super vague on the details of what you've been up to. And OH MY HOLY GOSH. Did you see what happened with Lawrence? That he was shot and killed? *Such* a tragedy. I actually cried when I heard about it."

"And *obviously* we'll be at the memorial tomorrow morning," the first girl chimed in. "Will you be there?"

"Kelly, Luna, hi." Archer's smile was friendly but guarded.

He gestured across the table and added, "This is Ridley. You might remember her from Wallace."

"Oh. Hi." Luna jerked to the side as if surprised to find someone sitting beside her. Ridley remembered both girls from Archer's class two years ahead of her own, but neither girl seemed to recognize her.

"I'd love to catch up," Archer continued, "but Ridley and I were actually about to leave. We need to meet someone, and we're already late." He pushed his chair back and stood. "I'll see you around."

"Uh, yeah, sorry about that," Ridley said as she stood. Archer walked away from the tables, and she followed quickly. "Wait, the bill," she added, pulling her commscreen free. "I'll just go inside and scan the—"

"It's fine, I paid at the bar when I got the drinks. Come on, or we'll lose him."

"Oh, did you see him leave?" Ridley pushed her commscreen back into her pocket as she and Archer stepped onto the street. "I thought you just didn't want to talk to your old friends."

"I saw him walk past just as Kelly and Luna sat down. Perfect timing."

"Great. So ... which one is Malachi Hollings?" she asked, her eyes scanning the people walking ahead of them.

Archer nodded toward the dark-skinned man with a backpack over both shoulders who was about to turn a corner into the next street. He glanced back once before disappearing around the corner, giving Ridley a brief glimpse of his face. She guessed he was in his early twenties.

"Don't hurry," Archer said as she edged ahead of him. "Keep it casual. We don't want to talk to him until we're somewhere quieter."

"I know, I know, I just don't want to lose him." She pushed her hands into her jacket pockets and forced herself to slow to a stroll beside Archer. They turned left into the next street, and Ridley was relieved to see Malachi hadn't vanished. He was walking a little faster though, and soon he turned another corner. Ridley linked her arm with Archer's and pulled him along as she increased her pace. "We need to move quicker, and I don't want to look like I'm running away from you, so we need to walk *together*."

"You do realize," Archer said as a fine drizzle began to fall, "that if we happen to lose him we can just come back tomorrow night, right?"

Ridley sighed and reached back with her free hand for the hood of her jacket. The rain was little more than mist right now, but it could change at any moment. "This would be so much easier if I were on my own," she said. "I could become air, follow him without anyone knowing, then appear only when it's safe and he's completely alone."

"That sounds a lot more stalker-ish than what we're doing."

"I could actually hide us both," Ridley continued, ignoring the stalker comment. "Like I did when we went into Brex Tower to look for Lawrence. I can't do it *now*, of course, since there are other people around." She threw a look over her shoulder at the group of giggling young women crossing the street. "But perhaps we can do that next time."

"Maybe," Archer said as they turned the next corner into a residential street. It was quieter and darker now, with only the regular street lamps and no bright restaurant signs or billboard screens. Aside from a man hurrying out of an apartment building with his commscreen to his ear, Malachi was the only other person on this street. And he was even further ahead now, already rounding the corner at the next intersection.

"Crap, come on." Ridley let go of Archer's arm and broke into a jog. As she approached the corner, she prepared to shout out for Malachi. But his name died on her tongue as she rushed around the corner.

He stood there, facing her, his backpack on the ground and his fists balled at his sides. Ridley skidded to a halt. A second later, Archer stopped beside her. "I don't know what the hell you're doing following me," Malachi hissed, "but I'm not interested."

"Um, hi," Ridley said. "Sorry about the creepy following thing. We just want to talk."

Malachi's gaze moved to Archer. "I know who you are, and if you come any closer I will *kill you*!"

"Whoa, jeez." Archer raised his hands. "That's not necessary. Look, man, we just want to talk. It's really—"

But Archer never got to explain what he wanted to talk about because Malachi's arm flashed forward, his fist connecting with Archer's face a second later. Archer stumbled backward. "Hey!" Ridley yelled, but Malachi didn't stop. He lunged at Archer and slammed into him with the full weight of his body, sending them both crashing to the ground.

CHAPTER 7

ALL RIDLEY COULD MAKE out was a confusion of swinging arms and clenched fists. Then, just to make the scene even more dramatic, lightning flashed overhead. "YOU KILLED MY FATHER!" Malachi roared, aiming for Archer's face again.

"What the *hell*?" Archer demanded, his arm up to protect his face.

"Your father—" punch "—fired my father—" another punch "—and we were still mourning my mom and sister. Your father *ruined* mine with his lies and accusations." Malachi paused for a moment, breathless, and Ridley was about to yell at him to get off Archer when he finished with, "So he committed suicide," and threw another punch, this one directly to Archer's abdomen.

Ridley hadn't witnessed a great many fist fights in her life, but she knew enough to be fully aware that Archer wasn't fighting back. He was strong—she'd felt the muscles across his back the night she'd wrapped her arms around him and hidden them both with magic—so she figured he could easily take on Malachi. But he wasn't even trying. "Hey!" she yelled again. Archer might feel the need to take a beating for whatever his father had done to ruin Malachi's father, but that didn't mean she had to stand by and watch. "Malachi, stop!" Malachi paused at the sound of his name, his arm pulled back long enough for Ridley to grab hold of it. She tugged as hard as she could, but he resisted instantly, and though years of indoor rock climbing had given her great upper body strength, Malachi was clearly far stronger.

"Get off me!" he yelled, ripping free of her grip. He swung his elbow back at her with way more force than she expected, striking her stomach and shoving her backward into the nearest wall. Her head smacked against the bricks, and pain rocketed through her body.

"Hey!" Archer shouted. Ridley blinked and gasped for breath, but she couldn't seem to get any. With a wordless cry, Archer finally kicked Malachi off and struggled to his feet. "Touch her again and you're dead." Clutching his ribs and wiping one hand across his bloodied face, he lurched toward Ridley. "Are you—"

Malachi launched himself at Archer's legs before he could finish speaking, tackling him to the sidewalk again. "I'm dead? *I'm* dead?" He went for Archer's face again with renewed fervor.

Ridley raised one hand to the back of her head as she sucked uselessly at the air that refused to fill her lungs. She couldn't feel anything wet in her hair, which was a good sign. She'd probably just end up with a painful lump on the back

ELEMENTAL POWER 101

of her head. She tried again to breathe, managed a cough and a groan, and then finally pulled a small breath into her lungs. "Dammit," she wheezed as the two guys struggled with one another on the ground.

"I am not my father!" Archer yelled.

"You're just as bad!"

"NO I'M NOT!"

Enough! Ridley shouted inside her head, since shouting out loud was still impossible. She may not be able to physically pull the two guys apart, but that didn't mean she was completely useless. She looked both ways down the street, confirming there was no one else around, then up at the windows in the buildings on both sides of the street. Those that were illuminated were covered by curtains or blinds. As far as she could tell, no one was watching. It was a risk, but it might be the only way to get Malachi off Archer before one of them seriously injured the other.

She breathed in another few shallow breaths, then pushed her aching body away from the wall, letting her magic rise to the surface of her skin. She imagined air, and as she threw herself at Malachi, her body vanished. Her magic swirled around him in glowing blue wisps as she collided against his side and clung tightly to him. Together the two of them spun away on the evening breeze.

He cursed loudly in her ear and tried to shove her away. She let go of both him and the air that concealed them, and a moment later, the two of them landed hard on the ground. "What the hell?" he gasped, scrambling to his feet and backing away from her. His sweater was rumpled, and blood oozed from his split lip.

"Yeah, I'm just like you," she said, straightening and rubbing the part of her backside that had hit the ground. "That's what we want to talk to you about. Now will you please stop attacking us?"

"Ridley, are you okay?" Archer asked as he staggered toward them, which was a ridiculous question considering the state of his face.

"I'm fine," she said. She'd feel it later, no doubt, but for now, the immediate pain of being thrown against a brick wall was beginning to recede. "Malachi, we need to talk."

He cursed beneath his breath as his eyes, wide and bright against his dark skin, darted around the empty street and up to the windows. Soft rain pattered onto the hood covering Ridley's head as she waited, her gaze switching between Malachi and Archer. The latter was making his way toward them, his steps uneven and his arm wrapped around his chest. Ridley's stomach turned at the sight of all the blood on his face. Hopefully it looked worse than it was.

"Fine," Malachi said eventually. "Follow me." He hurried past Ridley. She rushed forward, took Archer's free arm, and helped him to walk a little faster. Around the next corner, Malachi ran up a few steps to the door of a residential building and punched in a code. The door swung open. Once they were all inside, he shoved the door shut and hissed, "Why the hell would you do that out there? You could get us both killed."

"And how is that any different from what you were doing

to Archer?" Ridley asked as she pushed her hood back. "You actually used the words 'I will kill you.'"

"Yeah, but I wasn't *literally* going to kill him."

"How was I supposed to know that? And I checked before using magic. There were no people around and no drones flying by. If there was someone in a window too high up for me to see, then that means he or she would have been too far away to see our faces. We'll be fine."

With another curse, Malachi turned away from the elevator and stairs toward the passage on the left. "Come on, my apartment's right here."

"Thank goodness," Archer groaned. After passing two doors, Malachi unlocked the third and hurried inside. Ridley followed as fast as Archer—still hanging onto her arm—would allow. As Malachi shut the door behind them, Archer let go of Ridley. She glanced around the small studio apartment, quickly taking in the unmade bed on one side, the well-worn couches in the middle, and the kitchen on the other side, before turning her attention back to Malachi.

He met her gaze and stared for several silent moments. Lightning flickered outside, brightening the dim apartment for a moment. Malachi exhaled slowly. "Okay. Wow. You're ... I can't believe this. You're like me. And here I was thinking I was the only magical freak in existence."

Ridley allowed herself to smile for the first time since coming face to face with this guy. "I know, me too. I only found out a few days ago that I'm not the only one. I'm Ridley, by the way."

Archer dropped onto the nearest couch with a groan, one hand pressed against his ribcage and the other gingerly prodding the swollen skin beneath his right eye. "Sorry," Malachi said to him, though he didn't sound all that apologetic. "You might need to go to a hospital."

"I'll survive," Archer answered.

"I'll fix him up later," Ridley said. "I know a few conjurations that'll help."

"You do?" Malachi's eyes snapped back to hers. "Where'd you find those? Weren't all the books and everything destroyed? I've scoured the net, but I haven't found much."

"I just remember a few things from before," Ridley said, not wanting to reveal that she'd found a book containing certain conjurations in her father's antique store. "Things my parents made me memorize. Anyway, this is why we're here." She removed the letter from inside her jacket and handed it to him. "I received one of these, but the guy who delivered it died before he could pass on the rest of the letters. So I figured I should probably do it."

"Um, thanks." Malachi unfolded the paper, and Ridley watched in silence as his eyes scanned the words.

"Go into the *wastelands*?" he muttered before looking up. "That's suicide."

"Apparently it isn't," Ridley said. "But you don't actually need to do that. That's the reason I wanted to talk to you as well as give you the letter. Not everything in there is true anymore. That information they're talking about that was stolen? It never reached the Shadow Society. We destroyed it. So, I mean, you can go looking for the elementals out there if you want to, but you don't *have* to leave the city. We're in the same amount of danger we've always been in, living here."

"I see. Um ... okay." He looked at the letter again as he ran one hand over his buzz cut. "This is all just ... a lot to take in."

"I know. I've had a little bit of time to process things, but it was a shock at first." She crossed her arms, flinching as pain radiated across her shoulders and back.

"Hey, uh, I'm sorry I hit you," Malachi said, probably noticing her expression. "I wasn't really thinking, and when you pulled my arm, I just automatically fought back."

"Sure, yeah, I understand. I'll be fine. It's just a few bruises."

"Dude, I think you have rage issues," Archer mumbled from the couch.

Malachi's eyes narrowed as they focused on Archer again. "I have my reasons."

"What exactly happened with your family?" Ridley asked. "I mean, unless you don't want to talk about it. I'm just trying to understand where the, uh, rage comes from."

Malachi moved away from the door, looking briefly at the letter again. Then he folded it and placed it on the kitchen counter. "So, uh ... my mom and sister were outside the city during the Cataclysm, so they didn't make it. And my dad ... he just couldn't get over the pain of losing them. Then he got fired—and not just fired, but falsely accused of fraud. He went to Alastair Davenport himself and tried to explain his side of things, and the bastard called security in and had him dragged away in front of all his colleagues and friends. He was facing a trial and possibly time in prison, plus there was the shame of it all, and the pain of losing half his family, and he just ... couldn't take it."

Archer leaned forward on the couch and stared at the floor. "I'm really sorry," Ridley said. "I lost my mom in the Cataclysm, but at least I still have my dad."

"I'm sorry too," Archer said quietly.

"Yeah, anyway. I realize that logically it had nothing to do with you," Malachi said to Archer, "but grief doesn't leave much room for logic. I've hated your family ever since."

"Understandable," Archer answered. "I kind of hate them myself sometimes." Ridley frowned at him. Surely he didn't mean that, did he? He met her eyes—or tried to, at least, but she guessed he couldn't see much through the one that was almost closed. "Not Lilah," he added. "But my parents. My dad. I totally get where Malachi's coming from."

Malachi leaned against the kitchen counter and crossed his arms. "I guess I didn't really expect that. I'm actually starting to feel bad about hitting you so hard."

"Well," Archer said. He pulled his jacket sleeve further down over his hand and used it to dab at parts of his face. "We can pretend you hit my dad instead."

Ridley was about to say it was time to leave—the more time that passed, the worse Archer's face looked—but Malachi spoke first. "So what else do you know? About people like us?"

"Uh ..." Her gaze shifted to Archer again.

"It's fine, you can talk." He gestured to his face and added,

"This looks worse than it is."

"Um, okay." Ridley sat on the arm of the couch and told Malachi, as quickly as she could, everything her father, Mrs. Lin and Grandpa had explained to her. Malachi interjected here and there, and she answered as best she could, but when she was done, she stood and said, "I know you've probably got more questions, but that's all I know, and we really need to go now. Archer's in a bad way. I need to get him fixed up."

"Oh, well why don't you just heal him here?" Malachi pushed away from the kitchen counter and moved closer. "I'd love to see the conjurations."

"Um ... I don't actually remember all of them," Ridley admitted. She needed to get home and pull the conjuration book out from the back of her wardrobe. She didn't want to tell Malachi that part though. He'd probably ask to see the book, and then she'd have to come back here, which was not part of her plan. "My dad knows some of them," she said instead, which, now that she thought about it, might actually be true. "So I'd rather take Archer to him."

"Oh, okay." Malachi's face fell, but he nodded as Archer stood. "I understand. Can I get your number? We should obviously stay in contact."

Ridley's eyes flicked toward Archer as she remembered her father's warning. "Uh ... I'm not sure. I think that might be a little dangerous."

"Why? It's not like we're going to use magic in public. It's just ... you're the only person I know who's like me. It would be great to hang out. And what if something changes? What if someone does find out who we are and we need to leave the city? If I discover something, then I'll need to tell you."

Ridley scooped her hair away from her neck and pulled it over her shoulder, twisting it as she tried to figure out how to be both polite and safe. From the corner of her eye, she saw Archer shaking his head. She lowered her hands to her sides and said, "I'll think about it."

"You'll think about it?" Malachi repeated. "And if you decide you don't want to stay in contact, then that's it? I don't ever see you again because I have no way of finding you? Seems a little unfair that you know all about me, but I barely know anything about you."

"Okay fine. You can have my number. But I'm not telling you where I live."

Malachi laughed. "You can keep your home a secret if it makes you feel safer. We can hang out somewhere else."

"Ridley ..." Archer said, a warning tone to his voice.

"It's fine," she told him as she raised her hands. Electric blue wisps were already rising away from her skin. She did a simple conjuration—one of the simplest there was; just three quick hand movements—then wrote her number in the air with her forefinger. Her magic followed her finger, leaving glowing blue numbers hanging in the air between her and Malachi. "Know that one?" she asked, lowering her hand.

"Obviously," he said with a smirk. "I was almost in high school when the Cataclysm happened. I knew all the basic conjurations by then."

Ridley shrugged. "I probably don't have much to teach you then."

"Well, perhaps I can teach you a thing or two."

With a groan, Archer directed Ridley toward the door. "Time to go."

CHAPTER 8

AS QUIETLY AS POSSIBLE, Ridley unlocked the door that led from the alley into the back rooms of Kayne's Antiques. "I probably should have asked this earlier," Archer said, "but that part about you taking me to your dad wasn't true, was it?" He was speaking oddly now, almost in a ventriloquist sort of way. Probably trying to keep his swollen jaw from moving too much, Ridley realized.

"No," she answered as she eased the door shut and turned the key. Her jacket was damp from the pattering rain they'd hurried through. She pushed her hood back and pulled the jacket off, then hung it on the back of the door. "But I do need to check my conjuration book for some of the movements," she added. "The one I memorized the other day when I came to find you in the hospital was for broken bones. I need to look up the ones for bruising, swelling and surface cuts." She nodded past the stairs and added, "You can go through to the store and I'll bring the book down here. Dad should be asleep now, and I don't want us to wake him. If he sees you, he'll want to know what happened to your face."

"Wait." Archer caught hold of her arm as she placed one foot on the lowest step. "Are you sure your dad will be asleep? Wouldn't he have stayed up to make sure you got home safely?"

"He would have—if he'd been aware that I left."

"You snuck out?"

"Yes. I said goodnight, shut my bedroom door, and climbed out my window."

"You have magic that can make you appear as invisible as air," he said in his strange, almost slurred manner, "but you chose to climb out your window instead?"

Ridley sighed, turned away, and headed up the stairs. "Wait for me in the store." Once upstairs, she paused near Dad's bedroom door and listened for his quiet snoring to confirm he was asleep. Then she quietly pushed aside the shoes and old school files on the floor of her wardrobe until she located the scarf-wrapped conjuration book.

Downstairs, she found Archer examining the items arranged on an ornately carved mahogany table. His jacket, which was probably just as damp as hers, hung over the back of the desk chair. Perhaps it was the shadows cast by the few lamps he'd turned on, but his face looked even worse now. Ridley stopped beside the desk at the back of the store, hugging the book to her chest. "Remember how you insisted you accompany me so you could make sure I was safe?"

Archer looked up. "Yes."

"I'm pretty sure tonight's meeting with Malachi would have gone a whole lot smoother if you hadn't been with me."

"A horrible coincidence." Archer said. "It probably won't

happen again. Everything would have been fine if he hadn't held an extremely personal grudge against me."

"True. Let's hope there aren't any other elementals holding extremely personal grudges against you." She walked around the front of Dad's desk, moved a few items out of the way, and pushed herself up to sit on the edge. "Get over here. You need some serious conjuration help. I don't know how you can talk at all right now."

"My whole head is basically one giant mass of throbbing pain," he said as he came toward her. "That doesn't really change whether I speak or not."

Ridley shook her head as she opened the book on her lap.

"What was that head shake?" Archer asked. "Disapproval?"

"Indeed it was." She turned a few pages, looking for the conjurations that had to do with healing.

"How can you *disapprove* of this? It's not like I punched my own face."

"No, but you're at least partly responsible for the state you're in, considering you didn't fight back until after Malachi knocked me into a wall. Which, by the way," she added as she looked up, "you could have done *without* telling him he was dead if he touched me again."

Archer made a sound that was probably supposed to be a chuckle. "You think that made things worse?"

"Definitely. I mean, it was sweet and everything, so thanks for that, but you really didn't need to get your pretty face smashed up even worse just for me."

"My pretty face?"

"Sorry. Handsome face? Does that make you feel more manly?"

"More like warm and fuzzy." He moved closer, placed one hand on either side of her on the desk, and attempted a goofy smile. "Ridley Kayne thinks I'm handsome."

Her heart did some kind of irregular beat thing, which was probably just her body signaling its annoyance at having someone right up in her personal space. She lifted one knee and slowly pushed Archer away with her foot. "You're such an idiot."

"A handsome idiot."

"Not right now, you're not. Your face is such a mess I don't even recognize you." She returned her gaze to the book and carried on flipping pages. "Let's work on fixing that so you can be a handsome idiot again."

"Look, I'm sorry if it upset you," he said quietly. "I know you can take care of yourself and don't need anyone getting all protective, saying things like 'Touch her again and you're dead.'" She looked up and found him focusing somewhere on the surface of Dad's desk to her left. "It's just ... if there's one thing that's been hammered into my brain this past year, it's that people like you are vitally important to our world, and I should do whatever I can to make sure you survive."

Ridley bit her lip and shifted a little, hanging onto the book to make sure it didn't slip off her lap. Thinking of herself as *special* made her uncomfortable. "But ... why are we any more important than people who aren't born with magic pulsing through their bodies? Surely *all* people are important?"

"Yes, but there are far less of your kind than there are of my kind. If the society knew the location of all the elemental communities around the world, they could easily wipe them out. Elementals would be close to extinct. And there's something so utterly wrong about that. The things you can do ... the way people like you used to live so in sync with nature instead of always *taking* ... That's the way the rest of us should live. We can learn so much from you, and that's never going to happen if there are none of you left."

There was a passion in his voice Ridley had never heard before. But beneath it, there was something else she couldn't quite identify. Envy? Before she could stop herself, she asked, "Do you wish you were like me?" Then, realizing what an intensely personal question that was, she shook her head. "Sorry, forget I asked that. It's totally none of my business. Here I am wasting time on personal questions, and you're still very much in pain." She hastily flipped through the pages of the old book. "I really should have marked this section a few days ago when I first looked up these conjurations. I should have known I would—Ah, here they are." She smoothed her hands over the pages, flattening the spine a little to keep the book open.

"Is the whole book full of medical conjurations?" Archer asked.

"No. The common theme is the movement type. The book starts off explaining this one simple hand movement, and then expands into all the conjurations that use that particular movement. The further you get into the book, the more complex the conjurations become."

"I see. Looks like that page you're on is past halfway."

"Yeah, apparently there's no such thing as a simple heal-ing conjuration. Okay, just give me a few minutes ..." She peered closer at the step-by-step pictures for the conjuration that was supposed to heal bruises. The following page had one for relieving swelling, and the next one was for minor cuts. All similar conjurations, but with a few key differences. She'd looked at them numerous times before but hadn't made a point of memorizing them until now. She reminded herself of the movements, her fingers trailing through the air above the book as she practiced them. "Okay, come closer," she said eventually.

Archer took a step forward but left a few inches of space between them this time, which Ridley was grateful for. She raised her hands. Magic pulsed beneath her skin, showing up as glowing blue lines where her veins were close to the sur-face, or, on other parts of her skin, as patches of pulsing blue. Her earlier conversation with Archer came to mind, and she wondered just how weird she would look if she let go properly and her entire body glowed blue. But that wasn't necessary for ordinary conjurations, so she pushed the thought from her mind. "Okay, so remember I have to do each conjuration at least three times, and there are three different conjurations."

Archer nodded. "I'm not going anywhere."

She quickly gathered up the wisps of her magic by scoop-ing at the air. Then, with the magic concentrated between her palms, she began the movements. Her palms touched, then curved away from each other, then came back around as her fingers danced in wave-like patterns. Without ceasing the motions, she managed to glance down at the book every few moments, just to be sure she was following the correct order. After sweeping her hands toward each other for the final time, she pushed the wisps of magic toward Archer's battered skin.

"Please stop looking at me," she said as she positioned her hands to begin the second iteration.

"Um ... you're right in front of my face," he said. "Where would you like me to look?"

"Close your eyes."

"Why?"

"It just makes me feel weird that you're watching me while I'm trying to do this."

"Okay, sorry." His eyes closed. "It's just ... I think you look cool with magic under your skin."

"Mm hmm." Ridley didn't want to argue when she was trying to concentrate. She performed the conjuration a second time, watched the resulting magic drift over Archer's face, then began a third time. "Okay," she said when she was done. "Next one." Returning her gaze to the book, she scanned the pictures for a quick reminder of the movements in the next conjuration.

"So I can't open my eyes yet?" Archer asked.

"Nope, sorry. We're only a third of the way through this."

"Can I talk?"

"You can," she said as she raised her hands again, "but don't expect me to reply while I'm trying to concentrate."

"So—"

"And do not make a comment about women and multitasking."

Archer pressed his puffy, blood-smeared lips together. "I'll be quiet," he whispered.

And, true to his word, he didn't say a thing throughout the second and third conjurations.

"Okay, I'm done," Ridley finally said. She snapped the book shut and placed it on the desk beside her.

"Thanks." Archer opened his eyes and raised one hand to prod carefully at his cheekbone.

"Feel any better?" Ridley asked.

"Um, I think so." He moved his jaw from side to side. "That doesn't feel so sore anymore."

"Your eye that was half closed is looking a little more open."

"Great. Is there a bathroom down here? I'll wipe all the blood off, and then you'll be able to see better if everything's healed."

"Yeah, back there." Ridley jabbed her thumb over her shoulder. "The door opposite the stairs." As Archer left the room, she let her eyes travel across the contents of Dad's desk. Her gaze fell on the carved wooden box her mom had given him years ago. The one with the tree carving on the lid. The same tree shape that had been drawn on the outside of her letter. With her forefinger, Ridley carefully traced the pattern, thinking again of all the secrets her father had kept for so long. She imagined him and Mom talking about her when she was little, discussing whether or not they would ever tell her about the other elementals. Had Mom agreed with Dad that it should always remain a secret? Or had she planned to tell Ridley one day?

Archer's footsteps interrupted her thoughts, and she twisted to look behind her as he walked back into the store. "Much better." She smiled. "You look almost normal."

"I feel almost normal. Except for—" He straightened, breathed in deeply, then grimaced and pressed one hand against the right side of his ribcage. "Yeah, except for that."

"Bruised ribs?" Ridley asked.

"Probably." He rounded the desk. "I think I got kicked a few times."

"You did. I can fix that too if you want."

He stopped in front of her as a smirk appeared on his lips. "You just want me to—"

"Oh my goodness, you are so predictable," she said with a laugh. "Fine, yes, if it'll boost your confidence, *I just want you to take your shirt off.*"

He pretended to pout. "It's not as fun when you say it."

"Sorry. I'll let you say it next time, okay?"

"Thanks. Though hopefully there won't be a next time that involves me getting kicked in the ribs." He reached for the back collar of his T-shirt and pulled it upward, wincing and bending to the right slightly as his arms stretched over his head. He draped the T-shirt over one shoulder, and though Ridley did an excellent job of keeping her expression neutral, she had to admit inwardly that she was impressed. Whatever

Archer had been doing to keep himself busy while living with the elementals in the French Prealps, it clearly involved some form of upper body physical activity.

"Right, let's start again," she said, looking away from his defined muscles and quickly raising her hands before he could make any stupid comments about her checking out his abs and arms.

"Hey, we don't have to do this all over again if you want to get to bed," he said. "I know you've got school in the morning."

"Oh, no, it's fine. Don't worry." She pulled at the wisps of magic that had risen away from her skin. "There's probably a conjuration that can make me less tired."

"You think?"

"I don't know." She paused, her hands frozen in the air between them. "That was a joke, but now I'm thinking I should try to find out. It would be amazing if I could give myself more rest without actually having to sleep."

She went through the movements of the conjurations for bruising and swelling, and, once done, she nudged the magic toward the splotchy red marks on the side of Archer's chest. The area didn't look too bad yet, but she was guessing it would be a mess of black and blue the following day if this conjuration didn't work. She sat back and lowered her hands. "Okay, that should do it." Looking up, she found Archer's eyes on her face already. "Hey, you weren't supposed to be watching."

"Sorry." He gave her a sheepish smile as he reached up for his T-shirt. "I can't help it. You're fascinating."

"Wow, thanks. I've always wanted to be stared at and called *fascinating* like some kind of weird, abstract artwork."

He pulled the T-shirt over his head, and Ridley relaxed now that she didn't have to avoid looking at the naked chest that had been directly in her line of sight. "That is definitely not what I meant when I said fascinating," Archer told her.

"Well, anyway." She looped her hair behind both ears and decided not to ask exactly what he meant by 'fascinating.' "Um, I'll let you out now?"

"Thanks. Oh, wait," he added before Ridley could jump off the desk. "I wanted to tell you something. I checked my commscreen while you were upstairs fetching the book." He removed the device from his pocket. A crack was now visible down the center of it, but it still lit up at his touch. "It's about the next person I thought we should try to speak to. Callie Hemingway. She was a singer before the Cataclysm. Do you remember her? She became famous as a teen, singing country-pop or something, and her career continued into her twenties."

"Her name sounds vaguely familiar," Ridley said, twisting a few strands of hair around one finger.

"Well, anyway, she's retreated from the public eye in recent years. I can't figure out where she lives. She seems to have hidden that pretty well. But there's an event this Friday—a birthday party for Jurenza, that singer with the super weird fashion sense—and my mom and Lilah are organizing it."

"Because your mom and Lilah are such great friends with Jurenza?"

"Apparently. Lilah said they hung out over the summer. So she and my mom have been talking about the guest list for days, who's RSVP'd and who hasn't, and how rude it is to not reply when the RSVP date was weeks ago. Blah, blah, blah, drama. Anyway, when I looked at the list, Callie's name jumped out at me immediately because I'd just been reading about her. She hadn't confirmed yet, but I see there was a message from Lilah to Mom earlier tonight." He peered at the device as he thumbed it again, adding, "She likes to copy my dad and me in on these things, in case we have any major objections to any of the guests. But my point—"

"Which you seem to be taking a long time to get to," Ridley muttered.

"Right, sorry. My point is that Callie's on the final list. Let me confirm I wasn't seeing things earlier ..." He tapped and scrolled a few times. "Yes, her name's definitely there." He lowered the commscreen. "Great news, since she seems to be somewhat of a hermit these days. Who knows when she might attend a public event again."

Ridley pulled her jacket tighter around herself and crossed her arms over her chest, ignoring the ache across her back and shoulders. "So you're breaking our agreement already and doing this one on your own? Because that's not how this is supposed to—"

"No, that's not what I was planning. I figured you'd insist on coming with."

"Oh. Good. And no one will have a problem with me being there?"

He gave her a quizzical look. "Why would someone have a problem with you being there? People usually have a date for these sorts of things. Lilah's already got my name down with a plus-one next to it. I'd be conspicuous if I *didn't* take someone."

"Right. Of course." Ridley unfolded her arms and pushed herself off the desk. "How could I forget about the endless string of girls always attached to young Mr. Davenport's arm?"

"Well, it's generally only one girl at a time who—"

"Yeah, okay, whatever." The last part of 'whatever' was swallowed up in a yawn, which Ridley managed to cover with the back of her hand. She blinked a few times and added, "Okay, I'll let you out now." Archer followed her, grabbing his damp jacket from the desk chair on the way. In the back room, Ridley glanced out of the window beside the door to the alley, remembering the moment she'd looked out and seen Archer and the man who'd ended up murdered. Had that only been last week? So many things had happened since then. Her entire world had shifted. "Earlier this evening," she said, turning to face Archer, "one of your friends mentioned Lawrence's memorial is tomorrow. I assume you'll be there?"

"Yes, along with the rest of my family. We have to show our support for the Madsons. According to the media, our families are close."

"And in reality?"

"My mother doesn't like the mayor's wife. Which means my dad isn't allowed to like her either. But it's a secret," he added in a whisper, "so don't tell Mrs. Madson."

Ridley chuckled. "I'll be sure to keep that one to myself next time I sit down for tea with her." She reached for the key in the door, her expression turning somber as she added, "I haven't heard much about the investigation into Lawrence's murder."

"Probably because no one knows much," Archer said. "As you and I are both aware, the guy who did it is long gone, and I guess the cops haven't found anyone else to pin the blame on yet."

Ridley nodded as she quietly turned the key, her thoughts turning to Shen. She tried to imagine where he might be, but her mind came up blank. How could she picture what her friend might be doing right now when it felt like she barely knew him?

"So, the party on Friday ..." Archer said.

"Mm hmm?"

"Do you think you can manage to look the part?"

Ridley pulled the door open, then turned a deadpan expression toward him. "I'm not *completely* unfamiliar with that way of life, in case you've forgotten. I think I can manage to fit in for a few hours."

"I don't doubt that. I just mean ..." His dark eyes bored into hers before looking away. "Nothing." He stepped outside, draping his jacket over his shoulder. Clearly the chilly air didn't bother him the way it bothered her. "I'll see you then."

"Okay," she answered, the word slipping out on a sigh. There was definitely something Archer wasn't saying, but it was late and she was tired, and if he didn't want to spit it out, she wasn't about to force him.

"Hey, wait, one more thing." He leaned back inside. "Are you sure you're okay? You hit that wall pretty hard earlier tonight."

She raised her hand to the lump on the back of her head. One or two of the conjurations she'd used on Archer would probably work to get rid of it. "I'll be fine," she told him, moving her hand to stifle another yawn. "See you Friday night."

"Yeah, okay. See you."

Archer's quiet footsteps disappeared into the night as Ridley shut the door. After making sure it was securely locked and bolted, she almost turned away. But something held her back. She peered out the window, leaning to the side so she could watch Archer walking away until he disappeared from view.

She realized there was a small smile on her lips, which she hastily banished before returning to the store to turn off the lamps. She had no business smiling like that for someone like Archer Davenport. With him gone from her mind—sort of, maybe not entirely—she finally headed upstairs to bed.

CHAPTER 9

RIDLEY MADE IT TO FRIDAY afternoon without anything going wrong. She didn't accidentally give away any secrets to Meera, Dad didn't find out she and Archer were looking for elementals, and no one tried to kill her. All in all, a perfectly normal few days.

She sat at the kitchen table with a mathematics textbook open on her commpad as she diligently worked through her homework. Her world might have tilted on its axis recently and never quite realigned itself, but she still had a scholarship to maintain if she was hoping to make it through the rest of the year as if nothing had changed. At least, that's what she was planning to tell Dad if he walked in and asked why she was working so hard on a Friday afternoon. But in the back of her mind, she was hoping she and Archer would be able to spend the weekend tracking down the other elementals. If that happened, there'd be no time for homework.

Her commscreen pinged, and she paused to read a message from Malachi. He wanted to meet up the following day to see what conjurations they might be able to teach each other.

He used the word 'skills' instead of conjurations, which Ridley was grateful for; she never knew if her messages were as private as she wanted to believe. She stared at the screen for a while, trying to figure out what to say. This was the kind of thing Dad had warned her about. This was why he'd said it would be better to stay away from other elementals. If they hung out together, the temptation would be to play around with their magic, and that only increased the risk of getting caught. In the end, she dictated a quick reply saying she'd let him know the next morning.

It was a little after five when Ridley finished her home-work. *Not bad*, she thought. The rest of senior year would probably *not* be this chilled. She gathered her notebooks, pens and commpad and carried them to her bedroom. She'd just checked her commscreen for the details of tonight's party when she heard footsteps—lighter than Dad's—in the living room. "Ridley, I'm here," someone called out to her.

Meera? Confused, Ridley hurried out of her bedroom and along the passage. Walking into the living room, she found Meera, also still in her school uniform, placing her commpad and notebooks on the upturned crate. Ridley hadn't heard a knock on the back door; Meera must have come in through the front of the store, which Dad was currently manning. "Um ... hi?" Ridley said.

Meera looked up. At the sight of Ridley's confused expression, her face fell. Her hands moved to her hips. "You forgot, didn't you."

"I, um ..."

"We made a plan to get started on the literature assign-ment. After you told me you couldn't do it on Tuesday night because you were busy with your dad. Remember? We said we'd do some work this evening and then get pizza and watch a movie."

"Right, yes."

Meera's thick eyebrows climbed a little higher. "So when I left for Debate Club after school and said, 'See you later,' and you were like, 'Yeah, okay,' were you just ... not even think-ing?"

"I guess not? Crap, I'm so sorry. I, uh ..." Ridley scrambled for an excuse, but she was so tired of all the secrets she al-ready kept from Meera. Maybe this one could remain as close to the truth as possible. "I have a date," she admitted.

Meera's mouth dropped open as her eyes grew even larger behind her glasses. "Oh my goodness, why didn't you tell me? Is it Derek? Did you change your mind about him?"

"No. I didn't tell you because I didn't think you'd approve."

"Oh dear." Meera screwed her face up as if she'd just tast-ed something unpleasant. "It's not that library monitor guy with the mole, is it? The one who kissed you at that horrible club you dragged me to last year?"

"That club was not horrible. It was just a bit loud. The wind dancing tunnels were seriously cool."

"Yeah, okay, whatever." Meera plopped onto the couch. "So who's the guy?"

Ridley crossed the room and joined Meera on the couch. Her lips stretched into something that was more grimace than smile. "Archer Davenport."

Meera was silent a moment too long. Then she started laughing. "Okay. Funny. Who is it really?"

Ridley folded her arms and leaned back against the cushions. "I am honestly attending a party in the Opal Quarter with Archer Davenport."

Meera's smile slowly faded. "You're being serious?"

"I am."

"But ... he's *Archer Davenport*."

"Yeah, so?" Ridley asked, feigning ignorance.

"So," Meera said, "aside from all the stuff the net articles say—billionaire playboy with nothing better to do than waste his parents' fortune—there's the fact that *you don't like him*."

Ridley shrugged. "He's actually not that bad. We've spent a little time together recently—"

"You have? When?"

Crap. More secrets she couldn't share. "Just, I don't know, here and there," she said vaguely, bending forward to pull her school socks a little higher.

"Have you forgotten how he framed Shen for that murder?" Meera demanded.

For a moment, Ridley couldn't say a thing. She'd lived with the truth for several days now, and hearing the version of the story that Meera believed—that pretty much everyone else in the city believed—was jarring. "That wasn't Archer," she told Meera. "It was his lawyers and his father. He didn't know what they'd done until afterwards. And he told the truth about it in the end, remember?"

Meera exhaled sharply through her nose. "So what are you saying? You like him?"

"Not in the way you mean," Ridley said, partly to Meera and partly to herself. Her subconscious needed to understand this so it wouldn't mess around with her dreams again like it had on Tuesday night after Archer had left. She would have been totally fine with a restful, dreamless sleep, but her brain decided to replay Archer standing with his hands braced on the desk on either side of her. Getting inappropriately close and invading her personal space. Which, for some reason, the dream version of herself hadn't seemed to mind at all. The dream version of Ridley had actually reached out, fisted a hand in his T-shirt, and pulled him closer. Perhaps because dream-Archer's face was utterly perfect, not a bruise or blemish in sight, and dream-Ridley had had the crazy urge to kiss that beautiful face.

"This date is more of a friends thing," she continued, shoving aside the memory of her dream. "It's a party his mom is hosting. He needed someone to go with, and I happened to be around when he was making plans. I don't know, it just sort of happened." She shrugged. "It's not a big deal."

"Oh. Okay." Meera looked around the room. "Well ... can I at least help you get ready? We can pretend we're still friends for a little while longer."

"Meera!" Ridley launched across the couch and tackled her friend in a giant hug against the cushions. "Obviously we're still friends. What are you talking about?"

"Well if you're hanging out with people like Archer now—"

"Don't be so silly!" Ridley grabbed one of the cushions and smacked the side of Meera's head. "There. Did that knock some sense into you?"

"Hey, my glasses!" Meera's hands flew up to protect her face.

Ridley pulled away and lowered the cushion to her lap. "Your glasses are fine."

Meera adjusted the enormous frames so they sat a little straighter on her nose. "Is it something I did?" she asked. "Please just tell me that. Because you've been distant for days, and I still haven't heard anything directly from Shen, so now I'm wondering if maybe *I'm* the problem, and neither of you—"

"Do you want me to smack you with the cushion again?" Ridley asked. "Because clearly it didn't work the first time." She placed one hand over Meera's and said, "There is *nothing* you did wrong. I'm just ... I don't know, everything's been a little weird since that man died outside my home."

"Understatement of the year," Meera muttered, which Ridley couldn't agree with more.

"Look, I can't speak for Shen," she told Meera, "but you and I will always be friends, okay?"

Meera let out a long sigh. "Okay. Good. But I can't promise I will ever like Archer Davenport, so don't expect us to go on any double dates or anything."

Ridley couldn't help laughing at that ludicrous idea. "There will never be any double dates, because Archer and I will never be dating."

"Good to know." Meera leaned down toward her bag and

removed a large hair clip from the strap. As she twisted her shiny black hair into a knot and fastened it with the clip, she asked, "So what are you wearing? I know you have a few dresses for Wallace Academy events, but they're not the glitzy, glam, figure-hugging, red carpet type dress you're probably supposed to wear to an evening event hosted by Aurelia Davenport."

Ridley raised an eyebrow. "You've been streaming too much of that entertainment news show."

"Hey, give me a break, it's my one guilty pleasure. And thank goodness one of us watches it, or you'd show up in the wrong kind of dress. You're probably *still* going to show up in the wrong kind of dress because I know you don't own anything that looks like what I've seen on Celeb News Nightly."

"You're right, I don't," Ridley said. "But my mom had plenty of dresses like that."

Meera paused. She'd clearly been about to say something else before Ridley mentioned her mother. "Your mom?" she asked carefully.

"Yes. So, I know this might sound weird, but part of my dad's wardrobe still has a bunch of her stuff, including her fancy dresses. I don't really have any other option, so ... I thought I'd wear one of them. Obviously the styles will be a bit outdated, but if I pick something that's sort of simple and classic, then it should be okay, right?"

"Okay," Meera said slowly. "That could work. If you don't feel super weird about it."

"Well, it does feel weird. But also ... maybe ..." Ridley lifted her shoulders. "Kind of cool? To wear something that used to be hers?"

"Yeah, definitely." Meera nodded, but Ridley could tell she was still a little uncertain about the idea. "Are the dresses still in good condition?" she asked.

"I think so. I don't actually know, but they're inside those special garment bags, so they're probably fine. Do you want to go look?"

"In your dad's bedroom?"

"Yes."

"He won't mind us being in there?"

"No, I don't think so." Ridley didn't admit that she hadn't actually asked her father. But he'd given her Mom's scarves when she asked, and he'd never told her she *couldn't* touch any of Mom's other things. Ridley's reasons for not asking about the dresses had more to do with not wanting to dredge up old memories that would cause Dad pain. And also because she hadn't told him about tonight's party. She was hoping she'd be able to sneak out without Dad seeing her and let him think she was spending the evening at Meera's.

"Okay, cool, let's have a look," Meera said, sounding a little more enthusiastic than she had at first.

They walked into Dad's bedroom, and Ridley stopped in front of the side of the wardrobe he never used. She gripped the handle, paused, and took a steadying breath before pulling it open to reveal several garment bags, two coats, a scarf hanger, and a few shoe boxes. Then she wrapped her arms around her middle, simply staring, working up the courage to remove the garment bags from the wardrobe.

"Ridley?" Meera asked quietly.

"Yeah, I'm okay." She uncrossed her arms and stepped forward. She removed the bags one at a time and handed them to Meera, who lay them out on Dad's bed. There were eight in total, which was only a fraction of the dresses Ridley remembered her mom owning. She wondered what had happened to the others. Then she wondered why Dad had kept any of them at all. "Okay, let's look inside." Her fingers trembled just a little as she reached for the zip at the top of the first bag.

Memories flooded her mind as she opened each bag: Mom getting dressed and styling her dark, glossy hair in her expansive bedroom up on the hundred and fifty-second floor of Aura Tower. Mom twirling in front of the floor-length mirror in the apartment's entrance hall. Mom's smooth, powdered cheek brushing against Ridley's as she said goodnight before leaving with Dad for whatever event they were attending. Ridley could almost smell Mom's perfume, could almost feel her arms wrapping around her.

"Ridley?" Meera asked again, and Ridley realized she'd been standing motionless with her arms at her sides, staring at the four dresses she'd revealed so far.

She inhaled deeply before clearing her throat. "Yes?"

"What about this one?" Meera asked, pointing to the bag she'd just opened. The gap in the garment bag revealed glittery, powder blue fabric. "Blue looks good on you," Meera continued. "And the style seems to be fairly simple." She unzipped the bag fully and removed the dress. "Yes, it's just long and strapless. Nothing too dated about it." She lifted the dress and turned it around. "And it laces up at the back, so that's good. Makes it slightly adjustable, in case you're not exactly the same size your mom was."

Ridley nodded. "Yeah, that looks good." She opened the remaining bags to see what her other options were, but Meera was right. The blue dress was the best. She returned the other garment bags to the wardrobe and closed the doors as Meera draped the blue dress and its bag over her arm. "I'm gonna have a shower before getting ready. If you don't want to wait around, I understand. You can—"

"Of course I'm going to wait, silly," Meera said as she followed Ridley out of the room. "Who's going to lace you up if I'm not here?"

"Oh, right, I didn't think of that."

"Exactly. Go shower. I'll catch up on Celeb News Nightly."

When Ridley was done in the shower, she found Meera lounging on her bed with a commpad propped against a pillow. "I still can't believe you watch that stuff," she said as she quickly pulled on some underwear.

"Yeah, well, I'm tired of watching documentaries and the news and other intellectual stuff. I keep seeing the same story about Lawrence Madson's murder, because apparently there's nothing else to report."

Ridley paused while removing the dress from its hanger. "Oh, has there been some new development?"

"Yes, something about an eye-witness coming forward yesterday." Meera paused her celebrity show and looked at

Ridley. "Some guy who said he was on the private balcony next to the one Lawrence was murdered on. There was something that partially obstructed his view—plants or whatever—but apparently he saw part of what happened."

An icy finger of fear trailed down Ridley's spine. "Really?" she asked, her voice slightly higher than usual.

"Yeah, but it's probably just someone looking for attention," Meera said. "I mean, why did it take him four days to go to the police with this information? That sounds suspicious to me."

"Yeah, maybe," Ridley said, feeling a tiny bit better. Hopefully Meera was right. She couldn't remember being able to see onto the balcony next to Lawrence's one. Wasn't that the point of having *private* balconies? So that no one could see what was going on?

She did her best to push her concerns to the back of her mind as she stepped carefully into the dress. Meera climbed off the bed to help with the laces at the back. After what seemed like a whole lot of tugging and adjusting, Meera said, "Okay, I think that's fine."

Ridley turned both ways in front of her wardrobe mirror as she tried to see herself from all angles. "Do you think it fits properly?" she asked, sliding her hands down her sides and over her hips.

"Um, yes." Meera pushed her glasses up her nose and moved to Ridley's side. "Mostly. It's just the bust that looks a little loose. Your mom must have had bigger boobs than you."

Ridley laughed. "Yeah, she did. It's fine, let me put on my

other strapless bra. It has more padding."

"Okay great. 'Cause I don't think I can lace the dress any tighter than it already is. Ugh, wait." Meera made a face at her. "This means we have to do the laces all over again, right?"

Ridley gave her an apologetic smile. "Yes, sorry."

After the bra-switch and redoing the laces, Meera decided Ridley looked a little better in the bust department. She returned to the bed, and Ridley moved on to her hair next. Fortunately, she'd attended enough stuffy Wallace Academy events that she could pull of a half-decent hairdo when the need arose. While other girls went to a salon to get their hair done, Ridley and Meera had spent a number of hours during their first year at Wallace watching DIY hairstyle videos online.

"That looks good," Meera said from Ridley's bed, pausing Celeb News Nightly as Ridley finished pinning her hair into a loose French twist that left stray pieces of hair framing her face.

"Thanks." Ridley turned her back to the wardrobe mirror and held her commscreen up, using it as a second mirror to check the back of her head. "A-plus for hair," she decided.

"Oh my gosh, if only it were a real course at school," Meera said. "I feel like we would ace it. We've certainly learned way more than all those girls who hire stylists to come to their homes or book their salon appointments before every Wallace Academy event."

"Definitely. Okay, just makeup, and then I'm done." Ridley headed to the tiny bathroom she shared with Dad and opened the second drawer of the cabinet beneath the basin. She removed the bag with her small makeup collection and set about applying as little as she figured she could get away with.

She was almost done when her commscreen, sitting on the edge of the basin, lit up and started singing as it displayed Archer's face. With one half of the mascara container in each hand, she tapped the screen with her pinky finger. "Hey, what's up?" she asked as she leaned closer to the mirror and carefully dragged the end of the mascara wand over her lashes.

"Are you there?" Archer asked, and Ridley realized the only thing her commscreen could see was the bathroom ceiling.

"Yeah, sorry, I'm here." She waved the mascara wand over her commscreen before bringing it back to her eyelashes. "Just busy."

"Oh, hey. Um, what time shall I come pick you up?"

"Pick me up?" Done with the lashes on one eye, she began applying mascara to the other. "I'll just meet you there. It's inside Aura Tower, right?"

"Yes, the ballroom level. But if you're meeting me here, that means you have to walk down a grimy street and sit in a grimy bus while you're all dressed up."

"So?" She lowered the mascara wand and leaned over the commscreen. "You know I've been doing that for years, right? How do you think I get myself to every Wallace Academy event?"

"Uh …"

She screwed the mascara cap back on and dropped it into the makeup bag. "Not something you've ever thought about, obviously."

"Just let me bring one of our cars. It's not a big deal."

"*One* of our cars?" Meera shouted from the bedroom, and Ridley realized she was listening in on the conversation.

"What was that?" Archer asked.

"Nothing," Ridley told him, trying to keep her laugh to herself. "Look, don't be weird about this, okay? I'll see you there." She swiped at her commscreen to end the call. Looking up, she saw Meera in the mirror's reflection, leaning in the doorway. "Are my calls more entertaining than your celeb show?" Ridley asked, one brow arched.

Ignoring the question, Meera said, "I can't believe that Archer-freaking-Davenport has your number and just, like, casually calls you."

Ridley shook her head, but there was a smile on her lips as she returned her makeup bag to the cabinet. "He's just a guy. Once upon a time he was an annoying little boy who teased his sister and her friends and tried to gross us out with things like mud and frogs and snot. He even flashed his bare butt at us once."

Meera slapped a hand over her mouth as she burst out laughing. "That did *not* happen," she said between snorts of laughter.

"True story." Ridley turned to face Meera. "It's hard to think of Archer Davenport as this superior, intimidating celebrity when you've seen his seven-year-old ass."

Meera tilted her head back, laughter consuming her. But as she recovered, her smile slowly slipped away. "Sometimes I forget you had this whole other life before I met you. The kind of life you and I make fun of now."

"Well, fortunately, I don't have that life anymore," Ridley said, "or it would be kind of awkward for you and me to make fun of it."

A small smile returned to Meera's lips. "Yeah. Anyway, you look amazing. I wasn't sure about this dress idea when you suggested it—I thought it might be weird—but it really is special to wear something of your mom's."

"It is," Ridley agreed, pushing aside the small part of her that wanted to cry every time she thought about Mom never seeing her like this. She checked the time on her commscreen as she walked out of the bathroom. "I'll probably leave in about twenty minutes. Wouldn't want to be too early. That would be awkward."

They spent the next twenty minutes watching more Celeb News Nightly, Meera lying on the bed and Ridley sitting uncomfortably upright in her desk chair. When it was almost time to leave, she removed an appropriate purse from the top shelf of her wardrobe and, while Meera wasn't looking, slipped a copy of the letter inside.

Meera paused the show, scooted to the edge of the bed, and stood. "Okay, let me just grab my things." They walked through to the living room, where Meera quickly packed her commpad and notebooks back into her school bag.

"Can I ask one more favor?" Ridley asked. "Can you leave

just before me and go through the front of the store?"

Meera raised an eyebrow. "So you can sneak out the back without your Dad seeing you?"

Ridley pressed her lips into a guilty smile. "Maybe."

"So he doesn't know?"

"He thinks I'm spending the evening with you."

Meera groaned. "You know I can't lie. What if he asks me something? And won't he think it's weird that you're not leaving with me now?"

"You don't have to say anything. He'll just think I'm joining you later."

"Ugh, okay. I'll try to leave as quickly as possible."

Meera descended the stairs, and Ridley tiptoed—slightly difficult in heels, but she made it work—a few steps behind her. "Thanks for your help," she whispered just as Meera reached the bottom step.

"You're welcome," Meera whispered back, looking over her shoulder. "I hope it's a fun evening." Then she crossed the back room and walked into the store. "Bye, Mr. Kayne," she said loudly, and it sounded to Ridley like she might almost be running—a risky activity in an antique store with narrow aisles between overloaded tables, cabinets and shelves. Ridley tiptoed down the last few stairs, listening for a crash. When it didn't come, she figured Meera must have made it to the other side of the store. She hurried as quietly as possible across the room toward the back door. She inserted her key—

"Ridley?"

She froze, then slowly turned around. Dad stood at the

back of the store beside his desk. For several moments, the two of them simply stared at one another. Ridley's heart pounded wildly, and her hand tightened around her purse. Her father's expression was unreadable. Eventually he said, "That's ..."

"Mom's dress," Ridley quietly filled in when it seemed Dad couldn't finish his sentence.

"Where are you going?" he asked. She still couldn't read his expression. He didn't seem angry, which was a relief, but she worried he might be feeling something worse.

"Archer invited me to a party," she said, the idea of making up some story not even crossing her mind. She'd told Meera the truth—most of it, at least—so she may as well tell Dad the truth too.

A frown creased his features. "I thought you didn't like Archer."

"I thought you didn't like him either," she replied.

"Is that why you didn't tell me about this party?" He walked into the back room and stopped in front of her. "You didn't think I'd approve of you going out somewhere with him?"

"It isn't like that," she said, skirting the question. "It isn't a *date*. Just a birthday party his mother is organizing for someone, and she expects Archer to be there. I somehow ended up agreeing to go with him. And, I mean, he's not that bad. He's ..."

"Not the same person who left the city over a year ago?" Dad asked, arching an eyebrow.

"Sounds stupid, I know," Ridley said with a brief eye-roll. "But I guess with everything he's ended up getting involved in, he couldn't help but change."

Dad nodded. "I agree. It was a shock to me when he turned up several months ago, needing a place to hide. But he quickly convinced me he was on our side." Dad scrubbed one hand through his unkempt salt-and-pepper hair. "We spoke a lot then, and he isn't the person I thought he was. Or at least, he isn't the person he's always allowed the media to portray him as. Anyway. I, uh ..." He cleared his throat and lowered his arm. "Well, I know we've never had any serious discussion about boyfriends—"

"Oh, gosh," Ridley groaned.

"—because you've never found anyone you wanted to go out with more than a handful of times."

"You know why."

"Yes, because it's hard to keep the whole magic thing hidden when you're getting *that* close to someone, but—"

"Dad, please." Ridley's face was just about on fire by now.

"But Archer already knows, so if you *do* feel that way about him—"

"Dad!" she interrupted. "Remember when I said it's not like that? It's really not like that."

"Right, of course, I'm sorry." Dad smiled and placed a hand on her shoulder. "You look ..." He sighed and shook his head. "This dress is perfect on you."

She swallowed, pressed her lips together, and asked, "You don't mind? It isn't, like, completely weird?"

"No, it's ... I can't really describe it, but I know your mother would have loved to see you looking so glamorous and grown-up in one of her dresses. She would have—" His voice hitched, and he cleared his throat once more. "She would have had so much fun helping you get all dressed up."

Ridley inhaled deeply, blinked a few times, then wrapped her arms around her father. "I love you," she whispered.

"Love you too, Riddles." He held her tight for a moment before letting go. "So where will you be tonight?"

"Aura Tower. Ballroom level."

Dad nodded, the corners of his eyes crinkling as he smiled. "Fancy schmancy. Just like the old days."

"Yeah. Not really inside my comfort zone, but I'm sure I can handle it."

Dad laughed. "Of course you can. Hopefully you'll actually enjoy it."

Ridley turned back to the door, unlocked it, and pulled it open. Outside, the evening air was cool against her bare arms and shoulders. She thought about going back inside to get a scarf or a coat, but it would be warm inside Aura Tower's ballroom, and she didn't have to survive long until she got there. Hopefully it wouldn't start raining.

She dropped her key into her purse, then lifted the lower part of her dress so it wouldn't touch the dirty street. She'd barely taken a few steps forward when she looked up and stopped. A resigned sigh escaped her lips. Parked right at the entrance to her alley—despite what she'd repeatedly told Archer—was a shiny, dark blue vehicle.

CHAPTER 10

RIDLEY WOULD HAVE BEEN wary of the car if not for the smartly dressed young man leaning against the side of it. Archer's hands were pushed casually into the pockets of his pants as he stared down the main street, watching something Ridley couldn't see. He was ridiculously good-looking in his perfectly tailored suit. If Ridley had been a different type of girl, she might have stood there drooling. *But I'm not*, she reminded herself. *Do not be that kind of girl.* So instead she crossed her arms. "Seriously?" she called out. "I told you not to worry about bringing a car here."

He turned his head toward her, and a wide smile spread across his face. He straightened, removing his hands from his pockets. "It was no problem."

"I would have been fine on the bus," she said as she approached the vehicle. It looked like one of those driverless ones with only one door on either side. "You really didn't need to worry about me."

"Okay, well let's say I did it for selfish reasons then. I didn't want to have you walking beside me through Aura Tower with dirt on the hem of your dress and a chocolate wrapper stuck to your butt."

Ridley managed to hold in a snort. "When was the last time you took a bus? The chocolate wrappers are on the floor, not the seats."

"Never," he told her as he opened the car door for her. "I've never been on a bus."

She ducked her head and slid onto the leather seat. "I guess that's not surprising," she muttered as she shut the door. Archer walked behind the car and climbed in the other side. Between the two front seats, which were turned to face the seats Ridley and Archer sat in, was a raised console with a screen. Archer leaned forward, tapped through several menus on the screen, then settled back.

"You look lovely, by the way," he said to her.

"Um, thanks. You don't look too bad yourself." He looked swoon-worthily gorgeous, to be more accurate, but he was probably aware of that already, and Ridley wasn't about to increase the size of his ego. "No paparazzi following you today?" she asked lightly as the car pulled away from the curb. "This would make a wonderfully scandalous headline, don't you think? 'Billionaire Archer Davenport Dating Girl From City Slums.'"

"Nope, haven't seen a single one." Archer peered out of the window on his side of the car. "I'm disappointed. Clearly they don't like to hang around this part of the city."

"That's because people like *you* don't hang around this part of the city."

He turned away from the window to look at her. "This district is hardly a slum," he said, as if that part had only just registered in his brain.

"Yeah, but it makes a snappy headline."

"True. Also, I'm not a billionaire. That would be my father."

"Details," Ridley said. "You know the tabloids never get them right."

His expression sobered. "I am all too aware of that."

Remembering what Meera had told her, Ridley asked if Archer had seen the latest development on Lawrence's case.

"Yes, but I'm not worried," he said. "I would definitely have been recognized if I'd been seen, but I haven't been hauled in for questioning. And no one's come looking for you either. So I'm guessing we weren't seen. Or if we were, this guy didn't see us clearly, so he couldn't give the cops a good enough description." Archer's hand brushed over hers for a moment. "Don't worry about it."

"Yeah, okay. You're probably right."

The conversation turned to Lawrence's memorial, and after that, Ridley asked about the other elementals on their list. Archer said he'd found various online public profiles for each of them, so he'd confirmed the faces that matched the names, but he hadn't discovered where any of them lived or worked. Ridley almost suggested he ask Lilah for help before remembering he wasn't aware of his sister's hacking expertise. At least, that's the way it had seemed.

The buzz of a scanner drone reached her ears, and Ridley

turned her frown toward the window. The drone, flying unusually low, soared past the window before stopping to hover over a taxi in the next lane over. Ridley toyed absently with the two cylindrical pendants on the silver chain around her neck, watching as the drone glided smoothly away and disappeared. When she looked at Archer again, his eyes were on her necklace. "Do you ever get nervous?" he asked.

She lifted one shoulder in a casual shrug as she lowered her hand to her lap. "Maybe a little. Sometimes. But it's always worked. No scanner has ever detected a problem."

"And the necklace has never fallen off?"

"No. But it wouldn't matter if it did." She hadn't told him before about the illegal second copies of her AI1 and AI2, but she had no reason to keep the information from him now. "I have backups," she admitted.

His lips lifted into a smile. "Of course you do. I should have known you wouldn't place all your trust in a necklace. Where do you keep the backups?"

Ridley extended her right leg and pulled the dress high enough to reveal her ankle and the silver chain encircling it. "Sexy," Archer said, his grin still in place.

"Totally," Ridley said with a roll of her eyes. She looked out of her window just as the car stopped in front of the steps leading up to the entrance of Aura Tower. Archer pressed a button on the center console, and both car doors opened. Ridley climbed out and smoothed the wrinkles of her dress. She turned to close the door, but Archer was already there. "You really don't need to do that," she told him.

"I know," he said, closing her door anyway.

Together, they ascended the stairs, Ridley's hand tight around her purse and her heart thudding faster than usual against her ribcage. It was always strange to return to Aura Tower, but returning for an event like the one she was about to walk into was even stranger. She couldn't help thinking that if the Cataclysm had never happened, nights like tonight would most likely be a normal part of her life.

As they crossed the sweeping foyer, Ridley's heels clicking against the marble floor, they neared two men shaking hands. Ridley's breath caught in her throat when she realized one of them was Mayor Madson. He let go of the other man's hand. Then he turned and moved toward them, his eyes meeting hers. Time seemed to slow, and it felt to Ridley as if he could see right into her. That somehow he *knew*. She sensed the truth seeping out of her and writing itself all over her face: *I'm an elemental. I'm the thing you want to rid the world of. I was there when your son was shot. I know who killed him.*

Then the moment was over, and Mayor Madson released her from his cold, almost lifeless gaze. He gave Archer a small nod as he walked past them. Ridley let go of the breath she'd been holding. "Everything okay?" Archer asked, looking sidelong at her.

"Yes. Just a moment of paranoia." She smiled at him. "But I'm fine."

They stopped in front of one of the elevators. "Have you been inside the ballroom here before?" Archer asked. The doors slid apart and they walked forward. Another couple joined them in the elevator, dressed just as smartly as she and Archer were.

"Once, I think," she answered as Archer pressed the button for the hundred and fortieth floor. "But I don't remember much. I was only about six or seven. It was an early evening event, and children were allowed to attend."

"The views are stunning," he said. "It's situated on a corner of the building, so two of the four walls are entirely glass."

"That sounds vaguely familiar." Ridley focused on the man and woman standing in front of her as the elevator began to ascend. They hadn't selected a floor, which, along with their attire, suggested they were attending the same party she and Archer were headed to. They held hands, their fingers laced together, and Ridley watched as the man's thumb brushed slowly against the woman's.

She looked away, feeling as though she were intruding on a private moment. She tried to think of something to say, but no safe topic came to mind. Did she and Archer only ever speak about things that were meant to remain secret?

Before the silence inside the elevator could swell to an uncomfortable level, a ping sounded and the doors slid open. The man and woman walked forward into a wide corridor with an arched ceiling, and Ridley and Archer followed. A plush red carpet lined the marble floor. Ridley smiled to herself as she imagined Meera's squeal when she told her about this. "There was an *actual* red carpet?" she would say.

They followed the corridor around a corner, where it came to an end in front of an open set of double doors. Gold lettering above the doorway spelled out the words Mannheimer Ballroom. Just inside the doorway stood a man in a suit with a commpad in his hand. The couple walking ahead of Ridley and Archer paused to give their names and waited while the man checked his commpad. After a nod from him, they walked forward. Ridley was about to stop as well, but the man smiled at Archer and said, "Good evening, Mr. Davenport."

Of course, Ridley thought. She shouldn't have expected anything else.

The ceiling rose high above, while a grand stairway led downward into a vast room filled with beautiful people, soft lighting, tastefully decorated tables, and two walls made entirely of glass. Here on the upper level, a balcony encircled the entire room, perhaps so that people could have quieter, more private conversations while still enjoying the ambience of the ballroom.

"This way," Archer said, leading her toward the left instead of down the stairs. "Let's check things out from up here. Hopefully we can spot Callie."

"What does she look like?" Ridley asked. Archer pulled out his commscreen and showed her a photo. Callie Hemingway looked to be in her thirties, with caramel skin, blond hair that was more golden than Ridley's, and a heart-shaped face. "Okay, got it," Ridley said. She leaned against the balcony railing and looked down, noting two security guards in suits at the bottom of the stairs. "Do your mother's events tend to get a little wild?" she asked, nodding to the two men.

"A *little* wild?" Archer said. "It'll be like a circus in here once things get going." For a moment, Ridley thought he might be serious. Then he started laughing. "Nope, no wild parties for Aurelia Davenport. They're not wild in the least, but every now and then you wind up with one or two people who drink too much and get unruly. Those kinds of people will be swiftly removed."

"Noted," Ridley said with a nod. "I'll try to hold back on the punch." She moved further along the balcony, her eyes scanning the crowd below for Callie Hemingway. She thought she might have spotted her wearing a green dress, but it was impossible to tell when the woman moved a little further to the side and ended up partly hidden behind a giant crystal vase containing an arrangement of exotic flowers. Though it was hardly a priority right now, Ridley couldn't help but take a moment to appreciate the flowers. She knew they must be real. Aurelia Davenport would never use fake flowers, and the fact that they would have cost a not-so-small fortune wouldn't have deterred her.

Not important right now, she reminded herself silently. Leaning a little further over the railing, she tried to see past the flower arrangement. "I can't tell if that's her behind the flowers," she said to Archer. "Can you see her?" When he didn't answer, she straightened and glanced over her shoulder—and caught him for a moment with his eyes aimed downward before they darted up to meet hers. "Are you kidding me?" she asked. "You're seriously checking out my butt instead of looking for Callie?"

"Well, not *just* your—"

"You can't even tell me you're making sure there's no chocolate wrapper stuck there, which is an excuse you could have tried if you'd let me take the bus."

An amused smile pulled at his lips. "I wasn't planning to go for any fake excuse. You look amazing. I have no problem telling you that."

After a moment of silent astonishment, Ridley turned away to hide both her frustration and her flushed cheeks. "I thought we were supposed to be looking for Callie."

"Yes, that's her in the green dress. Behind the flowers."

"That's what I was asking you," Ridley replied with a groan. "Anyway, it's good to know she's definitely here. But we can't talk to her in this room. We need to get her out somehow."

"Yes, definitely."

"Also," Ridley added, "I think I should talk to her alone."

Archer leaned sideways against the railing and looked at Ridley. "You think she might hold a personal grudge against me, like Malachi?

Ridley shrugged. "There's always a chance."

"Highly unlikely, but you're probably right about talking to her alone. It'll look strange if both you and I accompany her out of the ballroom. If it's just you, then you can probably wait till she goes to the ladies or something. Find her there, then tell her you need to talk outside. Definitely don't say anything important while you're still in the bathroom."

Ridley folded her arms and fixed her gaze on Archer. "I'm not a complete amateur."

"Sorry, just making sure."

"Okay." Ridley looked down into the ballroom again. "Shall we head downstairs now?"

"Yes. Let's go and *mingle*. That's what my mother would—Ah." Archer paused, his gaze focused on the room below once more. "Speak of the devil. There she is, along with the rest of my perfect family."

Ridley followed his gaze and saw Mr. and Mrs. Davenport greeting a politician whose name Ridley couldn't remember. Lilah was at their side, smiling politely. Like Archer, all three of them were dark-haired and dark-eyed. Aurelia Davenport's hair was up in a glamorous style, while Lilah's dark locks fell in voluminous curls around her face, pinned back on one side with a sparkly clip that was probably encrusted in diamonds. Alastair Davenport wasn't the tallest man in the room, but he exuded the kind of confidence that made him appear to tower above everyone else.

They were, as Archer had said, the picture of perfection. Sophisticated. Refined. And yet, for a moment, Ridley couldn't help remembering an evening long ago when she and Lilah had raced through the penthouse dressed up like superheroes in capes while Archer and his friend chased after them with wooden swords and Mr. and Mrs. Davenport laughed as they sat curled against one another on a couch. "Did you really mean what you said about leaving the city without telling them where you're going?" Ridley asked. "And never returning?"

"Yes." Archer nodded toward the stairs, and together they headed back that way. "I can't live the life my father's planned out for me."

"Can't you do something else that involves you helping people like me while also staying in the city?"

He grinned at her. "Worried you're going to miss me?"

She smacked him with her purse. "Be serious."

With a sigh, he looked forward again. "No, I can't do that. My father won't let me. In his mind, the only option for me is to take over his company one day. And aside from that, he's just ..." Archer shook his head. "We disagree on too many things."

"You could move to another building," Ridley suggested as they descended the stairs. "You don't necessarily have to leave the city and disappear completely. You could still do some kind of work to help those like me, but here in Lumina City."

Archer shook his head again. "I'll never be truly free as long as he knows I'm alive."

Well, that sounded sinister. Ridley sensed there was something deeper and more complex going on between Archer and his father, but it didn't feel right to ask about it. She might be on friendly terms with him now, and they had shared many secrets in the past week or so, but this felt like something off-limits.

They reached the base of the stairs, and Ridley looked around the ballroom. Women in designer dresses and men in tailored suits mingled between the tables and around the dance floor. Ridley figured the birthday girl herself, popular singer Jurenza, must be around here somewhere. But Callie

Hemingway was the one Ridley was here for, so she kept her eyes peeled for golden locks and a green dress as Archer directed her through the crowd. They ended up on the far side of the room near one of the glass walls, and Ridley sucked in a breath at the sight of the glittering city spread out around them. "Incredible," she said to Archer. "I know your place is even higher, but there's something about standing at such an enormous window with such a high ceiling that makes this view seem so impressive."

"I know," he answered, staring out. "It almost feels as if there's nothing separating you from the world out there. As if you could step forward and just fall into the night."

Just let go and fall into it. Grandpa's words whispered at the edge of Ridley's mind. She shivered at the idea. No way in hell would she be falling from this kind of height while letting go of all control. Maybe her magic would automatically take over, but what if it didn't? "Well, anyway," she said, turning away from the window. "I wish we could watch the city all night, but we need to watch Callie instead." She scanned the ballroom, her eyes meeting those of a young blond man nearby. She gave him a polite nod, her gaze moving on until she picked out the green dress. "Looks like Callie's talking to someone else now. We should get closer."

They wandered casually between the tables, Ridley asking random questions about random people to make it appear as though they were in conversation rather than following someone around. "Is that the girl who got caught skinny-dipping in the school pool during an awards ceremony one year?" she asked, catching sight of a familiar face framed by vibrant red hair.

"Yes, that's the one," Archer replied. "The skinny-dipping may or may not have been related to an ongoing string of dares that I ... well, may or may not have been part of."

Ridley laughed. "I think I'm relieved we were never friends at school." Her eyes moved on from the redhead and landed on the same blond man from a few minutes before. He still appeared to be watching her. "That guy behind the skinny-dipper keeps looking at me," she told Archer. "It's weird."

"Well, as previously noted," Archer said as he followed her gaze to the young man, "you do look lovely, so there's nothing weird about him checking you out. Perhaps he's working up the courage to ask you to dance."

"I don't know. He doesn't look happy."

"Probably because you're with me." Archer swung an arm around Ridley's shoulders. She swatted his hand away as she smothered another laugh.

"Why don't you go find us something to drink?"

Archer smirked. "So your admirer can talk to you without feeling intimidated by me?"

"No, so I can speak to Callie. It looks like she's just finished talking to that old lady. So you go do something else—" she turned him in the direction of the nearest waiter "—and I'll make up an excuse to talk to her."

"Yes, ma'am." He gave her a lazy salute, then walked away before Ridley could tell him exactly how she felt about being called 'ma'am.' She sighed and stepped around two men in the midst of a heated debate about commscreen brands—only to see that Callie was now chatting with someone else. Apparently, when you spent most of your time being a recluse, lots of people wanted to catch up with you when you finally did venture into the real world.

"Crap," Ridley muttered beneath her breath. She turned away, and almost smacked into Archer's mother. "Hi, um, Mrs. Davenport." Ridley took a step backward, putting a respectable amount of space between her and the party's host, and noticed then that Lilah was standing there too.

"Ridley?" Mrs. Davenport asked with a frown. "Ridley Kayne?" Her eyes darted around as if she might find an explanation for why a girl from a family she no longer associated with was standing in the middle of one of her glitzy events. "Are you … in the right place?" she asked.

Lilah's piercing gaze swept the full length of Ridley's body. "I don't think she is," she told her mother before Ridley could reply.

"She's with me," Archer said, returning to Ridley's side at that moment. He had a champagne glass in each hand, both of which he placed on the table beside them before facing his mother.

"Archer, darling." A strained smile appeared on Mrs. Davenport's lips. "What do you mean?"

"I mean she's here as my date." He slipped one arm around Ridley's back and pressed a quick kiss to her temple as if it were the most natural thing in the world. "We've reconnected since I returned to Lumina City."

"I—that's—lovely," Mrs. Davenport said, and Ridley thought it was probably the only time she'd ever heard the woman stammer over anything. It was entirely worth the strange sensation of Archer's lips on her skin just to see the horror in Mrs. Davenport's eyes and written all over Lilah's face.

"Oh, I need to greet Madeline," Mrs. Davenport said hastily, her eyes landing on someone behind Ridley. "Lilah, you must thank her for putting you in touch with that professor."

"Actually, I'd like to speak to—"

"Don't be rude," Mrs. Davenport hissed, gripping Lilah's arm and pulling her away.

Ridley faced Archer and raised one hand delicately to her forehead as she fanned herself with the other. Archer frowned. "You okay?"

"Just a little dizzy," Ridley said. "I mean, a week ago I hated you, and now we're dating? Can you blame me if my head's still spinning?"

Archer's concern vanished as he realized she was joking. "I have that effect on women."

A most unladylike snort escaped Ridley's lips, and she clapped one hand over her mouth as a man standing nearby shot a frown in her direction. "I'm not sure it's a good thing that you make people dizzy," she said once the man looked away. "But the kiss on the temple was a nice touch. Good job with that."

"Smooth, right?" Archer nodded agreement. "My improv skills are stellar."

"Next level indeed."

"What the hell is going on?" a voice demanded, and Ridley turned to find Lilah right in front of her, glaring at both of them. Whatever she'd needed to say to Mrs. Davenport's friend, it clearly hadn't taken long. She took a step back as Lilah looked at her brother and added, "You've been acting weird ever since you got back. I know the two of you aren't here on a *date*. No way would either of you put up with each other's company if it weren't for some mutually beneficial reason."

Archer's arm was suddenly around Ridley again. "You mean like our mutual affection for one another?"

Lilah narrowed her eyes. "Don't make me sick. I'm calling security. I know you're both up to something. I have no idea what it is, but I won't have you ruining this event." She spun around and marched toward the entrance.

"Wonderful," Archer said. "My lovely sister really is going to get us thrown out of here."

"Crap," Ridley muttered, her eyes following Lilah as the dark-haired beauty walked up to one of the security guards at the base of the stairs. She exchanged a few words with him before throwing a triumphant smile over her shoulder at Ridley.

"Please don't slap me," Archer said. "That would really ruin the act."

"What?" Ridley's eyes snapped back to him just as his hand rose to her chin. Without a word, he tipped her face up toward his. Then, before she could find the breath to protest, he kissed her.

CHAPTER 11

THE KISS WAS OF THE innocent close-mouthed variety, but slow and lingering in a way that made heat sizzle across Ridley's skin and a shiver race up her spine and into her hair. Her eyes drifted closed of their own accord, then flickered open again as the warmth of Archer's lips vanished from hers. She took in a shallow breath as her eyes found his. Then he pressed a second soft kiss to her lips. Quicker than the first. Easy, natural, as if they shared brief kisses all the time. He paused then, his face mere inches away from hers. Close enough that she was still breathing in his cologne or aftershave or whatever that intoxicating scent was. "You're good," he whispered.

Ridley sensed heat rising up her neck, but she refused to let him know he'd affected her. As smoothly as she could, she said, "Thanks, I know. I've been told before."

One side of his mouth pulled up. "I meant your acting skills."

She gave him what she hoped was a knowing smile. "Sure you did."

He laughed, his eyes zeroing in on her lips, and she was

certain he was about to kiss her again.

"Hey!" a loud voice interrupted, ruining the moment. "Seriously?" Lilah asked as Ridley and Archer broke apart. "You're really here together?"

Ridley let out a breathy laugh. "We are."

Lilah's fiery gaze burned into her. Then her hand flashed forward—but she was aiming for her brother, not her former best friend. She grabbed a fistful of Archer's shirt and tie and tugged him closer. "You're unbelievable, you know that?" she hissed into his face. "After everything you said about her after the Cataclysm, now you bring her to one of our events on your arm? You're such a hypocrite. And *you*?" She shoved Archer away and sneered at Ridley. "I thought you had at least *some* dignity left, but now you're just like every other girl who's ever thrown herself at my brother's feet." And with that, she pushed her shoulders back and sauntered away.

"Well," Ridley said quietly. "That was pleasant."

Archer was quiet for several moments before saying, "She doesn't know that I've—"

"Changed?" Ridley said, her tone light.

"Yes." He sighed. "I know it sounds stupid—"

"It's fine." She patted his arm and gave him a reassuring smile. "Really, it is. This isn't a real date, remember? You don't have to explain anything."

"I know, but—"

"Anyway, maybe you should talk to Lilah while I'm talking to Callie. You can tell her ... I don't know. That things probably won't work out with me. Tell her whatever she wants to hear. Because if you're leaving soon, then you don't want the last few days or weeks of your time at home to be filled with fighting."

"True," Archer said quietly as his eyes followed Lilah. Ridley watched her sashay back toward the stairs. Not to speak to the security guards this time; she was all smiles and charm as she greeted another couple that had just arrived. The Davenports were nothing if not exceptional in the acting department.

"Do you ever wonder if the two of you would still be friends if the Cataclysm had never happened?" Archer asked, drawing Ridley's attention back to him. "If it hadn't ruined your dad's business, and you were still living here in Aura Tower?"

"And if you'd never told Lilah to ignore me?"

"Well—"

"Sorry, I shouldn't have said that. You apologized, I'm over it, it's in the past." Ridley took a deep breath, her gaze wandering across the ballroom and its occupants. "I do wonder sometimes how different life would be. Not just because magic would never have been outlawed, but my mom would still be alive too. But if everything had remained the same, then ... I don't know, maybe I wouldn't be a nice person. Maybe I'd be just as much—" She silenced herself before finishing that sentence. It probably wasn't helpful to say things like 'Maybe I'd be just as much of a bitch as Lilah if we were still friends.'

"Just as much what?" Archer asked.

"Nothing." Ridley mentally shook off her negativity and

tried to picture the imaginary situation the other way around. Maybe if things hadn't changed, Lilah would still be the fun, friendly girl Ridley had loved being around when they were little. "Yes," she said, pulling a smile into place. "Perhaps Lilah and I would still be friends if the Cataclysm had never happened. I would have spent almost every afternoon for the past decade hanging out at your place, and your parents would probably be sick of me."

Archer laughed. "Or they'd love you. If they were around enough to get to know you, that is."

"*You'd* be sick of me."

"Or maybe we would have been friends too."

"True." She tilted her head and gave him a thoughtful look. "That's a possibility."

"In fact," Archer continued, "that would have been the *best* part for you. You would totally have loved spending all that time around me."

She laughed at him and his ever-present cockiness. "Right, and maybe we would have found ourselves exactly where we are tonight, except it would be genuine instead of fake." At that, Archer raised an eyebrow. "That was a joke," she added hastily. "If all those things were true, then you'd probably see me as an annoying younger sister just like Lilah, so you and I *definitely* wouldn't be here together."

Archer smiled at her in a way that did strange things to her insides. "Highly unlikely. The sister part, I mean. Not the together part."

Ridley opened her mouth, planning to respond with

a clever comeback, but not a single one came to mind. She cleared her throat. "Um, anyway. None of that happened, so here we are. In our crappy post-Cataclysm world." As she looked around the room, wondering where Callie had got to, she sensed Archer's eyes still on her. "Oh, look, Callie's heading out," she said, grateful for an excuse to divert Archer's attention elsewhere. She nodded toward Callie, who was moving toward one of the doorways leading off the far side of the ballroom. "Are the bathrooms that way?" Ridley asked.

"Yes, I think so."

"Great, okay, I'll catch her there. Then hopefully I can convince her to speak to me somewhere a little more private." She walked forward, and Archer fell into step beside her. "Um, what are you doing?" she asked.

"Going with you. Not all the way to the ladies, of course. I'll hang out somewhere nearby. I think they have a few of those platforms with the glass floors along this side of Aura Tower. I'll pretend to stare down at the city far below and watch out for you in case something goes wrong."

"What, like she attacks me in the bathroom for asking to have a private conversation with her?"

"You never know."

They reached the doorway at the edge of the ballroom and continued into a wide passageway. To their right was a plain wall, while on their left were numerous enclosed platforms jutting out over the ground a hundred and forty floors below, like glass cubes stuck to the side of Aura Tower. Ridley could still see Callie up ahead, walking with a causal stride, her arms swaying at her sides and a purse clutched in one hand.

"Won't you miss this when we're done?" Archer asked.

"What, stalking people?"

"Actually, I meant more ... you and me hanging out to-gether."

"Oh." For a moment, Ridley imagined she could feel his lips on hers again. And then the memory of that stupid dream from a few nights before resurfaced. The one where she was sitting on the desk, and he was standing too close, and her hand had grasped his T-shirt to tug him closer. "Like as friends, right?" she asked as a flush crawled up her neck and into her cheeks. What the hell was wrong with her? She refused to prove Lilah right: she would not be joining the long line of girls who'd pined after Archer Davenport.

"Yes, as friends," he said, just as Ridley saw Callie walk through a door on the right. "Unless you've decided you still hate me. But I was kind of hoping we'd moved past that."

"We have. So, uh, yes. We could hang out. But you're leaving."

"I am."

They reached the door Callie had gone through—a door with a simple gold symbol of a stick figure in a dress stuck to it—and Ridley paused to ask, "So how are we going to hang out then?"

"Weeeeell ..." Archer drew the word out and gave her a knowing look.

Ridley shook her head. "You heard my dad. We're not leaving." She raised her hand to the door and pushed it open.

"See you a bit later."

The bathroom was preposterously large, with glossy floors, soft lighting, and enormous mirrors, some of which had cushioned stools in front of them. Three of the stalls appeared to be closed, but Ridley couldn't be certain they were all occupied. She washed her hands and took a rolled-up white towel from the pyramid of towels sitting on a silver platter. After drying her hands, she pretended to adjust her hair.

Behind her, a toilet flushed, and a stall door opened. A glance in the mirror told her it was Callie. As the woman moved to one of the basins on Ridley's left, Ridley opened her purse and fished inside for her lipstick. She was about to remove the cap when the lipstick slipped—intentionally, of course—from her fingers. "Oh!" she exclaimed as it hit the floor and rolled toward Callie.

"Oh dear, let me—"

"No, it's fine, don't worry," Ridley said as she moved closer. The lipstick came to a halt beneath the basins, and she crouched as low as she could in her form-fitting dress. "Okay, this dress was *definitely* not made for this kind of activity," she said with a laugh as she wobbled while trying to reach for the lipstick.

"Oh, sorry, here—" Callie grasped Ridley's arm to keep her from toppling over.

"Thank you!" Ridley's fingers finally reached the lipstick. "Thank you so much," she said as Callie helped her to stand. "I'm sorry, that was so silly."

"No, I'm sorry, my hands are still wet." Callie grabbed one

of the rolled-up towels from the platter and handed it to Ridley before reaching for a second one to dry her hands.

"It's totally fine," Ridley said with another easy laugh, just as a second toilet flushed. "I really don't mind." After drying her upper arm, she quickly dabbed some lipstick on. In the mirror's reflection, she watched a woman walk out of another stall. Callie headed for the door, and Ridley quickly returned the lipstick to her purse and followed her. "Oh, thanks," she said as Callie realized someone was behind her and held the door open. "So how do you know Jurenza?" she asked.

"Oh, we had the same singing coach, back in the day," Callie said. "We performed together a number of times when we were both getting started." She walked beside Ridley as they headed for the ballroom. "What about you?"

"I don't actually know her at all," Ridley admitted. "I'm a plus-one."

"I can introduce you if you'd like," Callie offered.

"Thanks, that would be so cool." After a pause, Ridley took a breath, made sure there was no one walking toward them and no one within earshot behind them, and decided to go for it. She had little time left before they reached the ballroom. "Callie," she said, and the woman's head jerked toward her.

"How do you—"

"I need to talk to you about something important, so it would be great if we could go somewhere we can't be overheard."

"Um ..." Callie turned her eyes forward and increased

her pace, but Ridley kept stride with her. "Okay, look, I don't know anything about you, so I don't think—"

"Please don't run away or scream when I say this," Ridley said.

"Why would I need to scream—"

"I know about your magic."

Callie came to an abrupt standstill. Ridley, already a few steps ahead, stopped and turned back. "How dare you accuse me of something like that?" Callie whispered. "You have absolutely no proof—"

"I don't have proof, but I have a letter with your name on it. I received the same letter." She hesitated, then added, "Because I'm just like you."

Callie gathered her skirt and rushed past Ridley. "Leave me alone."

"Wait!" Ridley hurried after her and grabbed her arm. "Let me at least give you the letter." Two people stuck their heads out of the nearest viewing platform, and Ridley let go of Callie's arm. Crap, this was so not how she'd wanted to reveal this information to her. "I can't say anything more here," she said in a low voice, "but this is important, so please just take the letter." She turned her back to the platform side of the corridor, removed the folded piece of paper from her purse, and held it out to Callie. "If you want to talk once you've read it, meet me at the top of the stairs. And if you don't, then just know that not everything in the letter is true anymore. The threat the letter talks about is no longer a threat. You don't have to leave the city if you don't want to."

"You're insane," Callie said faintly, but her fingers wrapped automatically around the letter when Ridley shoved it toward her.

"Don't go back to the ballroom if you're going to read it now," Ridley said. "Go somewhere private. Back to the bathroom if you have to. But we can't talk there in case someone overhears us." She looked back that way and noticed Archer leaning against the wall opposite the opening onto one of the platforms. "Meet me at the top of the stairs," Ridley repeated, then turned and continued toward the ballroom.

Once she was back inside the crowded room, she slipped between people and around tables, chairs and waitstaff. She dodged the arm of a particularly animated old man explaining fly fishing to a group of young teens, before almost walking right into someone. "I'm so sorry," she said automatically, only realizing a moment later that it was Lilah.

"What is *wrong* with you?" Lilah demanded, her tone venomous. "How hard is it to look where you're going?"

Ridley almost shoved past her without replying. Then she remembered what she'd told Archer and forced herself to say, "Archer's looking for you. He's down that corridor by the viewing platforms. He feels bad about earlier and wants to talk to you." Before Lilah could reply, Ridley stepped around her and continued toward the stairs. She climbed them slowly, giving Callie time to read the letter. Time to decide whether she wanted to talk to Ridley.

At the top of the stairs, Ridley stopped. She placed her hands on the banister and looked back down at the ballroom.

She couldn't see Lilah anywhere, which hopefully meant she'd gone to speak with her brother. She couldn't see Callie either, so—

Ah. There she was, walking out of the corridor that led to the bathrooms. She paused, glanced up, and from across the ballroom, her eyes met Ridley's. She stood there for several moments, and though Ridley couldn't make out her expression, she imagined Callie was deliberating. Then, after a glance behind her, Callie began making her way across the ballroom. She ascended the stairs, and when she reached Ridley at the top, she asked, "How do I know the letter is real? You might have made it all up."

Ridley sighed, deciding that maybe this was becoming more trouble than it was worth. She had delivered the letter, so perhaps it was time to walk away. She could move on to finding the next elemental before she wound up in trouble for aggravating one of Mrs. Davenport's guests. "Okay look," she said. "I took a risk by bringing you that letter. The person who was supposed to deliver it is dead, and I could have ignored the rest of the letters, but I thought maybe you'd want to know the truth. But if you're not interested in believing me, then that's fine. I've done my part." She stepped around Callie, planning to return to the ballroom below.

"Wait. Okay." Callie looked back over her shoulder, then toward the ballroom entrance where the man with the commpad stood talking to a woman who seemed to be dressed for a business meeting rather than a glamorous party. "Let's go that way," Callie said, nodding to the far corner of the balcony that protruded over the ballroom. "There's no one else up here."

Ridley would have preferred to get away from the ballroom, but Callie was probably afraid to accompany someone she didn't know—and was clearly still afraid of—away from a public space. Besides, there was no way anyone would overhear them way over there on the corner of the balcony high above the rest of the ballroom. "Okay," she said, "but can you try to look natural as we walk that way? Not like you're terrified to be in my presence."

After a pause and a deep breath, Callie relaxed her shoulders and linked arms with Ridley. She laughed at an imaginary joke as they wandered along the balcony. Tall windows to their right revealed the night sky and the twinkling city lights, while the ballroom lay below on their right. They stopped in the corner where two windows met each other. Callie stood with her back to the glass and, with brown eyes still wide with uncertainty, she said, "Show me."

"Show you what?" Ridley asked.

"Your magic. You said you're like me. I'm not listening to a thing you say until you show me you're telling the truth."

"*Here?* Are you crazy?"

"Nobody can see as long as you keep facing me."

It was true, but that didn't make Ridley feel any more comfortable about it. But if it was going to help Callie believe she wasn't alone, then perhaps it was okay to quickly reveal a little bit of a magic glow. Ridley hunched her shoulders over and kept her hands pressed right up against her body as she let magic rise to the surface of her skin. Blue color pulsed across her fingers and palms, but before any wisps of magic could escape her body, Ridley smothered the glow.

"Incredible," Callie breathed, her eyes fixed on Ridley's hands. "This is amazing. I always dreamed of finding someone else like me, but I thought that's all it would ever be: a fantasy." Her gaze moved down as she raised her own hands. Vibrant blue patches appeared all the way up her arms, and then suddenly it was glowing in her eyes and cheeks as well.

"Don't do that *here*," Ridley said, alarm shooting through her. "Someone might be able to see past me."

"I know, I know, I'm sorry." The glow faded from her face. "It's just that it's been so long. I never use it. I try to pretend it doesn't exist. But it feels so good, so right, to finally let go."

"Callie, seriously." Ridley moved a little closer to try to shield the woman's arms and hands with her body. "Do you *want* to get caught? Do you want us both to wind up dead?"

"Okay, okay." The blue slowly vanished from Callie's arms, leaving only her hands glowing. "So—so you said we're not in danger? We don't have to leave the city? Because that part about going into the wastelands sounded completely crazy."

"No, we don't. And why are your hands still blue? You need to—"

The sound of hurried footsteps reached Ridley's ears over the music and chatter. Fear squeezed instantly around her heart, even before she looked over her shoulder and saw the police officer running toward her. "Hide your magic!" she whispered as she spun around.

"Excuse me, miss?" The policeman slowed as he neared her.

"Uh, yes?" She tried to smile, but it felt far from natural.

"I've been looking for you." He stopped a little too close and reached for Ridley's arm. "You're wanted for questioning in connection with the murder of Lawrence Madson."

Ice drenched Ridley's body. She swallowed, and her brain registered a second police officer approaching them. "W-why? What did I do?"

"We have a witness who says he saw you from the adjacent balcony on the night of the murder. If you refuse to come quietly, I'll have to—Ho-lee ..." His jaw went slack as his eyes grew wider. "Is that *magic*?" Ridley's heart almost stopped, but the man was no longer looking at her. She twisted around and realized Callie's hands were still glowing blue.

"Don't move," the man said, his voice hoarse. He let go of Ridley and reached for his gun.

Unbidden, the memory of a woman falling to the street with a bullet in her chest flashed across Ridley's mind. A woman who'd used magic. A woman shot down by the police.

Crapcrapcrap! Ridley acted on instinct. Still clutching her purse, she launched herself at Callie. Her arms wrapped around the woman as her own magic rose away from her glowing skin. Her momentum knocked Callie sideways, and together they fell. But they were invisible before they hit the floor.

CHAPTER 12

THEY WERE AIR, THEY WERE wind, they were flying just above the floor, and then up and over the police officers. Someone shouted, Callie was screaming in Ridley's ear, and then came the crack of a gunshot. Confusion muddled Ridley's senses. The room spun around them, and she barely knew which way was up or down. All she knew was that if she stopped moving, if she let the two of them fall out of the air, they'd both be dead.

They were high up near the ceiling now, and Callie let out another yelp as Ridley directed them back downward a little too fast. They spun another few times before Ridley managed to slow down and move forward instead of around and around. Some small part of her mind remembered that this wasn't supposed to be about control, but how could she *not* attempt to control this?

They gusted along the balcony area, the windows flashing by—and Ridley suddenly realized the top of every window was partially open. They could easily slip out that way. But they were a hundred and forty floors up, and the mere thought was terrifying. *Just let go and fall into it.* Nope. No way would she be 'falling' a hundred and forty floors. *You've survived eighty-four floors*, she reminded herself. But this was worse. Way worse. She sped by without considering it again, aiming for the ballroom's main entrance.

Then they were out, and the carpet was a river of red rushing beneath them. She knew before reaching the elevator that they'd have a problem getting out that way. So she blew right past it—and there was the door to the stairs, standing slightly ajar. She whirled back around, and they slipped through the space—a gap neither of them could have squeezed through in human form—and then over the stairway railing and straight down the gap in the center of the stairwell, Callie screaming in Ridley's ear the entire way.

As they burst into the foyer, Ridley heard the startled gasps around them. Not because people could *see* them, but because of the unexpected flurry of wind. Skirts billowed and hair fanned out as she and Callie fled across the foyer, through the open entrance, and into the night. They kept going, speeding away from the Opal Quarter between buildings and along streets, zigzagging, turning, tumbling, until finally they reached a darkened, deserted parking lot behind a warehouse.

Ridley's feet touched the ground as she pulled her magic back inside her body. She let go of Callie, who sank to the ground immediately, her dress puffing up around her. The world reeled around Ridley, and she dropped her purse and staggered to keep her balance. Now that they were safe, her mind took off at a million miles an hour trying to process what had just happened. The cops wanted to question her—but it had nothing to do with her magic. And then she'd gone and given away her biggest secret. *Yes, that actually happened*, she told herself, because most of her brain seemed to be trying to shove away this terrible truth. *That actually happened. It actually. Freaking. Happened.*

Her chest heaved in and out as panic began to set in. She shouldn't have done it. She shouldn't have overreacted. She should have … *what*? As her thoughts tumbled over one another, she realized that every course of action she might have taken would have ended with the police discovering her secret. Whether she ran and they caught her, or she calmly agreed to answer their questions, they would eventually have used one of those little palm-sized scanners and found there were no amulets behind her ear.

"I'm gonna be sick," Callie moaned beside her. She was sitting across one of the faded white lines that marked out a parking bay, her head hanging over her lap as she inhaled shakily. "I … I've never done … I didn't even know …" She shook her head, swallowed, then climbed awkwardly to her feet. "What the hell have you done?" she demanded of Ridley. "I was fine until now. I've kept this secret my entire life, and now *everybody knows*!"

"I-I'm sorry," Ridley stammered. "But I kept telling you to hide your magic. You would have been fine if you'd done that. That cop was after *me*, not—"

"I couldn't!" she wailed. "It's been so long since I let

the magic out, and my emotions were heightened, and I just couldn't suppress it properly. My hands—my stupid hands—they just—" She stared down at her palms where there was no trace of magic left now.

"I have to go," Ridley told her. "I have to get home before they—" Panic tightened her chest and stole her breath as the horrifying truth slammed into her yet again. Her secret was no longer secret. She and Dad would never be safe again. "I have to get out of the city. So do you. You can come with me."

"What?" Callie backed away, shaking her head fiercely. "No way. I'm going home."

"But they'll find you. Now that someone knows, it's only a matter of time before every cop in the city comes after both of us."

"No. They don't know where I live. And my home is secure. I made sure of that a long time ago. Just—just leave me alone." And with that, Callie lifted her skirt away from her feet and took off across the shadowed parking lot.

Ridley didn't chase her. Getting home to warn Dad was the only thing that mattered now. She picked up her purse, let go of the hold she had on her magic, and vanished into the air within seconds. *Let go, let go, let go*, she told herself. She could travel faster if she made this work. A hurricane-speed wind could carry her all the way home. But how would the magic around her know where home was if she didn't consciously direct her movements? She tried not to *think*. She tried to simply *fall into it* and let it take her. She was aware of herself spinning up and over the warehouse. Tumbling, whirling, plummeting, rising. *It's okay, just trust the elements*, she told herself. But she couldn't. She had to know which way she was heading, because what if it was the *wrong* way?

She set herself down onto the nearest flat roof and took several moments to get her bearings. She located Aura Tower, rising like a glittering spire from the city center, and took note of the orientation of the buildings around it. Her heart sank as she figured out where home was: miles away on the *other* side of Aura Tower. "Dammit," she hissed between her teeth. Had she been this far from home in that parking lot? She wasn't sure, but it felt like she'd wasted precious time trying to do what Grandpa had instructed.

She raced away through the air, above the lower buildings and between the taller ones. *Faster, faster*, she coaxed her magic, ignoring the creeping tiredness at the edge of her mind. Eventually, she swept over the last roof and down into her alley, only becoming visible when she was right in front of the back door. Exhaustion settled over her, and she felt the start of a headache somewhere behind her eyes. Grandpa and Archer would have said that wasn't supposed to happen, but maybe they didn't know what they were talking about after all. Maybe this was just the way Ridley's magic worked.

She fumbled with her key, all thoughts of the exact technicalities of her magic fleeing from her mind. She bolted the door behind her the moment she was inside. "Dad?" she shouted as she clattered up the stairs in her heels. "Dad!"

She found him sitting in his favorite armchair in the living room, blinking rapidly and mumbling, "Hmm, yes, what, I'm awake." He met Ridley's eyes, then pushed himself up from the chair. "What's wrong? Did something happen?"

"I ..." For a moment, she couldn't bring herself to admit what had happened. She couldn't bear to disappoint her father so deeply. He'd done everything he could to keep her safe, and now she'd ruined everything. Their lives would never be the same. "Someone saw me," she eventually blurted out, and she saw from Dad's expression that he knew what she meant: Not just 'Someone saw me,' but, 'Someone saw me *use my magic*.'

"The Shadow Society?" he asked immediately.

"No. A police officer. Someone reported seeing me on the balcony where Lawrence was murdered. He wanted to take me in for questioning. And then the woman I was talking to at the time ... she was ..." Ridley squeezed her eyes shut, letting the truth pour out of her in a rush. "I was talking to one of the elementals. That's why I went to that party tonight. I knew she'd be there. And I know you didn't want me looking for them, but I thought they deserved to know the truth, and it wasn't supposed to be a big deal. Just hand over each letter, talk for a little bit, and leave. And Archer was with me, to make sure I didn't speak to the wrong person, and—"

"Stop," Dad said. "I already know what you've been doing." He stepped past her, aiming for the passage.

"You ... what? But how—" Her mind jumped to the only other person who knew, and the ache of betrayal hit her squarely in the chest. She hurried after Dad, saying, "Archer told you—"

"No, Archer didn't give away a thing," Dad said as he

walked into her bedroom. "He didn't have to. I'm not stupid, Ridley." He reached up toward the space on top of her wardrobe. After pulling down a backpack, he turned to face her. "Of course I didn't believe you. I knew you'd go looking for them. But I figured Archer would look out for you. That's why he came back here on Monday, right? He knew as well as I did that you wouldn't let it go." Dad held the backpack out to Ridley, and she reached silently for it, her mouth half open. "Not that he did a very good job," Dad added. "I was hoping he'd keep you away from this kind of mess."

"Wait, so ... you knew all of this?" Ridley asked. "And you let me believe I was being masterfully secretive?"

"Yes. It wouldn't have done any good if I'd confronted you. You would have gone after them anyway, and you might have done it without Archer's help." Dad sighed and added, "I know I'm no better than you. I've kept so many secrets. I fear I've taught you the same thing."

Ridley nodded mutely, her hands tightening around the backpack. Secrets had been part of her life for as long as she could remember, since the moment flames had erupted across her hand and her parents had told her she had magic inside her. Secrets had kept her safe. Secrets were key to survival. Both her parents had taught her that. But this was *Dad*. Why had she been keeping secrets from *him*? "We ... we should probably make more of an effort at being completely open with each other," she said quietly.

Dad nodded. "We should. Once we're somewhere safe. Right now, we need to pack whatever we can carry and get out of here."

"Yes. Wait, Dad," she added as he turned to leave. "I'm sorry. I'm so sorry. I know you wanted to stay here and live a normal life, and now I've messed everything up. But I had to protect her—the elemental I was speaking to tonight. She accidentally let her magic become visible, and the policeman saw her, and he was going for his gun, and I couldn't just stand by and wait to see if he shot her—" She cut herself off, telling herself to stop with all the excuses. "I'm just really sorry."

Dad moved forward and wrapped both Ridley and the backpack she was clutching in a tight embrace. "Sounds like it would have happened anyway. If the police have a description of you, they would have found you soon enough. It had nothing to do with you tracking down other elementals. Even though I would have preferred you hadn't done that." He stepped back. "Now we both need to pack."

"Yes. Got it."

Ridley tugged the laces at the back of her dress, loosening them as quickly as she could. When she was finally out of the dress, she changed into jeans and a long-sleeved T-shirt. Less than ten minutes later, she'd finished stuffing as many items as she could into her backpack, making sure there was space for the framed picture of her with Mom and Dad that had stood on her desk for years.

She dumped the backpack on the couch in the living room and was about to check the kitchen cupboards for small snack items when a loud pounding on the door downstairs made her jump. Dad rushed into the living room. "We're too late,"

Ridley whispered, her wildly thudding heart causing the ache behind her eyes to throb.

"Bring your bag," Dad replied. "Mine's packed. We can go out my window. You can use magic to—"

"It's me!" came a muffled shout from downstairs.

Ridley and Dad both paused, staring at each other with questioning gazes. "Archer?" Dad asked.

"I think so," Ridley said.

"Wait here. I'll check." Dad moved so quietly down the stairs that Ridley barely heard his footsteps. She stood frozen, barely breathing, listening as the bolt slid across. Quiet voices exchanged a few words, and then someone ran up the stairs. "Thank goodness," Archer said, appearing at the top still dressed in his suit. He crossed the room and swept Ridley into a hug. "I figured you'd be fine, but I was still worried." Ridley barely had time to be surprised by the hug before he let go, stepped back, and looked around for Dad. "You need to leave," he said the moment Dad reached the top of the stairs. "I don't know how long it'll take them to figure out who Ridley is, but they will."

"I know," Dad said. "We're ready to go. Just let me grab my bag."

"Wait. Your amulets. You need to get rid of them."

"They can track our AIs?" Ridley asked. "Surely that's—"

"Illegal? Yes. But that doesn't stop it from happening. It may take a few hours, but they'll soon have every scanner drone in the city searching for your amulets." Archer looked at Dad. "Yours too, I'm guessing. They'll assume you're help-ing her."

"So we should remove them," Ridley said. "But if we re-move them, then any scanner drone flying over us will detect us anyway for *not* having AIs."

"Still better not to have them," Dad said, prodding at the skin just behind his ear where his AI1 was still embedded. His AI2 was fused to the inside of his wedding ring—which meant, Ridley realized with a lurch of her heart, that he'd have to get rid of the ring. "We can leave them somewhere else. Any drones that detect our AIs will send an alert, and half the city's cops will end up there. It'll buy us a little time, at least."

"But the scanners detect body heat as well, don't they?" Ridley asked. "Or something like that. They'll know the amu-lets aren't attached to any people."

"We'll leave them inside a busy building. The scanners won't be able to tell the difference."

"And what about our commscreens?" she asked.

"They're fine if they're off," Archer said.

"Are you sure?"

"Yes, I've tested it myself."

"Okay, let me get my bag," Dad said as Ridley removed both her commscreen and commpad from the backpack. "One of you will need to cut my AI1 out once we're a good distance away from here." He turned and hurried back toward his bed-room. Ridley switched off her devices and returned them to the backpack. After zipping it closed, she lifted it onto one shoulder and turned to Archer. "What happened after I left? Do you know if lots of people saw my magic?"

"I'm not sure. I was down in the ballroom when I saw you on the balcony with Callie. But I couldn't see much through the railing. It was your dress that I recognized. I was halfway up the stairs when those two cops came in. By the time they confronted you, I was close enough to see what happened, but I don't know what people saw from down in the ballroom. Probably not much."

"Hopefully not," Dad said, returning with a bag over one shoulder. "Come on, let's go."

"Right behind you," Ridley said, rushing into the kitchen. She opened a cupboard and held her backpack in front of it. After unzipping the top, she swept the small collection of energy bars straight into the backpack. She pushed the contents down, forced the zipper closed, and ran out.

"Just getting a few things from my desk," Dad called as he reached the bottom of the stairs. He hurried into the store.

"Archer, did those police officers see you?" Ridley asked, following him quickly down the stairs. "I don't want you getting in trouble because they think you're connected in some way to me or Callie."

"They may have noticed me," Archer said, "but I was still near the top of the stairs, so I wasn't close enough to appear involved. They ran right past me as they were chasing after you. My mom came up then and wanted to know why two policemen had just rushed out of her party. I told her I had no idea. Then she asked about you, so I told her you were in the bathroom. I hung around a bit, pretending I was waiting for you, and then slipped out when my mom wasn't looking."

"Okay, that's good." Ridley jumped down the final two stairs and crossed the back room to peer out of the window beside the door. As far as she could tell, the alley was empty. "I don't think they knew who I was," she said, looking back at Archer. "That cop called me 'miss.' He didn't use my name."

"Yeah, I saw him talking to Harry on my way out."

"Harry?"

"The guy with the commpad who checks everyone's names against the guest list when they come in." Archer's hand moved to the knot of his tie, pulling it back and forth a few times to loosen it. "But your name was never on the list because I never told my mother and Lilah I was bringing you."

"So that cop will now be giving a description of me to your mom, or showing her my face on some Aura Tower surveillance footage from earlier tonight, and she'll be more than happy to give him my name."

"And she knows Kayne's Antiques," Archer added, "so she'll be able to send the cops straight here. Which she may have already done."

"Right, let's go," Dad said, returning from the store while zipping up his bag. Ridley barely had a moment to stare into the darkness of Kayne's Antiques and mentally say goodbye. It was so strange to think of leaving the store and the apartment above it forever. She'd hated it so much when she and Dad first moved here after the Cataclysm, but now it was her home. Unshed tears ached behind her eyes as she realized this was probably the last time she would see it.

"Come on, Riddles," Dad said, holding the door open. "We don't have time for goodbyes." Once the three of them were outside, he turned to lock it. Ridley shifted the backpack so she could get it onto both shoulders, then tugged downward on the straps to tighten them. The open end of the alley was still empty, the only movement coming from a chip packet as it skidded across the street on the breeze. Ridley glanced toward the other end, and her breath caught at the sight of two blue pinpricks of light glowing in the darkness.

"Oh." She exhaled as she realized what she was seeing. "It's just that cat. I thought you took it away," she said to Dad.

"I did. I left her near the wall on Monday evening when I was out. Kinda hoped she'd find her own way back out to the wastelands."

"I think she might be attracted to your magic," Archer said. "That's why she keeps coming back."

"Seriously? Is that a thing?"

"I think so. We had quite a few magic-mutated animals living with us on La Tournette. They always seemed to attach themselves to a certain elemental, following him or her around all the time. People guessed it was something about the animal's magic responding to a certain person's magic, but no one really knew."

"We need to move," Dad said, walking forward. "Without the cat."

"I assume you'll be going to the bunker?" Archer asked as he and Ridley fell into step beside Dad. Ridley threw a final glance over her shoulder at the cat, feeling a little bad to leave her behind, especially now that she knew the animal might feel some kind of connection to her. She faced forward, pressing her fingers to her temples and rubbing in small circular motions as she tried to relieve the ache pounding dully through her head.

"No," Dad said to Archer. "First we're hiding our arxium implants somewhere, and then we'll find another busy building filled with lots of people for us to hide out for the night. Any scanner drone flying overhead hopefully won't be able to detect that we don't have AIs."

"Why not the bunker?" Ridley asked. "Surely it's safer down there?"

"It's definitely safer down there," Archer said.

Dad shook his head. He stopped as they reached the end of the alley and looked both ways down the main street. "I don't want to get involved with them. You know how I feel about magical communities. It's safer to stay on our own."

"But we are going to leave the city, correct?" Ridley asked. "The police or the Shadow Society—or both—will eventually find us if we stay here, especially if we're not down in the bunker."

"Let's just get somewhere safe," Dad said, turning left. "Then we can discuss this."

"I wish we had time to say goodbye to the Lins," Ridley said, hurrying to keep up with Dad.

"I know, but we can get a message to them later. For now—"

"Wait." Archer stopped, reaching out to grab both Ridley and Dad. From somewhere nearby, the vroom of a high-speed vehicle grew rapidly louder.

"Back to the alley!" Dad said, launching past Ridley and tugging her with him.

No sirens? some distracted part of Ridley's mind wondered as they raced back. Probably because they didn't want to warn her of their approach. Within the shadows of the alley, the three of them slowed to a halt. "Quickly, before they see us," Dad said to Ridley.

"What?" Alarm sent her heart racing faster and her head pounding even worse.

"There's no other way out of here. We can't outrun them on the street, and this alley is a dead end."

Of course her magic was the only way out. She just hadn't stopped to think about it as they'd raced back this way. "What's wrong?" Archer asked.

"Nothing. I just—I used a lot earlier. My head—but it's fine."

"I'm sorry," Dad said. "I didn't realize you still got those headaches. Um ..." He glanced around at the buildings on either side of them. "I can try to—"

"No, no, it's fine," Ridley said. "I can do it."

"Ridley," Archer said, looking back as car headlights illuminated the street. "We have to hurry."

"I know, I know!" She wrapped one arm around Dad while reaching for Archer with the other. She tugged him against her side as her skin began to glow and the pounding of her head intensified. And then the cat—that silly, magic-mutated cat—leaped at them. Dad caught it in his arms, probably by instinct rather than any conscious intention. "Ridley, now!" he shouted as a car squealed to a halt at the mouth of the alley.

Air, she thought, and her magic responded instantly.

CHAPTER 13

IT WASN'T LONG BEFORE Ridley's head felt like someone was trying to split it open with a chisel and hammer, but she managed to get the three of them into the next district and onto the flat roof of an apartment building. "Sorry, I can't ... I can't go ... any further." She bent over, pressing her palms against her knees and breathing through the nausea.

"Are you sure you're okay?" Dad asked, resting his hand on her shoulder.

"I'm fine, I'm fine." She waved him away. "You need to get rid of ... your other amulet."

"Maybe you should sit down," Archer suggested.

"Yeah, okay." She sank into a sitting position and pulled her backpack off. Then, deciding that being completely horizontal would be even better, she shifted forward and lay down, using the backpack as a pillow. "It won't last long if I don't use magic," she told him. "Maybe just ... I don't know. A few hours." Her gaze rose to the clouds hanging above the city, where lighting—or magic; she always found it hard to tell the difference from down here—zigzagged across the night sky.

She squeezed her eyes shut against the bright light, flinching as pain seared through her eyeballs.

Sounds swirled around her: sirens in the distance, Dad speaking quietly to Archer, a bag unzipping. Dad said something about a blade and his arxium implant, and Ridley was relieved that Archer was helping him remove it. She didn't particularly want to slice open her father's skin to get his AI1 out. She also didn't want to think about how he would no longer be protected once it was gone. Ridley's own magic guarded her body from any harmful conjurations someone might want to use on her, but everyone else had an AI1 for that. Without it, Dad would be at risk. Not a *huge* risk, seeing as most people couldn't pull magic anymore, but Ridley would feel better once he got himself a simple old-fashioned arxium charm to wear around his neck or on his wrist. She wondered where one got such things these days. Many decades had passed since anyone had needed to wear them.

"Ridley?" a quiet voice asked.

She opened her eyes and blinked a few times, unaware of how much time had passed.

"I'm sorry, I think you fell asleep," Dad said as he crouched beside her. The cat sat next to him, watching Ridley with unblinking blue eyes.

"Did I? I can't remember." She sat upright and added, "My head feels a little bit better."

"I did a conjuration," Dad said. "Just a simple one we used to use for headaches all the time. I didn't know if it would help if what you have is more of a migraine."

"Well the pain's definitely not as bad, and I don't feel so sick."

"That's good."

She bent to the side and tried to look behind his ear. "Did Archer get your AI1 out?"

"Yes, all done." Dad turned his head so she could see the small adhesive bandage stuck to his skin. "Took a little bit of coaching," he added with a chuckle, "but he managed to do it without passing out."

"Hey, I think we need to get inside the building," Archer said. Ridley twisted around and saw him looking over the wall running along the edge of the roof. "I see some scanner drones coming this way. They might have been programmed by now to search for your AIs."

"Then we should get rid of them before we go inside," Ridley said, reaching behind her neck to unclasp the silver chain she'd been wearing since she was five years old. "Maybe we can throw them over to the next building."

"Yes, I can probably throw them that far," Archer replied.

"I'll use a conjuration," Dad said as Ridley rolled up the bottom of her jeans and removed the ankle chain with her backup amulets. "That'll easily get them over." He looked down at his wedding ring, and Ridley watched him pause before removing it. Then he stuck his hand into his pocket and retrieved another tiny piece of arxium. His recently removed AI1, Ridley realized. She climbed to her feet and stood in front of him, but his attention remained focused on the ring sitting on his palm.

"Mom would understand," she said quietly. "She wouldn't be mad at you. She'd want you to do whatever you have to do in order to stay—"

A loud buzzing cut off the remainder of her words. It came from behind them, soaring up and over the edge of the building. A single scanner drone none of them had seen or heard approaching. They raced across the roof, trying to get out of its path, and for a moment, Ridley thought they'd made it. But the drone stopped. Then a blinding spotlight shone down on them and a siren began blaring.

"Quick, before the cops arrive!" Ridley yelled, her hands already glowing. That pounding ache was back in her temples and behind her eyes, but as long as she wasn't blind with pain or puking up her insides, then she'd force her magic out.

Dad caught her arm. "Are you sure you—"

"Yes! I'd rather not die!" They ran to retrieve their bags, and the drone's spotlight followed them. "Archer!" Ridley yelled, holding one hand out to him as she lifted her backpack with the other.

"No, let's split up," he said as he reached her side. "I'll take your amulets and go into the building. I'll hide them somewhere. You get to safety."

"The bunker," Ridley said immediately.

"No." Dad shook his head as he handed the collection of amulets to Archer. "I have contacts who'll help us. We can—"

"Your contacts will probably end up dead for helping us, Dad," Ridley argued. "We have to get underground. It's the safest place for us to be. You can't avoid the magical community forever." She looked at Archer and told him, "We'll be at the bunker. Now go quickly!" As he took off toward the door leading into the building, she spun around, looking for the cat. It leaped at her, and she caught it clumsily. Dad groaned and muttered something Ridley couldn't hear properly over the sound of the siren and the pounding of her own head. He wrapped his arms around her as she squeezed her eyes shut. And, despite the pain slicing through her skull, they were both lifted into the air and whisked away on the wind.

Ridley barely lasted a few blocks this time. As she and Dad became visible in a deserted part of one of the train stations, the cat jumped free of her hands. "Ridley?" Dad caught her as she staggered. "Are you okay?"

Her stomach heaved before she could answer, but she hadn't eaten anything tonight and there seemed to be nothing in her stomach to throw up. "The dizziness ... from spinning through the air ... makes the nausea worse," she managed to say. "I can't seem to keep hold of the magic while my body is trying to throw up."

"At least we got away from that screaming drone," Dad said. "Here, sit down." He took the backpack from her and led her to one of the benches alongside the railroad track. "I'll do that conjuration again. It seemed to help a little, right?"

"Yes." Ridley leaned forward on her knees while Dad pulled magic from the air. It was still so strange to see him doing that. Before the other night on the Brex Tower balcony, she hadn't seen him use magic in years. He swept his hands through the air in a series of swift movements before pushing the resulting magic toward her. She shut her eyes as it drifted across her face. Moments later, the nausea began to subside and her head didn't feel like it was throbbing quite so intensely.

"Any better?" Dad asked.

"Yes. There's still some head-hammering pain behind my eyes, but it isn't as bad."

"I don't think you should use magic again," he said. "We can walk from here. If it's an emergency and we have to get away quickly, then you can make us disappear."

"Okay." Ridley looked around, but she couldn't tell which station they were at. "Do you know which way the bunker is from here?"

"Ridley, I'm really not sure about going there. You know it's dangerous to be around a large group of magic users. Anyone could discover them at any moment, and then their entire community will wind up dead."

"Dad, they've remained hidden for almost a decade."

Dad heaved a sigh. "True, but the risk is still there."

Ridley rubbed her forefingers against her temples. "I don't understand. We can't stay in Lumina City, right? We have to leave. And the only way for us to get to the other side of the wall is through that bunker. So we have to go there eventually."

Dad nodded slowly. "I know you're right. In the back of my mind, I know I'm only delaying the inevitable."

Ridley lowered her hands and focused on his face. His tired eyes, and the silvery gray in his dark hair. "It's really not that bad down there," she reassured him. "And we don't have to stay there long."

"All right then. I guess that's where we're headed."

Nothing went wrong on the way to the bunker, which Ridley took as proof that it was the right decision to go there. Dad knew how to get to Jasmine Heights, and, once they were there, he knew how to locate the passageway that ended with the door leading down to the bunker. Which was a good thing, because the only other way Ridley knew of was via a trapdoor in Ezra's apartment.

Dad knocked twice on the door, and it was only when it swung open that Ridley remembered the rose bush. With so many leaves, twigs, and thorns tangled around one another, it filled the space ahead of them and was impossible to see over. "Well, that's new," Dad said. "Last time I was here, this was a stone wall with a phoenix carving at the center. You had to know which of the phoenix feathers to touch in order to get the wall to disappear." He looked at Ridley. "Do you know what to do?"

Ridley eyed the many red roses. "The highest rose," she said. "That's what we have to touch. I think it's that one." She pointed to the spot she remembered Archer reaching up toward. Dad stretched upward, and the moment his fingers brushed the rose, the twigs began to retract. Green and red were replaced instantly by vibrant glowing blue, reminding

Ridley that the rose bush was nothing but a magical illusion. It flattened itself against the walls and ceiling, revealing the same two broad-shouldered men who had been standing guard last time: one with copper-colored skin and dark tattoos marking his arms, the other pale and bald with multiple piercings.

"Um, hi," Ridley said. Her headache had been lessening, but pain pulsed a little harder throughout her skull as her heart rate increased. "It's a coincidence that you're here again, right? I mean, you don't spend *all* your time at this door, do you?"

The two men looked at Ridley, then at Dad, and finally, at the magic-mutated cat sitting beside Ridley's ankles. But neither said a word. It was then that Ridley remembered Archer speaking some sort of pass phrase. "The, um, the moon is out—no, the moon is *hidden* tonight." The tattooed guy raised an eyebrow. "Look, if it's changed, I'm sorry," she continued. "That's the only one I know. You do remember me, right? It hasn't been that long since I was here."

"I remember you," Tattooed Guy said. His eyes shifted to Dad. "Don't remember him though."

"Christa knows me," Dad told him.

The two men looked at one another. "Funny how everyone says that."

"Look, you know the drill," Bald Guy said to Ridley. "We can't let him in until we've confirmed with Christa."

"Sure, yeah, okay. As long as you don't try to kill us like last time."

Dad's eyes snapped toward hers. "They tried to *kill* you last time? You told me it wasn't that bad down here."

Ridley rubbed above her eyebrows with her thumb and forefinger, attempting to massage away the last of her headache. "Technically, I think they were trying to kill Archer. I just happened to be with him."

Bald Guy let out a long-suffering sigh. "We weren't trying to kill him. We just wanted to incapacitate him and lock him in a room while we called Christa. Things would have been much simpler if he hadn't fought back."

"Things would have been much simpler if you'd just *told* us that."

"Can you please just fetch Christa?" Dad asked. "Without any attacking or locking in rooms? We'll happily wait back out there in the hallway." He jabbed a thumb over his shoulder.

"No need," Tattooed Guy said. "You can stand right where you are. We'll send a message to—"

"Actually," Bald Guy said, looking down at a commscreen in his hand, "she says it's cool. You can meet her in the beach rec room." He looked at Ridley and added, "She says you know where that is."

Ridley glanced up and around for any sign of a camera. "She's watching us, isn't she."

"Yes. She doesn't always have time, but tonight, yes. She's watching."

"Great," Dad said, and Ridley couldn't tell if he was being sarcastic or not. "You know where to go?" he asked Ridley.

"Yes." She led the way past the two men and down the

stairs, with Dad on one side and the cat on the other. There had been a lot of running, shouting, and offensive magic-use the last time she was down here, but without all that, it was fairly simple to get to the rec room she'd met Ezra in. Once they'd made it all the way down the stairs, they entered a cavernous tunnel with a canal running through it. A slow-motion replay of Archer falling toward it from high above flashed across Ridley's mind, but she pushed the memory aside with a shiver. It made her sick to think of what would have happened if her magic hadn't caught him.

She and Dad—and the cat, of course—crossed the bridge to the other side of the canal and walked through the conjured forest of trees and bushes that grew from the concrete alongside the water. The same luminous pink jellyfish she'd noticed last time pulsed through the water, and lilies floated at the canal's edge. Vibrant blue tinged the edges of their petals, the only visible sign that all of this was made of magic.

Ridley turned away from the canal and moved through the trees toward the arched doorways that stood at intervals along the wall. She looked into the first room, which didn't seem familiar, so she pushed past a few bushes to get to the next doorway. This room was also full of cozy couches, rugs, and a few tables and chairs, but it was the walls that told Ridley she was in the right place: they were covered in painted windows looking out onto a painted beach scene. Not a static scene, but one that moved in looping motion, depicting waves that appeared to roll up a sandy shore before sliding back into the sea. Paint infused with some sort of conjuration.

The room was empty except for a man lounging on a couch wearing headphones and a woman who'd just walked into the room from a door on the far side. "Maverick," she said, a smile spreading across her face as she approached them. Her long brown hair was twisted into a messy bun on top of her head, and she scooped a few gray strands behind her ears as she stopped in front of them. "It's been a long time," she said, holding her hand out to clasp Dad's. Then she turned her green gaze to Ridley. "It's good to see you again too. I had no idea when we met last weekend that you were Maverick Kayne's daughter. Ah, and you have an illegal pet," she added with a grin, looking down at the cat. "How fun."

"Christa, thank you for letting us in," Dad said before Ridley could answer. "We need to stay here for a few days, if that's okay. Do you have space?"

"Yes, I'm sure we can find an unoccupied room. You're both very welcome here."

"Thank you. It definitely won't be for long. We're heading out of the city. I'm sorry I didn't contact you sooner to make arrangements. Our decision to leave was very … sudden."

Christa cocked her head as her eyes returned to Ridley. "You're the other one they're looking for."

Ridley blinked, her head throbbing anew as her pulse ratcheted up again. "I'm sorry, what?"

"It's all over the news. Two women used magic at a party tonight. Very unusual, dangerous magic, though no details were given as to what exactly that means." Ridley remained quiet as she tried to decide whether to confirm or deny Christa's words. Dad shook his head almost imperceptibly, but before Ridley could come up with a lie, Christa said, "You're one of them, aren't you. An elemental."

Surprise flashed across Dad's face. "You know about them?"

"Yes. I don't know too much, but I'm aware of their existence."

"I see. Well, I ... I hope you'll forgive me for not saying anything when we used to know one another," Dad said. "You understand the need for secrecy, I'm sure."

"Of course, yes." Christa looked at Ridley again. "Does Archer know?"

"Um, yes."

"Oh, I wonder why he didn't tell me. Anyway, you'll be pleased to know Callie made it here safely."

"Callie?" Ridley repeated. "Callie Hemingway?"

"Yes, the other woman who used magic tonight. Weren't you with her when both of you ended up using magic?"

"Yes. But ..." Ridley shook her head. "She said she was going to hide out at home. That she'd be safe there. She had no interest in leaving the city with me. I didn't realize she even knew about the magical underworld down here."

"Apparently she's known for years. Her father discovered this bunker while it was being built. She was quite honest about never planning to come here, but apparently the police showed up at her house, so she had no choice but to run. She said she used magic in a way she'd never used it before. Something she didn't even know she could do."

"Air, perhaps," Ridley said quietly. "She screamed a lot when I did that earlier, so it's possible she didn't know she can become the elements."

"Well, then I'm guessing the two of you will have a lot to talk about." Christa's eyes sparkled as she smiled again. "Anyway, let's go and find you guys a room."

They left through the door on the other side of the room and entered a corridor. Some stairs and a few more corridors led them into what felt almost like an old house with wooden floors, a wooden staircase up ahead, and large, low windows on each wall. There wasn't anything real on the other side of the windows, of course, but the walls were painted with the same conjured paint that had been used in the rec room.

They climbed the stairs and stopped on the next landing up. The wall to their left and right each had two doors, as did the wall ahead of them, though one was open to reveal a bathroom. Ridley assumed the others were bedrooms. "Do you mind sharing?" Christa asked as she walked to the left and opened the first door. She flicked a switch on the wall, and an overhead light came on. "We don't have a lot of empty space left here."

"I don't mind," Ridley said.

Dad nodded. "It's fine. It won't be for long."

The room was only a little bit bigger than Ridley's bedroom at home. A narrow bed sat on each side of the room, separated by a single bedside table with a lamp on it. Squished into the space beside the door, against the only other available piece of wall, was a small wardrobe. What made the room a little more welcoming, though, was the scene painted behind the fake window above the bedside table. It depicted a lake at sunset with snow-capped mountains in the distance. The lake rippled, and the occasional bird soared low over the water.

"Someone went to a lot of trouble to decorate all the walls in this place," Ridley observed.

"Some people have been here a long time," Christa said. "They need to keep busy somehow."

"It's great, thank you," Dad said. "We appreciate this, Christa. I can't imagine what it takes to keep a haven like this running, and I don't want to take your hospitality for granted, so ... if there's some way we can contribute, some form of payment you'd accept, or—"

"Don't worry about it now," Christa said, a warm smile reaching her eyes again. "We can talk in the morning. See if there's any way you can help out before you leave." She clasped her hands together. "I hope you guys sleep well tonight. Oh, and the bathroom you saw out there—" she pointed over her shoulder with her thumb "—is for you to share with the others who live on this landing."

She left then, and the cat jumped onto the bed on the right hand side of the room. Ridley lowered her backpack beside the cat, wondering if she should come up with a name for the animal that seemed to want to follow her around. After retrieving her small toiletry bag, pajama bottoms, and a T-shirt, she went to the bathroom to change. Dad used the bathroom after her, and when he returned, Ridley was sitting up in bed, staring at her blank commscreen while the cat slept beside her.

"You didn't turn that on, did you?" Dad asked immediately.

"No." Ridley turned the commscreen over and over in her hands. "I just wish I could tell Meera everything that's going on."

"You can't tell Meera," Dad answered.

"I understand, Dad, I'm saying I *wish* I could. I feel terrible about vanishing with no explanation. She's already confused about Shen, and now I'm disappearing too? She's going to be so confused and upset. And there's the fact that you're gone too. She'll try to find out what's happened to us."

"Mei will come up with something," Dad said as he pulled back the duvet on his bed.

Ridley lowered her face into her palms. "That's even worse. Lies upon lies. They just never end. Oh," she added, looking up as she remembered something. "Malachi."

"Who?"

"The first elemental I found. I was going to meet him again tomorrow. I need to tell him I'm—"

"You don't have to tell him a thing, Ridley."

"I don't want to leave him hanging. He needs to know I'm leaving the city."

"No, he doesn't." Dad repositioned his pillow before lying down and pulling the duvet up to his chin.

"Dad, he *just* found out that he's not alone. He's excited, looking forward to spending time with someone who understands what it's like to be a freak, and—"

"You're not a freak, Riddles."

"I know that *now*, but I've spent my whole life believing I am—and so has he—and that doesn't just go away overnight. And now I'm just going to disappear without a word? That's not fair."

Dad turned onto his side to face her. "Ridley, you can't contact him. You *know* that. Someone might be trying to track your commscreen, so you need to keep it turned off. In fact, you should probably get rid of it."

"I'll keep it off," she promised, leaning over the side of the bed to slide it into her backpack. She couldn't face getting rid of it. That single piece of technology felt like her only remaining tie to Meera. As long as she had it, there was still a chance she'd be able to contact her friend at some point.

Dad reached over and turned the light off, and the dim orange glow from the painted sunset was now the only light in the bedroom. In an effort to ease the anxiety that was tightening its fist around her chest, Ridley stroked her hand gently along the length of the cat's body, from her head all the way down her back. *Ember*, she thought. *Is that a suitable name for a black cat?*

"Ridley," Dad said. "Why are you still sitting up?"

She exhaled slowly. Her eyes were heavy and an echo of her earlier headache still thudded dully at her temples. She really wanted to sleep, but ... "I'm worried about Archer," she admitted.

"I'm sure he's fine."

"But we left before he got into the building. What if he couldn't get inside? What if that door on the roof was locked?

What if he was stuck up there and the police found him?"

"I doubt a locked door would stop him," Dad said.

Ridley chewed on the tip of her thumb nail. Dad eyed her with a strange half smile. "What?" she asked eventually. "What are you smiling at?"

"Nothing."

"Fine, don't tell me."

"You need to sleep, Riddles. You're exhausted."

She lay down, but worry still ate away at her insides. The cat snuggled a little closer to her, and she didn't push it away. *Ember*, she whispered again inside her mind. Her thoughts drifted, and she wasn't aware of it when she finally fell asleep.

CHAPTER 14

IT WAS DISCONCERTING TO wake up in an unfamiliar bed, but it took Ridley only a few moments to remember everything that had happened the night before. At least, she assumed it was now morning. It was difficult to tell in a room that had the same amount of illumination coming through the window as it had when she'd gone to sleep. But she felt rested, so that was probably a good sign that it was now a new day.

She pushed herself up and looked across the small space—but Dad's bed was empty. Ember, the cat who didn't yet know she had been named, didn't seem to be around either. Ridley's eyes landed on the table between the beds where a small square of paper sat. She picked it up, recognizing Dad's handwriting.

Going to talk to Christa. Thought I'd let you sleep in a while longer.

Her stomach grumbled as she climbed out of bed, so she took her water bottle with her to the bathroom. Unsure of what the food situation was at the bunker and when she'd be able to eat again, she stood at the basin and drank a full bottle's worth of water while taking in her messy appearance in the mirror. She'd briefly washed her face the night before, but the makeup smudged beneath her eyes indicated she hadn't done a very good job. Her hair was in desperate need of a brush. And probably a wash too. The French twist was long gone, but she spotted pins here and there. Probably because she hadn't bothered removing a single one before climbing into bed last night.

She picked the hair pins out one by one, filled the bottle a second time, and then remembered the energy bars in the backpack as she opened the bathroom door. At the sight of someone walking toward her room, she stopped. "Archer?" He looked back over his shoulder. "Hey," she continued, a smile breaking out across her face as she walked toward him. "You're okay."

His expression turned to one of bemusement. "Me? Of course I'm okay. I'm here to check that *you're* okay. That you and your dad got here safely. Christa told me where you're staying."

"Yeah, we made it. I'm glad you're okay too." She tucked her bottle beneath one arm and rubbed her forefingers below her eyes, hoping to get rid of the dark smudges there. Archer, of course, looked perfectly presentable in jeans, a T-shirt and a jacket. His hair was slightly damp, as if he'd showered just before coming here, and that scent—his aftershave or whatever it was—took her right back to the moment he'd kissed her last night. Stupid aftershave.

"Rough night?" he asked with a mischievous smile.

She lowered her hands, guessing she was probably making the dark rings beneath her eyes worse. "Hey, I'll bet you looked just as bad before your shower this morning."

He nodded, his expression serious all of a sudden. "Yes, I always find it difficult to remove my, uh ... mascara?"

She walked past him, shaking her head as she laughed. "Mascara, yes. That's the one." She placed the water bottle and hair pins on the table and turned back, finding him standing hesitantly in the doorway, clearly unsure whether to come in or not.

"Um, I can wait for you in one of the rec rooms if—"

"What? No, it's fine, come in. I want to ask you about last night. Where'd you hide the amulets? And what happened when you got home? Did your parents question you? Also, don't mind me while I eat an energy bar to keep my stomach from digesting itself."

Archer stepped into the room as Ridley dug inside her bag and found an energy bar. Cranberry almond, according to the wrapper, though she knew it was made from zero natural ingredients. "I left the amulets about halfway down the building," Archer told her. "There was a pot with a fake plant in it on one of the landings, so I dropped them in there. As for my parents ..." He lowered himself to the edge of Ridley's bed.

"They must know by now that I'm the one the police are looking for," Ridley said. She climbed onto the bed, scooted back so she was leaning against the wall, and pulled her knees up to her chest as she unwrapped the bar.

"Yes, they know," Archer said. "First they asked where I'd disappeared to, so I told them I waited and waited at the party, but you never came out of the bathroom. I said I called your commscreen, but you didn't answer, so I sent someone in to look for you and it turned out you weren't there. So I left the party to try to find you, but I never did, so eventually I went home."

With her mouth half full, Ridley asked, "Do you think they believed all that?"

"They seemed to. My mother then took great delight in informing me that you're some kind of magical criminal, and that you abandoned me when the police came looking for you. Lilah was already in bed—or pretending to be, at least—but I'm sure when I see her later she'll say something along the lines of 'I told you so.'"

Ridley wrapped her arms around her knees without taking another bite of the bar. "Then you'll be able to tell her she was right. The two of you can be friends again, and you can part on good terms."

Archer shook his head, his dark eyes settling on Ridley's as he said, "I won't be telling her she was right. But I will try to patch things up with her as best I can before I leave."

Ridley nodded slowly, unable to pull her gaze from his. "Okay. That's good. I mean, you know I don't really like her, but I'm guessing it will suck big time for her when her big brother simply vanishes with no explanation. She'll go to school one morning, and by the time she gets home, you'll be ..." Ridley trailed off, her eyes slipping past Archer's as something occurred to her.

"Everything okay?" he asked.

"I just realized something," she said as a strange sense of loss threatened to overwhelm her. "I won't ever be going back to school."

"No, I guess you won't. Not in this city, at least." He paused, then added, "Why do you look sad? I would have been overjoyed to leave school a year early."

"It's just ... I worked so hard for that stupid scholarship. For the chance at a better life." She folded the wrapper over the remaining half of the energy bar and placed it on the bed beside her. She didn't feel so much like eating anymore. "You wouldn't understand," she said as she wrapped her arms around her knees once more. "You never needed—"

"No, I'm sorry." He rested one hand lightly on top of hers as he added, "I'm an idiot. I didn't think. Obviously it's important to you."

She looked at where his hand sat on top of hers. She was hyperaware of his touch, as if all the nerve endings in her body now existed in her hand. She thought about turning it over so they were palm to palm. So she could slide her fingers between his.

"I can't imagine how unsettling this is for you," Archer said, pulling his hand away. "At least I *planned* to leave the city. You had no idea this was coming."

Ridley inhaled deeply, immensely relieved that she hadn't embarrassed herself by doing that entwined-fingers thing.

"Well, yes and no," she said after she'd given her brain a few seconds to replay Archer's words. "Last week I had no idea this was coming. This week … well, ever since I got that letter, the possibility has been there in the back of my mind that we might have to leave suddenly. Dad said we wouldn't need to, but I know things can change in an instant."

"Like last night," Archer said quietly.

"Yes."

He was silent a few moments. Then: "What are your dad's plans for the two of you? Will you be staying here in the bunker for a while?"

"No. We're definitely leaving, probably sooner rather than later." She pulled her knees tighter against her chest. "It seems the only thing Dad dislikes more than the idea of heading out into the wastelands is the idea of living with a bunch of magic users."

"If you wait a few days, I can go with you."

"You're planning to leave that soon?"

"I have nothing to stay here for. I just need to get a few things in order, and then I'm out."

"Where are you planning to go? Back to France?"

He shook his head. "No, it's too much of a risk to try to travel in secret on the TransAt Train again. The first time I left, I obviously wasn't hiding. My parents knew where I was going. And when I returned this most recent time, I wasn't hiding either. I just didn't broadcast it to the world through all my social channels, and I kept a low profile on the train. But a few months ago, that time I snuck back into the city … well, I was *not* an official passenger on the TransAt."

Ridley's lips tugged up into a smile on one side. "Archer Davenport, how daring of you."

"Clearly I'm not as good at going unseen as you are. Being able to literally disappear into thin air would have been helpful. I almost got caught. When I leave now, for good, I need to do it properly. I don't want anything going wrong, and I don't want anyone to know where I'm headed. So I'll stick to this continent. There's an elemental community I know of. They told me about it when I was living on La Tournette. In fact, I know the location of most of the communities around the world, but this one's the closest. Probably a few weeks away from here on foot."

Ridley's eyebrows rose. "You're planning to spend several *weeks* out in the wastelands?"

"It's not as dangerous out there as you think, remember? You just have to be careful. Respectful. Don't take anything with arxium thinking it'll protect you. The magic out there will just fight back."

She tilted her head in thought. "You told me you were hiking in one of those hazmat-type suits made of arxium when you first found the elementals. Was magic attacking you then?"

"Yes. I didn't get hurt because I was inside the suit, but it was like trying to hike through a storm. We all got buffeted around a lot. That's how I ended up separated from the group." He let out a quiet laugh. "Best thing that ever happened to me."

"Okay, so if Dad and I go with you, then I don't have to worry about doing that whole 'look for the signs, listen to the elements' thing."

"What thing?"

"From my letter. That's what the elementals told me to do to find them."

"Oh yes. No, you wouldn't need to do that. I know where to go." He gave her that smile again, the one that stirred something deep inside her, and added, "It would be great if you came with."

She nodded, smiling. The idea of not having to say good-bye to him filled her with a comforting warmth. She was leaving behind almost every other part of her life, so at least she'd have this one thing—aside from Dad—that would feel like carrying a piece of home with her. She did a double take at that thought. Since when had she come to associate Archer Davenport with the idea of *home*?

"Oh, and the other benefit of us traveling together," Archer added, "is that it'll be much faster. On my own, I'll have to walk. But you can whisk us through the air at the speed of a gale force wind."

"Ah, I see." She cocked her head and gave him a teasing smile. "So you just want me for my magic, huh?" She expected him to respond in the same teasing manner, but instead he hesitated, his eyes burning into hers with an unusual intensity. "Um, so, it doesn't totally freak you out?" she asked hurriedly, before the moment could become awkward. "When I turn you to air?"

"No," he said immediately.

She laughed. "That was too quick to be true."

"Well, maybe I was a little freaked out, but mostly I thought it was incredible. It was such a rush, racing through the air like that." He moved as if he were about to push himself to his feet, then stopped. Looking back at her, he said, "I wasn't going to admit this, but ... remember you asked me if I wish I was like you?"

"Yes?"

His eyes moved across her face as a small smile made its way onto his lips. "I do. I wish I was like you."

She had no idea what to say to that. It was completely absurd that someone like Archer, who appeared to have everything in the world, wanted to be like her.

"I wonder if anyone is ever truly happy with the hand they're dealt in life," he continued quietly, "or if everyone's always wishing for something they don't have."

"Or wishing they *didn't* have something they do have," Ridley answered.

For several moments, they simply stared at one another. She couldn't tell what he was thinking, but her brain was backtracking, trying to figure out when this conversation had turned so serious.

"Do you really mean that?" he asked. "Do you wish you didn't have magic?"

"Well ... maybe not so much anymore. But for a long time, yes. I just wanted to be normal. I didn't want to have to worry all the time that someone might find out what I could do. Even after I decided to use it to help me get into people's homes and steal things, I still had to hide it from, well, everyone. Even Dad. He never wanted me using it. He always reminded me how dangerous it was."

Archer watched her for another few seconds. "So you feel guilty when you're using it?"

"Well, yeah. Dad never wanted me to use it—he'd probably *still* prefer it if I didn't use it—so of course I feel guilty about it. Not that the guilt has ever stopped me," she added with a roll of her eyes. "Obviously. I just told myself I was doing something good, and that Dad didn't need to know about it."

"Hmm," Archer said, still watching her.

"Why? What are you thinking?"

"I don't know ... Your grandfather said you're trying too hard to control the magic, and that's what's giving you a headache. You didn't seem to believe that. But maybe it isn't just the exertion. You're feeling guilty every time you use magic, and anxious because you might get caught, and afraid because of what might happen to you if you fully give yourself over to the elements." She frowned at that last bit, but he added, "Yeah, I was listening to you that day you came to the hospital to heal me. When you told me you were scared of earth, and that water and fire are too volatile."

Ridley sighed and tipped her head back against the wall. "So basically, you're saying I get stressed out and scared and guilty, and that exacerbates the headaches until they feel like they're going to blind me and make me hurl my insides out?"

Archer shrugged. "Maybe."

"Wow, you make me sound like a total basket case."

"Look, I don't know. It's possible I'm talking total non-sense."

"You're probably talking total nonsense."

"But I've spoken to a lot of elementals over the past year," he continued. "And not everyone can just automatically interact with the elements from the get-go. Some people have to teach themselves how to relax. I imagine that if you're a control freak—"

"You're saying I'm a control freak?"

"—then you should probably, I don't know, meditate or something."

Ridley sighed. "That doesn't sound like something I'd be good at." Archer's smirk reappeared, and Ridley pointed a finger at him, hastily adding, "And don't say, 'Exactly.'"

He laughed. "I was just going to add that maybe you don't need to meditate now that the other factors aren't an issue anymore. You have nothing to feel guilty about now, right? Your father knows you're using magic. He's okay with it. I think? And the anxiety part ... well, once you're in a place where no one can see you—"

"Like the wastelands?"

"Yes. Then you'll have nothing to be anxious about. No one's going to arrest you and sentence you to death out there."

"And the fear of the elements ..." Ridley said quietly, no longer meeting his gaze.

"I guess that's up to you. You'll have to figure out a way to get over your fear. Maybe by letting yourself go and proving to yourself that it doesn't kill you."

Ridley snorted. "Great plan. What if it does? What if I end up stuck inside a rock forever?"

"I suppose you'll have to take a leap of faith at some point."

"Yeah, maybe ..." She pushed her hand through her tangled hair. "Anyway, what were we talking about before you decided to go and get all deep on me?"

"Um ..." Archer turned his gaze toward the painted scenery behind the window. "Oh yes. The possibility of you and your dad coming with me when I leave to join the elementals."

"Right, yes. I just have to convince Dad that it's a good idea, which isn't going to be easy. You know how he feels about us living with elementals."

Archer stood and said, "I can try to talk to him, if you think it might help."

"Sure, you're welcome to try," Ridley said with a shrug. "But he's pretty stubborn once he's decided something."

"I guess you had to get it from somewhere."

Ridley fought the upward tugging of her lips and decided not to respond to that. "Uh, before you go ... do you know what time it is? I'm finding it quite disorienting not being able to see outside. It could be lunch time for all I know." The thought of lunch—and the fact that she wasn't currently feeling depressed about ruining her high school career and future job opportunities—made her stomach grumble again.

Archer pulled his commscreen out. "Not too late. Just after nine."

"Okay. Does your commscreen work down here?" she asked as he put it away.

"No. Well, yes, it *works*—so I can see the time—but it doesn't connect to anything. You have to go up those stairs near the entrance. Remember where those guys attacked us when we came here last time? You can get a connection there."

"Oh, so it's safe if I turn mine on down here? No one can track it?"

"Well it can't connect to anything, so I don't think so."

"Okay. I just need to get Malachi's number off my commscreen." She scooted to the edge of the bed and leaned down to dig inside her backpack. "Can I ask you a favor?" she said as she turned the commscreen on. "When you get out of here, can you send him a message? I was going to get back to him about meeting somewhere today, but that's obviously not happening anymore. But I don't want to just leave him hanging, never knowing what happened to me. So ..." She looked up. "Do you mind doing that?"

Archer sighed. "Sure. He's not my favorite person, but I guess I can text him."

"Thank you." She stood and handed the device to Archer so he could copy the number. "Uh, anyway, I should probably go shower."

"Yeah." He returned the commscreen to her. "You're a total mess."

"Oh my goodness, it's not *that* bad," she said, dragging her fingers self-consciously through her hair again.

He laughed. "You're right. The post-party look is actually

really cute on you."

Her mouth fell open, but she had no idea how to respond to that. "Okay, you need to go," was all she could say in the end.

With another smirk, Archer turned and walked away. "Enjoy your shower, Ridley," he called back.

In her flustered state, it took her longer than it should have to gather up some clothes, her toiletry bag, and the towel hanging behind the door. It was only once she was in the shower with her stomach starting to gnaw on itself that she wished she'd grabbed the other half of the energy bar too.

CHAPTER 15

DAD WAS BACK IN THEIR room when Ridley returned from showering. It felt good to be clean again, but she couldn't enjoy the feeling while her stomach was loudly demanding a proper meal. She lunged for the other half of the energy bar on her bed just as Dad said, "There's a kitchen downstairs if you want to get some food."

"Oh, fantastic. How does that work? Do I need to, um ... pay for it?"

Dad shook his head. "It's okay. I've already worked things out with Christa. I made a contribution that should cover us for the next few days. It's different for everyone who comes down here. Some people can pay, some people can work. I offered to fix a few things—items that require some complex, intricate conjurations—and also gave her some money."

"Thanks, Dad."

"There are no set meal times or anything like that. You prepare your own food. There are a whole bunch of fridges down there, and a huge pantry. Some food's labeled, some isn't. Come on, I'll show you."

They left the room together, but not before Ridley grabbed the other half of the energy bar. She wasn't sure she could survive all the way to the kitchen without nibbling on something. "We'll need to buy some food and other supplies before we head out to the wastelands," she said as she peeled the wrapper back.

"Yes, but first we need to discuss where we're going. Then we can figure out exactly what and how much we need."

Ridley nodded. "Did Archer speak to you?"

"He did. But before we talk about anything, you should eat."

"Definitely."

About twenty minutes later, Ridley stood in the doorway of a large dining room with a bowl and spoon in her hands, feeling a little bit like the new kid entering the school cafeteria for the first time. Dad had gone to fix something for Christa, and Ridley was left to face the dining room alone. She'd expected to find it empty seeing as it was too late for breakfast and too early for lunch, but three of the tables were occupied. With a lurch of her grumbling stomach, she realized the woman sitting alone at one of the tables was Callie.

Ridley took a deep breath and walked toward her. On the table in front of Callie sat a mug and a plate with half a sandwich. But instead of eating, she had her chin propped on one hand while she traced patterns in wisps of magic above the mug with her other hand.

"Hi," Ridley said hesitantly, stopping across the table from Callie.

The golden haired woman looked up, surprise registering on her face. "Oh. It's you. I didn't know you were here."

"I only arrived here after you last night. Do you, uh, mind if I sit here?"

Callie leaned back and lowered her hands to her lap. "Um, no, I don't mind. You can sit."

"Thanks." Ridley slid onto the bench and placed her bowl of cereal in front of her. She might have been hoping for a proper meal, but there weren't many food items in the pantry that didn't have 'Don't touch!' or 'Hands off!' written on them, and she was so hungry that she was happy to eat cereal with some form of milk substitute—she couldn't remember what kind, exactly—poured over it. But first, there were a few things she needed to say.

"Callie, I am so, so sorry," she said. "I know you must hate me right now for ruining your life."

"Well, as you pointed out last night," Callie said as she lifted her mug, "I was the one who couldn't hide my magic."

"I know, but you would never have been using it in the first place if I hadn't gone to that party to speak to you. I thought I was doing the right thing passing on those letters. The person who was supposed to deliver them was killed, and since I ended up with them, it felt like my responsibility. I thought you—and the others—would want to know the truth. But—

"Hey, you can stop with all the teenage melodrama, okay? You didn't *ruin* my life." Callie sighed. "I don't exactly have much of a life to ruin."

Ridley raised her eyebrows at that. Clearly she wasn't the only one prone to 'teenage melodrama.' But she was supposed to be apologizing, so she decided not to say that bit out loud.

"I'm thirty-four," Callie continued. "I'm not married, I barely have any friends, and I spend most of my life hiding at home. I'm not exactly *living*. I thought it counted as living because at least I wasn't trapped underground in this place. I could breathe fresh air and feel the rain on my skin and see the sky. Well, on the odd occasion when it's visible through the clouds. But since I got here last night, I've used so many conjurations—just simple things I used to take for granted before the Cataclysm—that I feel … I don't know. Like I'm alive for the first time in years. As if I've been half asleep, and now something's woken me up."

Ridley couldn't help the grin that spread across her face as Callie spoke. "That's amazing. I'm so relieved you feel that way. Oh, wait, have you let people see that the magic you're using is coming from inside you?"

"No, no, no." Callie shook her head. "When I spoke to Christa last night, it seemed like even the people who live down here using magic have no idea that elementals exist. She told me to keep that part to myself, so that's what I'm doing. I've just been pulling magic from the air like everyone else around here, and even just to do that is so …" A smile lit up her face. "It's so incredibly liberating."

"So you don't hate me after all?"

"No, I don't *hate* you."

"Well, that's really great to hear," Ridley said, picking up her spoon and stirring her cereal. She shoveled some into her mouth as Callie sipped from her mug. Then she lowered it and crossed her arms on the table.

"Of course, it's all still a lot to take in," she continued, "and I feel like I left my old life very abruptly. I obviously didn't have time to put things in order. Like, how do I access my bank accounts now? They—the government, police, this *Shadow Society*—will be watching. So even though I'm excited, I'm also feeling completely disorganized. And also ... there's this voice in the back of my mind saying, 'Are you really going to stay here? You've never wanted to live underground. There's a world of people out there just like you. Why don't you go and look for them?'"

Ridley lowered her spoon and swallowed her current mouthful of cereal. "You're talking about what the letter said at the end? About going into the wastelands and looking for the elementals?"

"Yes. It's completely ludicrous, of course. I'd never survive out there on my own. But ... I don't know." She stared down into her mug. "It's like ... I've finally discovered what I really am, but I still have to hide what I can do, even here in this magical underworld. So what's the point in staying here? If I want to be free to live the way I was meant to live, then I should go out there and find the others."

"If you're serious about that," Ridley said, "you should talk to my dad. We're leaving soon. He doesn't want to find the elementals, but I do. If I can convince him that that's where we should go, then you can come with us."

Callie's soft brown eyes were wide now. "Really? So—that's—wow, you mean this might actually happen? We might actually be able to live with our own kind?"

"Yes. I hope so."

"Okay," Callie answered. "I'm definitely interested."

Dad seemed to keep himself busy for most of the day, and Ridley began to wonder if he was avoiding her on purpose. Avoiding having to speak about where they should go. It was late in the afternoon when she finally saw him again. She and Callie were in the beach rec room, playing around with various conjurations, reveling in the fact that they could pull magic and use it without bothering to check whether anyone was watching. *I don't have to be afraid*, Ridley kept telling herself. *As long as it's not my own magic that slips out.* Ember the cat was curled on the couch between them, pretending to sleep and occasionally swatting at wisps of magic. Callie had been a little freaked out when she first saw the animal's glowing blue eyes and second pair of ears. But after Ember had twisted around her legs a few times, Callie seemed to warm to her.

Ridley glanced up as someone entered the room. "Dad," she called, waving to him as he looked around.

"Oh, there you are," he said. He crossed the room and took

a seat on the almost threadbare armchair beside the couch.

Ridley was about to introduce him to Callie when Callie said, "Do I know you? You seem really familiar."

"Oh, uh, Maverick Kayne," Dad said. He leaned forward and rested his elbows on his knees. "Perhaps you remember me from before the Cataclysm when I used to design—"

"Yes! Oh my goodness. It's you. Of course I remember you." Callie beamed at him. "For my very first awards event, I wore these gold wrist cuffs you designed. They had this intricate filigree flower design, and each of the metal flowers—well, they were buds, I suppose—had gold petals that slowly opened and closed. They were absolutely exquisite."

"Ah, yes, I remember those," Dad said with a smile. "Each flower had a diamond at its center, so the cuffs sparkled when the flowers were open."

"Yes, those ones." Callie was sitting forward eagerly now. "I still have them. Well, they're at my house, so I suppose I don't exactly have them anymore." Her smile slipped a little. "Anyway, I'm Callie." She reached across Ridley to shake Dad's hand. "It's so amazing to actually meet you. Back in the day, everyone wanted to wear something designed by you."

Now Dad's smile was fading. "That hasn't been the case for years, I'm afraid."

Callie sighed. "Yeah, and I haven't sung in public or produced any new music in years. The Cataclysm pretty much ruined everything."

Dad nodded. Callie slowly ran her hand along Ember's back.

"Well, anyway," Ridley said in a bright voice, determined to banish the depressing mood that seemed to be settling over them. "Are you finished with all the things you needed to fix, Dad? You were busier for longer than I expected."

"Oh, yes, almost." Dad straightened and leaned back in his chair. "It was actually a watch that took up most of the afternoon. It belonged to Christa's grandfather and stopped working a few years ago. She asked if I could take a look at it."

"Okay. Well, uh, remember how we were going to discuss where we should go when we leave here?"

Dad sighed. "Yes, I remember."

"Perhaps we should do that now."

"Yes, I suppose we should. Shall we go up to the room and talk there?"

"Well, actually, Callie might want to come with us, so we may as well talk here." Dad's eyes moved to Callie, then back to Ridley. Hesitation was plain on his face. "She's like me," Ridley told Dad before he could argue. "She's the one I was speaking to at the party last night. She's the one the police probably would have shot if I hadn't got her out of there. She wants to find the—" Ridley paused, her eyes darting around the room. There weren't too many other people around, but it was always possible someone might be listening in. "Them," she finally said, because Dad would know who she was talking about.

"I see," he responded, still sounding reserved.

"Dad, please. I know you're afraid of living with a magical community. You're afraid we're going to end up caught because there are so many people in one place using magic together. But things aren't the way they used to be. The world is so fragmented since the Cataclysm. No one's going to find us out there in the wastelands. Sure, the Shadow Society might be looking, but they have no idea where to look. And I just ..." She reached out and took his hand. "I want to go somewhere I can be myself. I'm so tired of hiding who I am. I don't want to be afraid of it anymore. I just want to be ... me."

Dad looked away, but not before Ridley saw a sheen of tears glistening in his eyes. Moments passed before he finally looked at her again. "I know," he said quietly. "You're right. I can't keep ..." He shook his head and sighed. "We need to go to them. Seeing you in so much pain last night ... I didn't realize you reacted that badly to using your own magic. It isn't supposed to be that way, and I think it's my fault. I never taught you what you needed to know. I thought I was teaching you to be careful, but in the end, I was just teaching you to be afraid." His hand squeezed hers. "I'm sorry."

"Dad, it's ..." Ridley cleared her throat. "I don't blame you. I promise I don't. I know you were only trying to keep me safe." After a moment of quiet passed, she added, "So you're really okay with us going to find them? Going with Archer?"

"Yes."

Ridley scooted further forward and wrapped her arms around her father. "Thank you. Thank you, thank you."

As she sat back, Callie leaned across the couch toward them. "So, um ... I'm probably intruding on a private moment here, but I just want to check if I can come with."

Ridley looked at Dad. He nodded. "Yes, I suppose so. If you're also wanting to go, then you may as well travel with us."

"Yes. Thank you." She pushed her golden curls behind one ear as she grinned. "This is so scary. But so exciting. I thought the rest of my life would be exactly as it's been since the Cataclysm, and I'd probably end up dying alone in the same house I've been in forever, and now *everything* has changed. I can't believe—" She stopped, her eyes widening as they focused somewhere behind Ridley. "Is that *Archer Davenport*?"

Ridley twisted around and saw him walking into the room. Her stomach did a weird flip-flop thing as his eyes landed on her, which she decided to blame on hunger. After all, her lunch hadn't been much bigger than her breakfast, so hunger wasn't out of the question. "Back so soon?" she teased.

He grinned. "Yep, and I brought someone with." As he moved further into the room, Ridley caught sight of the person behind him.

"Malachi," she said in surprise.

"I heard you were planning a wild wasteland road trip, and I didn't want to miss out," he said.

Beside Ridley, Dad let out a quiet groan. "Uh, who is this?"

"Oh, Dad, this is Malachi," she said as Archer and Malachi reached them. "Remember I mentioned him last night? He's the first one I found."

"I told him where you were headed," Archer said. "*Probably* headed, that is, since I wasn't quite sure you'd decided yet. Anyway, he insisted on coming to talk to you."

"Yeah, I'd like to go with," Malachi said as he and Archer sat on the couch opposite Ridley and Callie.

"Are you sure?" Ridley asked. "Do you really want to leave behind your entire life here in Lumina City? Because unlike us, no one's looking for you."

"I'm sure," Malachi said. "I'm tired of hiding. Besides, I'm used to hitting 'restart' on my life. I can do it again."

"Ridley," Dad said quietly. "This is not how we were planning to do things."

"I know," she answered in a low voice, "but what's the difference if we have one more person?"

"Can I just get some clarification on something quickly?" Callie asked. "No one else is freaked out by the fact that there's a Davenport sitting right here? You know, from one of the most outspoken anti-magic families in the city?"

"Oh, it's fine," Ridley said to her. "He's with us."

"So when you said the name 'Archer' a minute or two ago, you were talking about *this* Archer?"

"I hope so," Archer said, fixing his dark eyes on Ridley and smiling in that slow, lazy way that instantly made her think of the moment he kissed her last night. Actually, the moment *after* he kissed her. Their teasing comments, their faces so close together, the way he'd looked at her lips and—

You're just like every other girl who's ever thrown herself at my brother's feet.

Lilah's words were jarring inside Ridley's head. She tore her eyes from Archer's magnetic gaze. *I'm not*, she argued silently. *I refuse to be.*

"Anyway, back to the part about me going with you guys," Malachi said. "If it's a problem, I could travel a little bit behind you, and we can pretend we're not together."

Dad sighed. "That's ridiculous. If you're certain you want to leave, then you may as well come with us."

"And he's coming too?" Callie asked, jerking her head toward Archer.

"I'm the one who knows where to go," Archer said. "Well, you could find your way there too, according to the letter you received, so I guess you don't technically need me. But I'm going anyway, so, as Ridley's dad said, we may as well travel together."

"Oh, you're Ridley's dad?" Malachi asked.

"Yes," Dad answered.

Ridley frowned. "Why?"

"No, nothing. I just didn't know how this old dude was connected to the rest of us. I mean, no offense, but you are older than the rest of us."

Dad let out a weary sigh. "Yes, I'm beginning to feel it."

"Okay, so we're doing this?" Callie asked. "And are we sure we're not going to be zapped into non-existence by the wild magic out there?"

"You three will be fine," Archer told her. "And Mr. Kayne and I should be okay too, as long as we don't carry any arxium with us. The magic out there *does* get violent sometimes, but as long as you don't resist, you'll be fine. It's just sort of ... testing to see what you're made of."

"Literally," Ridley muttered.

"What about food and stuff?" Callie asked.

"I'll get food and a few other supplies," Archer said. "We don't need much camping gear; there should be abandoned buildings along most of the route. And with the three of you and your, uh, unique magic—" he said that last bit in a lower voice "—we'll be able to travel much faster. It shouldn't take us more than a few days."

"I can't do that," Callie said immediately. "Just so you know. Well, I can to some extent. I did it last night, but it was definitely more instinct than anything else, and I was so scared and confused that I didn't get too far before I fell out of the air."

"I can do it," Malachi said, "but I've never experimented with speed. I don't know how fast I can go."

"Sounds like the wastelands are perfect for all three of you then," Archer said. "Ridley needs practice too."

Ridley remained quiet, grateful he hadn't said something about her being a basket case of guilt, anxiety and fear.

"Okay, final question," Dad said. He looked at Archer. "When is this happening?"

Archer didn't speak for several moments. Then he said, "Four days from now? That gives me time to get everything organized. I can also try to find the others whose letters we haven't delivered yet and pass those on."

"Okay." Dad nodded. "We leave four days from now."

CHAPTER 16

RIDLEY WOKE WITH THE sky above her. She peeled her heavy eyelids back and squinted at the gathering storm clouds far above. Dark purple rolling into gray, with electric blue zigzagging across the scene. She shifted her body, becoming aware of the hard, uneven surface she was lying on. She blinked a few times as her brain tried to catch up with what she was seeing. But her thoughts were sluggish, half-formed, confused.

She slowly pushed herself up as she tried to think back—and then saw, with a nauseating jolt, exactly where she was: Outside the city wall. In the wastelands. With rusty vehicles, cracked roads, and the crumbling, overgrown remains of buildings nearby, and Dad, Callie and Malachi lying beside her.

Her racing heart sent adrenaline shooting through her body, helping to scatter the fog in her mind. She was more awake now, but still horribly confused. How on earth did they get out here? It was tough to judge the exact distance, but they appeared to be several blocks away from the wall, still within the clear zone encircling Lumina City, where some of the ruins had been flattened and cleared while the wall was being built. The decaying remains of civilization began just a stone's throw behind her.

Maybe I'm dreaming, was her next thought. *I must be dreaming.* But her heaving stomach felt all too real. She leaned over as she gagged and almost vomited. *Not a dream*, she decided. She'd never felt physically ill in a dream.

As she sat with her hand resting against her stomach, breathing deeply, her brain struggled to rewind. Struggled to figure out the events that had led to this moment. She and the others had finished making plans. Archer had left the bunker, and the rest of them had hung out together before having dinner and going to bed. At least, Ridley had *intended* to go to bed, but she couldn't remember that part. Nor could she remember anything since then. Given that she was still dressed in yesterday's clothes—jeans, a T-shirt, and her favorite jacket with the hood—she'd probably never made it to bed. From the angle of the few rays of sunlight that managed to pierce the clouds, she determined it must be late afternoon. How had she lost almost an entire day?

"Riddles?" She looked down at the sound of Dad's voice. He blinked repeatedly as Callie stirred beside him. Then Malachi groaned something unintelligible and slung an arm over his face. "What happened?" Dad mumbled, pushing himself up.

"I don't know," Ridley said. A breeze nudged her hair back from her face. "I just woke up. I can't remember anything after … dinner? I think?"

"Yeah, I don't remember going to bed," Dad said, squinting past her. "And now, somehow, we're on the wrong damn side of the wall."

"What?" Callie squeaked. She rose to a sitting position, then clutched her stomach. "Ugh, I feel so sick."

"Dude," Malachi mumbled from where he was still lying down. "Someone drugged us."

Callie swallowed and whimpered, "Oh my gosh."

"You could be right," Dad said.

Ridley blinked and inhaled deeply, trying to further clear her senses. "Crap. Do you think they found us? The Shadow Society. Maybe because … because I turned on my commscreen yesterday morning to get your number?" she said to Malachi.

"You *turned it on*?" Dad demanded.

"But that shouldn't have made a difference," Callie said. "I asked about that when I first got to the bunker, and Christa said—" Her words cut off abruptly as her body heaved. "Ugh, sorry," she said when she'd recovered. She sucked in a few shaky breaths and continued, "Christa said it didn't matter if I left it on. You can't get a connection unless you're right up by the entrance."

"Besides," Malachi said, finally pushing himself up and looking around, "if they'd found us in the bunker, wouldn't they have just killed us there? What are we doing out here?"

Ridley's eyes scanned the silvery arxium-plated wall, searching for the gap that led to the canal and the bunker, but she couldn't find it. "Hopefully this means everyone else in the bunker is still okay. Hopefully Archer's okay."

"Maybe he's the one who gave us up," Callie said.

"That's definitely not true," Ridley replied.

Dad climbed to his feet. "Whatever's going on, we can't just sit out here." He held a hand toward Ridley, and she took it, letting him pull her to her feet. "Callie?" Dad said, reaching for her next. As he helped her up, Malachi rose shakily to his feet. Ridley looked beyond him into the ruins just as a flash of magic burst out from somewhere amid the collapsed buildings. Callie gasped and ducked her head as the magic shot past them. Ridley turned to watch it rebound off the arxium wall, explode in a burning flash, and disappear.

"I do not feel safe out here," Callie said.

"Magic isn't supposed to hurt us, right?" Malachi said, though his tone suggested he was far from convinced. At that moment, a particularly strong gust of wind howled past them, as if the elements had heard Malachi and wanted to remind him who was boss.

"Supposedly," Ridley said, bracing herself against the wind, which then died down almost instantly. "Dad?" she asked. "We need to go back, right? I know we were going to leave anyway, but Archer's not with us, and we have no food, no clothes, nothing."

"Yes, but we need to be very careful. We should avoid the bunker. Can you get us over the wall as air?"

"Yes." Already, she was letting go, watching her hands begin to glow and—

She doubled over as a fresh wave of nausea twisted her stomach and rocketed up her throat. Dizziness sent the world spinning around her. "I—I can't—" she gasped, leaning her hands on her knees as she struggled to remain upright.

"Ridley?" Dad's hand was on her back.

She blinked at the ground, vaguely aware of Malachi saying, "I can't either."

"Arxium," Ridley panted. "I've breathed it in before."

"*Breathed it in?*" Malachi repeated. "It's metal."

"Tiny particles. Something like that. They probably put it in ... whatever they drugged us with."

"Okay, I'm not even trying," Callie said. "I feel sick and dizzy enough already."

"Dammit, they've made us *useless*," Malachi groaned.

"It'll wear off soon," Ridley told him, still staring at the ground. "Soon-ish. I think. Maybe we can still pull magic from the environment even though we can't use our own? I don't know. I didn't try before. I was feeling too—"

"Oh, wonderful," Dad muttered, then added a few more colorful curses Ridley hadn't heard him use in years.

"What?" She looked up, and her eyes landed on a handful of people—three men and two women—striding toward them. None in uniforms; all of them armed.

"Crap," she said.

"Okay, I'm gonna try pull," Malachi said, an edge of panic to his voice. "I don't know if I know any conjurations that'll actually help, but—"

A dazzling flash of magic erupted past Ridley before Malachi could finish speaking. It separated into three blue fire-balls, all of which hit the ground just ahead of their pursuers, sending a shock wave through the air that launched the men and women off their feet. Ridley stumbled backward as the pressure change reached them, but the explosion had been far enough away that she managed to regain her balance. Beside her, Dad's hands were raised, magic wisps swirling around them as he pulled again at the air. His fierce and unflinching gaze, pointed directly at their pursuers, would have scared Ridley if she didn't know him.

Crack, *ping* and *smash* reached her ears from the ruins behind her, and she realized, just as Dad shouted "Get down!" that bullets were zinging past them. "Close your eyes!" he added as she dropped down to the ground, and she obeyed instantly. Even with her eyes squeezed shut, blinding white light almost seared the inside of her eyelids.

The next sound she heard was screeching and grinding. The ground beneath her feet and palms vibrated. As the bright light vanished on the other side of her eyelids, she dared a glance at what was going on around her. Rusted vehicles of various sizes were dragging themselves out of the ruins from both sides, skidding forward and crashing together to form a barrier between them and their pursuers.

"Okay," Dad said, sounding somewhat breathless as he lowered his hands.

"Wow," Malachi breathed. "Whatever the hell that was, I want to learn it."

"I'll show you later," Dad said, tugging first Ridley and

then Callie to their feet. "Right now, we need to run." They hurried toward the ruins, and Ridley caught Callie's arm as the older woman almost tripped.

"Everyone feeling okay?" Dad asked, and Ridley figured the question was probably for all of them.

"More or less," she answered, "as long as I don't try using my own magic."

"Feel a little like puking still," Callie panted as they climbed over a pile of moss-covered rubble that was blocking their way down a broken, cracked road. The overgrown, derelict remains of buildings surrounded them on all sides, the tallest of which had a giant letter K hanging about halfway down.

They darted past an upturned food cart with vines pushing through it, and Malachi asked, "Do you think they were society members?"

"Don't know," Dad said. "But I'm guessing they thought we'd be knocked out for longer. I'm sure whoever dumped us out here would have made sure we were properly immobilized if they thought we might be able to fight back."

"Whoa, stopstopstop!" Ridley cried, pulling Callie to a halt as Dad and Malachi stopped just ahead of them. "What the freaking heck is that?" She pointed to their right between two crumbling buildings, where a dome-shaped metal structure was rising from the ground.

"Please tell me that's not a gun on top of that thing," Callie moaned.

They hurried back a few paces and ducked behind a bus.

But the cylindrical metal shape on top of the dome swiveled away from them and pointed straight up at the stormy sky. A moment later, some form of whitish gray gas spewed into the air. "What on earth?" Callie muttered.

"I seriously hope that's not arxium," Ridley said. "Because it's about to be blown all over the place, and we won't—"

Nausea turned her stomach and sent her head whirling at the exact same moment the weather changed. The clouds darkened and swelled at time-lapse speed, and lightning fractured the sky into dozens of pieces. Thunder cracked and grumbled. The earth shuddered, but Ridley barely had a chance to feel the vibration rushing up into her body before she was knocked clear off her feet by wind stronger than any she'd felt before. She landed hard, her right palm scraping against the ground and pain racing all the way along her right side.

"You okay?" Dad called, and she rolled over to see that all four of them were down.

"I can't breathe properly," Callie gasped as she pushed herself upright.

"Damn ... arxium," Malachi hissed.

"Okay, we need to get inside somewhere," Dad said. "Away from this stuff." Wind raged past them, snatching away the end of his words. Ridley blinked through her dizziness and struggled for breath as she looked around.

"Dad," she said hoarsely, then tried to shout over the wind. "Dad! There." She pointed toward a storefront where the large windows on either side of the glass door were both still intact.

"I know there's a hole in the door," she said as she climbed to her feet, "but we can plug it closed with something."

The four of them leaned into the wind as they pushed toward the store with the faded words Walden Shoes across both windows. Ridley fought the urge to throw up. It was almost overwhelming, but they were so close now. Just one more crack in the road, then the crumbling sidewalk, and then—

And then a car—an entire freaking car—sailed through the air toward them. Dad's reaction was instant. His hands tugged, spun, and sliced through the air in movements too fast for Ridley to follow. He hurled the magic forward with a guttural cry. The car crumpled in on itself, then exploded in a display of blue fireworks. The sparks fell toward the road, becoming bright blue leaves that were swept away on the wind.

Malachi launched toward the door and tugged it open. He shoved Callie inside ahead of him, then motioned for Dad and Ridley to follow. Then he rushed inside, banged the door shut and turned to lean against it, covering the hole with his body. For a moment, there was no movement from any of them except for the rising and falling of chests. Then Malachi said. "Wow. *Wow.* Respect."

"Yes, well, turns out us 'old dudes' are useful for something," Dad said.

Callie lowered herself to the floor and hung her head between her knees. "They didn't teach us conjurations like that at school," she mumbled.

"They haven't taught conjurations like that *anywhere* in a

long time," Dad said. "Not officially, anyway." Ridley started pulling her jacket off to plug the hole in the door, but Dad stopped her. "You'll need that later, and then it'll be covered in arxium particles. I'm sure a few pairs of socks should do the job." He moved to the sock display, and Ridley followed him. Dust rose from the fabric as they removed the socks from their cardboard packaging, and Ridley worked hard to keep from coughing. If she started coughing now, she would almost certainly throw up.

"Okay, you can move," Dad said, walking toward Malachi with a few rolled-up pairs of socks in his hands. Malachi stepped forward, and Dad stuffed the socks into the hole at the center of the door.

"Ugh, man, arxium is *evil*," Malachi groaned, leaning forward and pressing his palms against his knees. "I feel like I want to hurl out everything inside me." Ridley watched him reach one hand forward and shakily claw at the air a few times until glowing wisps began to form. "On the plus side," he said, "pulling magic like any average non-elemental still seems to work. So normal conjurations are still an option."

"That's good," Ridley said. "At least, it's good if you're conscious enough to do it. The first time I breathed this stuff in, it was concentrated enough to knock me out for a little while."

"So ... can we go back to the part where a car just flew through the air?" Callie mumbled, her face still pointed at the floor. "Was that magic, or are we in the middle of a tornado now?"

"Magic, I think," Ridley said, remembering her first time on the wrong side of the wall. "It seems to like grabbing hold of things and throwing them around."

"And that arxium gas machine thing?" Callie looked up, her eyebrows pinching together. "What the hell is that doing out here? And why didn't they point it directly at us if they're trying to kill us?"

"Maybe they couldn't see us," Dad said. "Maybe they were trying to stir up the magic in the elements so nature would get rid of us instead. Did you see how the storm worsened almost instantly?"

"Yes," Ridley answered. "That gas or spray or whatever it was probably isn't meant to get rid of any elementals who flee into the wastelands. It's probably out here to mess with the weather. Maybe all those violent magical storms we get aren't natural at all. People are the ones causing them."

Malachi looked up. "Sounds like a conspiracy theory."

"Okay, what's your explanation?" she asked.

"I didn't say I disagreed with you."

"Guys, what's that rattling sound?" Callie asked, looking around toward the back of the store. She climbed to her feet as Dad walked between the shoe displays to a door with a 'Staff Only' sign stuck to it. He reached for the handle, then paused. Instead of opening the door, he bent to look through the keyhole.

"Okay, so ..." He straightened and looked back at them. "There's nothing on the other side of this wall. That part of the building's been demolished."

"Wonderful," Callie muttered.

"If the storm gets any worse," Dad added, "this wall probably won't last long." He rapped his knuckles against the door, and a hollow sound ensued. "I'm pretty sure it's not meant to be a permanent wall."

"Okay, so we'll have to go back out there and find something better," Ridley said. She walked to one of the windows and looked out. "I don't know, I feel like I can see right through every other building. Nothing's intact."

"We'll find something," Dad said. "We'll just have to run a little further through the storm. Or maybe it won't get any worse and we can wait it out here."

"Hopefully," Ridley said, standing on tiptoe as she tried to peer back past the bus they'd crouched beside. And then— "Oh, crap." Her stomach dropped. Amid the debris tearing through the air, she saw a figure. "Someone's coming."

CHAPTER 17

"I DON'T KNOW IF HE'S coming *here*," Ridley continued, "but he's definitely moving in this direction. He's ... wait." She squinted harder as Dad rushed to her side. "Is that ... Archer?" He was racing along the road, leaping over the cracked parts and dodging flashes of magic as something small and dark streaked ahead of him. "Ember?" Ridley whispered.

A few heartbeats later, Archer was skidding to a halt in front of the shoe shop and reaching for the door handle. There was a moment in which he looked through the glass and his eyes met Ridley's. Then he pulled the door open, Ember raced in ahead of him, and he tugged it shut swiftly behind him. Before Ridley's brain had a chance to catch up, she'd thrown her arms around him. He hugged her tightly. "How on earth did you find us?" she asked.

"I didn't," he answered breathlessly. "Your cat did."

Ridley pulled back and looked down at the magic-mutated animal pawing at her shin. "Ember?"

"If that's what you named her, then yes."

"That's—that's amazing."

"Okay, you can keep the cat," Dad said.

Archer let out a brief laugh. "I'm not sure you ever really had a choice about that."

Dad clapped a hand on his shoulder. "Do you have any idea how we ended up out here?"

Archer's smile vanished. "No. I went back to the bunker this morning but neither of you were in any of the rec rooms or in your bedroom. I asked Christa, but she hadn't seen you. I figured you must be around *somewhere*, so I searched pretty much the entire bunker and realized no one had seen any of you since last night. Christa found the cat wailing somewhere—I think it couldn't figure out how to get out—so she asked me if I could take it with me."

The cat in question wouldn't stop pawing at Ridley's leg, so she bent to let it sniff her hand and rub its head against her knuckles.

"Did you call her Ember?" Archer asked, and Ridley nodded. "Anyway, I was near the canal when Ember got away from me," he continued. "She ran into that tunnel the canal goes through. The one that ends up out here on this side of the wall. I almost let her go, but then … I don't know, then I thought about how she's been following you around. So I ran after her."

"And she actually found me," Ridley said in wonder as she straightened.

"Oh, and I grabbed your bags at some point," he added, and Ridley noticed for the first time that he had a backpack slung over each shoulder. "By the time I figured out you weren't there … I don't know. I knew something wasn't right. If you disappeared from the bunker, then somebody there must have been responsible, so I knew if I did find you, I certainly wouldn't be taking you back." He lowered both bags to floor.

"Thank you so much," Ridley said, thinking of the picture frame inside with the photo of her and Mom and Dad.

"You didn't happen to grab our stuff too, did you?" Malachi asked.

"I didn't actually take anything with me to the bunker," Callie said. "I left my home in kind of a rush."

"No, sorry," Archer said to Malachi. "I wasn't anywhere near your room when I grabbed these, and then once the cat got away from me … well, there was no turning back at that point."

"Ah, well. I guess it's just *stuff*, isn't it," Malachi said. "At least we're alive."

"Yeah, thank goodness for that." Archer's eyes met Ridley's for a moment before he added, "I sent a message for backup while I was still close enough to the wall to get signal, but I don't know when it'll be received, so it's a good thing we don't actually need it."

"A message to who?" Dad asked.

"It's a number I was given for the community we're heading to. A contact of theirs. I don't know where this person is based or how often he or she communicates with the other elementals. I was running after the cat, and I didn't have many options, so I just called and left a voice message saying we're outside Lumina City and need help. I thought the society might have caught you out here somewhere and that I'd need help getting you out. Kind of a long shot, since it could be days until they show up, but I was desperate."

"Maybe we'll meet them along the way," Ridley said. "I mean, if some of them do come to help us."

"Yeah. So you don't remember what happened?" Archer asked, looking around at each of them.

"We think someone must have drugged us," Malachi said. "We woke up just outside the wall with a bunch of people with guns coming toward us. We only got away because of Old Man Mr. Kayne here."

Dad sighed and muttered, "I'm going to get a complex about my age if this 'old man' stuff doesn't stop soon."

"They drugged us with arxium," Ridley told Archer. "And possibly something else—they would have had to give Dad something else, at least—but there was definitely arxium involved. We couldn't use our own magic."

Archer shook his head, a deep frown causing a line to form between his eyebrows. "Someone must have heard us talking yesterday. I don't think any of us said the word 'elemental,' but maybe we said enough for someone who knows about them to figure it out."

"But still," Callie said, "why would anyone who's part of that community want to get rid of us? Everyone's there because they want to be free to use magic, and elementals are no different."

"Unless the Shadow Society planted someone there to seek out elementals," Dad said.

"I guess that's possible," Ridley said. She pushed one hand through her hair, then pulled it back down quickly as she felt a sting across her palm. She'd forgotten all about landing on the road and scraping her hand. She lowered it to her side, telling herself she'd deal with it later. "I'm sorry, Dad," she said. "I know you never wanted to go to the bunker, and now this has happened."

"Oh, and don't forget the arxium gas machine thing," Callie added. She looked at Archer. "We were trying to escape among the ruins, and this dome-shaped machine popped up and sprayed arxium everywhere."

To Ridley's surprise, Archer simply nodded. "I wondered about that when the storm suddenly got worse. I've heard rumors about things like that."

"Really?" Dad asked.

"Yes, from a few people in the elemental community I lived with. Not from anyone in Lumina City. I'm sure most people have no idea those machines are out here."

"Machines *plural*?" Ridley asked.

"I think so. That's what I've heard. They're buried in the ground around all the surviving cities."

Ridley slowly shook her head, remembering an argument she'd had with Archer not too long ago. She'd reminded him that the government *wanted* to reclaim the wastelands. They *wanted* things to be safe out here so they could begin to rebuild the world. It seemed crazy that they'd go as far as to *manufacture* deadly storms in order to keep everyone and everything contained within cities. And yet ... it was starting to seem as though that might be the case. Unless it wasn't the government. Unless it was some other organization—like the Shadow Society—and those who now governed the world had no clue what was really going on.

"Okay, so that's all really crazy," Callie said, "but we can talk about it later. What about right now? What's our plan? Are we going to head into the wastelands with no clothes or food or ... anything?"

"When the storm clears and we've recovered from the arxium, we can actually go back," Malachi said. "Not to the bunker, but we can hide somewhere else. We can do that air thing to get over the wall and then get whatever we need."

"The wall is so high," Callie whispered.

Ridley thought of the eighty-fourth floor she'd leaped off with Dad and Archer not too long ago. She'd been so desperate to escape Brex Tower at that point that she'd barely thought of how high it was. Perhaps if she hadn't known how high the ballroom was the other night, she would have been able to jump from there too. "It isn't too bad if you don't think about how high it is," she told Callie.

"And we don't *all* have to go back," Dad reminded her, "if you don't think you can do it."

At the back of the store, the semi-permanent wall rattled louder, and everyone turned to look at it. "I don't think we can stay here much longer," Dad added.

"Surely being partially sheltered by whatever's left of this building is better than going out there to find somewhere else to hide?" Malachi asked.

"Well, maybe," Dad said. "I guess we'll find out."

"'Cause it looks like it's getting worse out there," Malachi added, moving closer to the window. It had begun to rain now, and droplets splattered fiercely against the windows and door.

"And the magic is making it even more dangerous out there," Archer added.

"You said magic wouldn't harm us," Callie reminded him, an accusing edge to her tone.

"It wouldn't usually, but all this arxium is aggravating it."

"I'm not looking forward to breathing that stuff in again," Malachi said. "My stomach hasn't recovered yet from the first dose."

"That part shouldn't be too bad now," Archer said. "The storm's been going on for a while, so it's probably blown most of it away. It's the actual magic out there that's just so ... wild and angry. Still raging against all that arxium they pumped into the air earlier."

"I remember you talking about it like that before," Ridley said. "As if it has some kind of intelligence."

He looked at her. "It kind of does, doesn't it?"

She was about to reply, but her words vanished from her mind as the wall at the back of the store was ripped cleanly away from the rest of the building. The wind swept through, sending shoes and boxes flying. Callie shrieked and jumped out of the way as a display shelf skidded across the floor toward her. Ridley was about to grab her backpack when a glance at the window revealed a metal pole hurtling toward the front of the store. "Get down!" she yelled. She dropped to the floor, shielding Ember with her body and covering her head with her hands. A moment later, she heard the smash and shatter. Glass rained over her as the pole clanged onto the ground somewhere in front of the store. Slowly, she looked up and around at the others on the floor. "Everyone okay?" she called as rain stung her face.

"Yeah, but we need to find better shelter," Dad answered, pushing himself onto his feet. Ridley pulled her bag hastily onto her back, scooped Ember up beneath one arm, and handed Dad his bag.

"I can take her if you want," Archer offered. "Or carry your bag."

"Don't worry, it's fine," Ridley said automatically. But as Ember's hair aggravated the grazed skin on her right palm, she decided it was okay to accept help. "Actually, thank you," she said, placing Ember in his arms.

Dad opened the door—what was left of it—and hurried into the street. Bracing herself, Ridley ventured out after him. She was half drenched within seconds. "There," Dad shouted as he pointed. "The Huntley Hotel. Do you see it?"

Lightning forked across the sky, brightening the storm-gray landscape for a moment, and Ridley could clearly see the double H on a building not too far away. "Yes," she shouted as she reached his side.

"It's the closest building that looks, well, mostly intact."

"Seems pretty solid from here," Archer shouted, and Ridley realized he was just behind her. She looked around and saw Ember zipped up inside the front of his jacket with only her head poking out. Some teeny, tiny part of Ridley's mind—the part that clearly wasn't worried about staying alive right now—thought, *Ah, how cute.* But she gave it a good mental smack and turned back to face the hotel.

"Okay, that's where we're going," she shouted to Malachi and Callie as they joined them in the middle of the street and started moving forward. "The Huntley Hotel."

"And if magic grabs hold of any of us," Archer said, "and we end up separated, don't stop. Just get to the Huntley. Got it?"

"I wish I could say no," Callie whimpered. "I feel like it wasn't that bad staying back there in the shoe shop."

"Hey, you'll be fine," Malachi told her, taking hold of her hand as they started running. "This is better than being killed by a high-speed shoe to the head."

"What about being killed by a high-speed *car* to the head?" Callie wailed. "Or pretty much *anything* else that's flying around out heeeee—"

Callie's scream was lost to the wind as a flash of magic snaked around her and Malachi like a lasso and whipped them into the air. Within seconds, they'd vanished into the storm. "Ohmygosh," Ridley gasped, stumbling to a halt. "They're—"

"They'll be fine," Archer said.

"You don't know that!" she shouted.

"We can't do anything for them!" Dad shouted, reaching back to grab her hand and pull her forward. "Just keep moving. They'll meet us there."

They'll meet us there? They'll MEET US THERE? As if

they'd merely taken a simple detour instead of being whiplashed through the air by magic? Ridley's mind filled with hysterical laughter as she ran behind Dad, catching her foot on a clump of grass that had grown up through the cracked road. Her hand slipped out of Dad's as she stumbled, but she continued running as soon as she'd caught her balance.

They squeezed between bumper-to-bumper vehicles that blocked most of an intersection, finally making their way beyond the pileup past more crumbled, weather-worn buildings. Rain lashed at Ridley's face and wind buffeted her from all sides as she dodged the flashes of magic as best she could. A table flew across the road, and she dropped to the ground to be sure she was out of its path as it soared overhead. Looking back, she found that Archer had crouched down too, with one arm wrapped around his middle, probably to keep Ember in place.

"All good?" he yelled as lightning illuminated his face for a moment.

"Yes, you?" she responded, blinking away the raindrops on her eyelids. Archer nodded. After a glance toward the sky to make sure nothing new was about to fly into her, Ridley stood and faced forward.

Dad was nowhere to be seen.

"What?" Her racing heart lodged itself somewhere in her throat as her eyes darted across the dimly lit landscape. "Dad?" she shouted. She wiped a hand across her wet face and squinted harder with every flash of lightning, hoping to see him somewhere nearby.

Archer's hand gripped her arm as he moved to stand beside her. "We need to keep moving, Ridley. We'll meet him there."

"But—no—what if he's—"

"Wait, that's him!" Archer pointed to the right beyond a taxi and a building that was nothing more than a pile of rubble. On the other side, someone who looked like he might possibly be her father was standing halfway down a staircase that jutted up amid a few low, broken walls. Ridley jumped up and down, waving wildly and yelling, "Dad! Over here!"

He seemed frozen for several long moments, until suddenly he began waving frantically with both arms. "Yes! He's seen us." Ridley lowered her arms as Archer made a waving motion toward the Huntley Hotel. Dad mimicked him before starting his descent down the staircase. "See?" Archer said, pushing Ridley ahead of him. "Stick to the plan and we'll meet him there."

"Okay," she answered, then yelped in fright and jumped to the side as a bolt of magic shot straight down and sizzled through the roof of the taxi. She paused to take a deep breath— and then the entire car burst into thousands of glowing blue shards that rained down around her and Archer, forming droplets of water that mingled with the rain.

"Holy WHAT?" Ridley gasped. "What the hell was that?"

"Just keep moving!" Archer said, turning her toward the Huntley and giving her a nudge. She hadn't missed the fear in his voice though. What if magic did that to one of them? What if it had already done that to Malachi and Callie?

No, they're elementals, she reminded herself firmly as she hitched her backpack further onto her shoulders and ran forward. *They're fine.*

She dodged a sign board skidding across the road, and then a car door. As she darted between and around the shrubs that had pushed their way up through the road, she looked ahead. Dad's path must have been clearer than theirs because he was almost there. Further down the road, on the next block, he was now running up the stairs into the Huntley. If Ridley had had enough breath, she might have laughed. Instead, she looked back over her shoulder to share her relieved grin with Archer—but he was gone.

CHAPTER 18

RIDLEY SLOWED AND TURNED completely, but Archer was definitely no longer behind her. "No, no, no," she gasped, her chest heaving as she tried to catch her breath. She wiped rain from her face again as she looked around. How long had he been gone?

Her eyes darted down as something scratched her leg: Ember. Was that good news or bad? If Ember was alive, did that mean Archer was alive somewhere too? Or did it mean Ember had squirmed away from him before something terrible had happened?

She picked up the cat, then turned fully on the spot, her heart thudding wildly. What was she supposed to do now? *Stick to the plan.* That's what Archer would tell her to do. *Stick to the plan, and I'll meet you there.* But what if he was hurt and couldn't get to the hotel? He was the only one of them who had no magic of his own. The wild magic out here might take one taste of him and spit him out from a great height. The thought stole her breath away and made her throat ache. "Please be alive," she said, staring desperately into the darkening ruins. She could barely hear her own voice over the wind, thunder and pelting rain.

She hugged the cat tightly and moved toward the hotel, turning in slow circles as she went, hoping for a glimpse of Archer making his way through the ruins somewhere. She reached the hotel steps and ascended them slowly, backwards, her eyes still searching. Stopping in front of the entrance— an area protected by a solid arch that had somehow survived years of violent weather—she continued to stare into the storm. She could hardly bear to leave Archer out here, but that was the plan, and she knew he wanted her to follow it.

Since when do I do what Archer Davenport wants me to do? Ugh, just follow the damn plan, Ridley!

She turned and tugged on the heavy wooden door with one hand, finally pulling it open. Inside the hotel's lobby, which was lit only by the blue glow of magic, she found Dad— and Callie and Malachi, she noted with relief. But they were all on the floor, and Callie was lying down, and Dad was pulling magic from the air. "What's wrong?" Ridley asked, rushing over and lowering Ember to the floor.

"Oh, thank goodness you're here," Dad said, glancing up at her. "I was starting to get worried."

"Callie?" Ridley asked, pulling her arms free of the backpack and dumping it on the floor.

"I'm fine, it's just this cut on my arm," Callie said, screwing her face up. Ridley shifted until she could see past Dad to the blood seeping from a long gash down Callie's upper arm. "From when we landed," Callie added. "But otherwise, it wasn't nearly as bad as I expected. The wind was violent, but we both became air, so we were fine when the magic dropped us. I was just dizzy and I tripped and got this stupid cut from a sharp branch."

"Where's Archer?" Malachi asked, but Ridley couldn't answer. Ice had begun to settle in the pit of her stomach as Callie spoke. Callie and Malachi survived because they could become air, but Archer couldn't do that. He might still be hurtling through the air right now. Or he might already be—

"I'm going back for him," she said, not allowing her brain to finish that last thought. She ran back across the lobby, shouting, "There's a book of conjurations in my bag if you need it."

"What?" Dad called. "Ridley, wait!"

"I'll be fine, I promise!"

"Ridley!" But she didn't look back. She pulled the door open with both hands—barely feeling the ache down her right side and the cuts across her right palm—and rushed back down the stairs into the storm. She ran back the way she'd come, though there was no knowing, of course, where exactly Archer might be. "Where are you, where are you?" she muttered repeatedly in a voice that was swept away before it could reach her ears. The rain had lessened, becoming a fine spray, but the merciless wind still buffeted her from every side, blowing bits of grass, sand, leaves and other debris at her.

And then a tree! Tumbling through the air, heading straight for her. For a split second, Ridley was paralyzed by panic. Then the instinctive thought—*air*—flashed into her mind, and a moment later, the tree blew right through her.

Through. Her.

She looked down, but there was nothing to see since she was made of air. She waited for the nausea, the whirling dizziness, but neither came. It seemed she'd recovered from the arxium she'd inhaled. Wind gusted past and whipped her away past endless crumbling buildings. She almost fought back, but the current was so strong, she doubted she had any hope of regaining control. Terror slammed into her as she realized she was utterly powerless. But at the back of her mind, a quiet voice pushed through her fear: *Maybe this is the way it's supposed to be.*

She *couldn't* control this, even if she wanted to, so why not let go completely? Why not let the magic around her take over? Perhaps it would even lead her to Archer.

There was a moment where the wind quieted, and Ridley sensed she was close to the ground. She could have materialized, could have dropped to her feet and continued on the ground. But she didn't. With a shiver that was more excitement than fear, she forced herself to let go of any control she thought she still had. She felt the tension leave her mind. *Take me wherever you want*, she told the magic crackling through the storm around her.

As she reeled above the wastelands, she sensed herself coming apart, as if every particle of her air-being drifted away and mingled with the storm and its magic. She felt the undulations of the clouds and the changing currents of the wind and the topography of the landscape beneath her. *I know you*, the magic said. Not in words, but Ridley *felt* that it recognized her.

A thrill of pure delight rushed through every particle of her being before she became aware once more of why she had let go in the first place.

Where is he? she asked. *Where did you take him?* The answer came immediately. *He's behind me,* she realized. Though she made no conscious choice to move that way, the storm carried her back around, dipping and soaring and swirling. *Near that building with the giant letter K.* The knowledge slipped into her mind effortlessly, like air flowing through the smallest crack.

As she swooped low, he suddenly came into view, limping past the building she'd been thinking of. She was so relieved to see him alive and so scared she might end up whipping right past him that she abruptly lost hold of the perfect balance she'd found. *Put me down, put me down!* she shrieked inside her mind. Fighting back against the current, she struggled to control the direction she was moving in. She spun dizzily before finally dropping from the air and landing too hard on her feet. She staggered forward and tripped onto her knees, then blinked and breathed and allowed a few moments to pass until the world stopped tilting endlessly.

Then she was up and running toward him through the pattering rain. "Archer!" she shouted. He swung to face her, and their eyes met just as a blue zigzag flashed straight at Ridley. She knew now that it wouldn't hurt her, but she still found herself throwing her hand out instinctively to protect her face. The magic snapped around her arm, like a crackling blue bracelet, zipping around and around before taking off behind her. As it left, she felt a whisper of something, a caress against her mind. A greeting of sorts.

She stood frozen for a moment, breathing heavily, wondering if she'd imagined the strange encounter. Just like she was probably imagining it when she noticed the sky wasn't as dark, and the howling wind had died down, and the thunder had become a quiet rumble instead of a boom.

"Ridley!" Archer shouted, bringing her attention back to him as he limped hurriedly toward her.

"You're okay," she said, rushing forward as a smile stretched across her face. She almost threw her arms around him, but something about his expression made her stop.

"What the hell are you doing back out here?" he demanded, pushing his wet hair back off his forehead. "You were almost at the hotel."

"I ..." The sudden anger in his eyes—and something else she couldn't identify—made her hesitate. "I came looking for you. What—"

"Why would you do that? You were supposed to get to the hotel and *stay* there."

"I did, but you didn't come back. I couldn't just wait there."

"That's what you were supposed to do!"

The ferocity of his tone startled her. She wrapped her arms around her soaking wet self. "Why are you mad at me? I thought you might be hurt, or—or worse."

"I'm mad because you almost got yourself killed for not following instructions."

"I did *not* almost get myself killed!" she yelled at him. It was quiet enough now that neither of them needed to shout, but Ridley couldn't help it. She'd been so scared he was dead and now he was *angry* with her for caring? "I'm an elemental, so why would magic kill me? That's what *you* said. You said Callie, Malachi and I should be fine. But you're not like us, so of course I wasn't going to follow instructions when you disappeared. How was I supposed to know you'd be okay? You could have been dead! You could have exploded into a thousand little magical pieces and I would never have seen you again!"

"Well how do you think I felt when you just *vanished* from the bunker?" Archer yelled. "I've been trying to keep you safe since I returned to the city and you keep getting yourself into danger!"

"THAT ONE WASN'T MY FAULT!" She blinked away angry tears. "Now can we please stop shouting? I'm trying to be happy that you're alive and you're making it impossible."

Archer moved closer, his chest rising and falling with heavy breaths. He didn't say a word as his eyes traveled her face, and Ridley finally recognized what she'd seen in his gaze—fear. Suddenly, her anger was gone. She couldn't figure out what, exactly, took its place, but it expanded inside her chest until it felt like it might burst.

She couldn't tell which of them moved first, but suddenly Archer's hands were in her hair, her arms were snaking around his waist, and their lips were pressed together. She dug her fingers into his back and kissed him as if this were the only chance she'd ever get. Their lips were slippery from the rain, and when his tongue moved across hers, it tasted like rain too. She pressed closer, desperate for more. Her heart thrummed and her skin grew hot, and when a shiver raced across her skin, it had nothing to do with being cold.

"I'm sorry I yelled," Archer said breathlessly against her mouth. "I was just scared."

In answer, Ridley kissed him harder. Another shiver coursed through her as his arms slid down her back and tightened, pulling her even closer. Some part of her registered that she needed air, and eventually she paused for long enough to suck in a shaky breath. "I was scared too," she said, kissing him again before adding, "I had to come looking for you. You know you would have done the same for me."

She felt, more than heard, his quiet rumble of a laugh. He brushed his lips along her jaw and pressed a kiss beneath her ear. "I didn't realize you knew me so well." He tipped his brow forward to lean against hers. She drew her arms back from around his neck and flattened each palm against his chest. Closing her eyes, she let out a long, shaky breath.

"This doesn't make any sense," she said. "I don't even like you."

He laughed again, a little louder this time. "Your current actions suggest otherwise."

She bit her lip, but she couldn't keep her smile back. She tilted her head to the side and kissed him again. Because he was right, of course. She liked him very much. The problem was that part of her still felt like she *shouldn't*. Part of her still remembered the old Archer Davenport. The one the net tabloids liked to write about. The one dozens of girls had thrown themselves at, as Lilah had so sweetly reminded her. And that part of Ridley was screaming at her to run far away and protect her heart before he crushed it. Fortunately, that part of her was tiny, and she easily stomped it down. Because the last thing she wanted to do was run. She wanted to be closer, she wanted his arms around her, and his fingers threading through her hair, and his body against hers.

But the storm wasn't over, and at that moment, lightning struck so close that Ridley could almost feel the static crackle in the air. Her eyelids sprang apart, and she pulled her head back to look around. Archer's grip around her waist eased. His hand moved to take hold of hers. "The wind isn't as violent as it was before. Can you get us back to the hotel as air?"

"Yes. Actually—" She looked at him as a smile formed on her lips "I didn't tell you before when we were yelling at each other, but ..." Her smile stretched wider. "I did it. I let go properly. I had no idea how to find you and so I just ... let go. Surrendered myself. I felt like I was everywhere at once, as if I inhabited the entire storm." She almost added that the magic in the elements had told her it recognized her, but that sounded a little too weird.

Archer's hand squeezed tighter around hers. "Well done. See? Your grandfather and I weren't making things up."

"I kind of panicked at the end, but until that point, it was great." She beamed at him. "So we can get back to the hotel that way. It doesn't matter if it's too windy. I'll just let go and the elemental magic can take us."

Archer shook his head. "I can't do that. You can wrap air around me, but the other thing—the part where you said you felt like you were everywhere at once—that won't work on me."

"Oh." Disappointment settled over her. "I'm sorry. Okay, then let's just be air like normal." She smiled and rolled her eyes. "Not that that's normal, but you know what I mean." She looped her arms around him, and together they vanished.

It was a bit of a struggle working against the wind, and Ridley expected she'd probably end up with a headache later, but it didn't take too long to get back to the Huntley Hotel. They ascended the stairs hand in hand, but she let go just before reaching the door. Her brain had barely caught up with what had just happened; she didn't think she was ready to share it with anyone else just yet.

She heaved the wooden door open and walked in ahead of Archer. He limped inside behind her, and she asked, "What happened?"

"Just twisted it when the magic dropped me. I landed at a weird angle, I think."

"Okay. I'm sure we can fix it with a conjuration or two."

She expected to find the others in the lobby still, but it seemed they'd moved. As Archer pushed the front door shut behind them, darkness descended. The only illumination was a subtle glow emanating from a doorway on the far side of the lobby. Quiet voices reached Ridley's ears, and she figured that's where Dad, Malachi and Callie were.

Since she could barely see a thing, and she obviously had

no torch or commscreen with her, she allowed her hands to begin glowing. Magic rose away from her skin in wisps. In the eerie blue light, Archer reached for her right hand and inter-laced his fingers with hers. She felt his eyes on her, but she couldn't bring herself to meet his gaze. The more she thought about it, the weirder this felt. She'd kissed *Archer Davenport*, of all people! How could this *not* be weird?

"What, now you don't want to look at me?" he teased.

She dared a glance at his beautiful dark eyes before look-ing down again. "It's just …" She laughed and shook her head. "This is just very strange, that's all."

"How about I keep kissing you until it stops feeling strange?"

She pressed her lips together, but her smile refused to be contained. "I guess that wouldn't be the worst thing in the world," she told him.

His thumb brushed against her palm, and she was vaguely aware of the stinging pain from her grazed skin. Interesting how she'd paid *zero* attention to that pain as she'd pressed her hands hard into Archer's back. The memory caused heat to crawl up her neck.

"Ridley?"

She tugged her hand out of Archer's and stepped back as Dad shouted her name. Hurried footsteps sounded from the direction of the staircase beside the elevator door. "Down here," she called, moving toward the stairs.

"Ohthankgoodness," Dad said, his words rushing out of him in a single breath as he reached the bottom of the stairs.

He crossed the lobby and scooped Ridley into a tight hug. "What were you thinking going back out there?"

"Magic took him, Dad," she murmured as she returned his embrace. "I couldn't just leave him out there."

"Are Callie and Malachi here?" Archer asked.

"Yes." Dad removed his arms from around Ridley. "They're in a lounge back there," he added, nodding to the soft light Ridley had noticed radiating from a doorway. "I healed that cut on Callie's arm, but she wasn't feeling great after seeing her own blood dripping everywhere, so Malachi took her to lie down on a couch. I went upstairs to see if I could spot you through any of the windows."

"Did you see us out there?" Ridley asked, trying to hide the anxious edge her voice had taken on. She had no idea how high Dad had been, or how far he could see through the storm, or whether there was even a direct line of sight between this building and the one she'd found Archer in front of. Not that it would be so terrible if he'd seen the two of them kissing. She just didn't feel ready for him to know.

"Yes," Dad said. "I was looking down when you materialized from the air by the front steps."

"Okay." Ridley exhaled in relief. "Um, I suppose we should all change out of our wet clothes. But maybe we should talk first. About what we're going to do in the morning. You know, who's going to go back for food and all that."

Dad nodded. "Yes, although I thought you might want to tell me first about that highly illegal book of conjurations that's in your bag."

"Ah. That."

"That," Dad said.

Ridley glanced at Archer, then back at Dad. "There isn't much to say except that I found it among a pile of old books in the store and decided to keep it and not tell you about it."

"Right." Dad sighed. "This is the part where I should be shocked and horrified that you kept something so dangerous a secret from me, but ... well ..."

"You're totally not shocked and horrified," Ridley supplied.

"No. I'm thinking it could even be useful." He placed his arm around her as they crossed the lobby. "It might contain some conjurations I don't know."

"And it's not highly illegal out here in the wastelands," Archer pointed out.

"Because there are no laws out here," Ridley finished. Archer was walking on her left, and the back of his hand brushed briefly against hers. Warmth shot into her body from the point of contact, and for a moment, it seemed as though the glow of magic from her hands brightened. As they walked into the lounge behind the lobby, she focused on pulling the magic back inside her body.

"Oh, I'm so glad you're both okay," Callie said, looking up from the couch she was lying across. In the wing-back armchair beside her, Malachi reclined, playing with the wisps of magic curling around his hands. The lounge was filled with numerous couches, armchairs and elegant chaise longues. A long bar stretched across one side of the room, and on the other, stood a grand piano. Situated around the edges of the room were large pots that presumably had once housed living plants. "It doesn't look too bad in here," Ridley commented. She could almost imagine they were back inside Lumina City's walls, rather than out in the wastelands.

"Yeah, except for the ten years' worth of dust that crept in through whatever gap and crevice it could find," Malachi said. He leaned toward the empty armchair beside him and smacked the cushion. A cloud of dust rose into the air.

"Malachi," Callie groaned. "Would you please not do that?" A dark shape separated itself from her side, and Ridley realized Ember had been curled up against her on the couch. The cat leaped gracefully to the floor and sauntered over to rub her head against Ridley's legs.

"We should probably keep the light to a minimum," Dad said, removing his arm from around Ridley and striding forward. "It's fine in here; there don't seem to be any windows. But be careful in any of the exterior rooms. Just in case people are still out there searching for us."

"With this storm still going on?" Malachi said. As if to illustrate his point, a groan of thunder shuddered through the hotel. "I hope not," he added. "They probably think we're all dead by now."

"Probably, but we should still be careful," Dad said.

"Want to sit?" Archer asked Ridley, his hand landing lightly against the small of her back. An image of his arms encircling her as he pulled her tightly against his body while they stood beneath the pouring rain flashed through her mind. Her face grew warm, and she was thankful the only light in the room was the glow from Malachi's magic. *Stop being inappropriate!* she mentally scolded her imagination.

She cleared her throat and said, "Um, yes." Walking forward, she noticed her backpack was on the floor in front of Callie's couch. She crouched beside it, unzipped the top, and asked, "Anyone else hungry?"

"Yeah, now that the arxium-induced nausea has passed," Malachi said, "I'm famished."

"Me too," Callie added.

"Good thing we're inside a hotel," Malachi said. "Whatever canned food was here when the Cataclysm happened might still be good."

"Ten years later?" Callie asked, the doubt evident in her tone.

"Don't those things last forever?"

"I can offer you an energy bar instead," Ridley said, finally retrieving one from inside her backpack, which, fortunately, had lived up to its promise of being completely waterproof. "But that's all I've got."

"Oh, yes please. Definitely." Callie pushed herself up and scooted over to one side of the couch. "I'll take one of those."

After passing around the energy bars, Ridley sat beside Archer in the spot Callie had vacated. Archer rested one arm along the back of the couch, and as the five of them discussed who would return to the city the following day to get supplies, Ridley did her best to ignore the heat along the back of her neck, and the fact that Archer's leg was almost, *almost* touching hers, and the way he occasionally, surreptitiously, brushed his thumb across her shoulder.

And failed. Of course.

CHAPTER 19

AFTER THEIR DINNER OF energy bars—everything they found in the hotel's pantry had expired years ago—Ember disappeared and everyone else went one floor up to the side of the hotel where there was minimal damage to the windows. The beds in most of the rooms were covered in dusty linen, which they removed and replaced with clean linen. Well, as clean as they could find in the hotel's laundry, where things smelled musty and were covered in a very fine layer of dust.

Ridley offered some of her dry clothes to Callie, but Callie searched the entire ground level of the hotel until she located a small shop containing clothes. It was filled mainly with bathing suits and fancy dresses, but she managed to find some articles of clothing that would be comfortable enough to sleep in. Then, since three of their party were elementals, it was easy for them to fill a basin or a bath with their magic and will it into water. "I never realized what a perk it would be to be able to produce water on demand," Malachi said. "I'm appreciating my own magic more and more."

After saying goodnight to everyone, Ridley climbed be-

neath the covers of the bed in her very own Huntley Hotel bedroom and stared through the cracked window at the
stormy night. Though not as violent as it had been when it
began, the storm still tossed debris through the air, splattered
rain against the windows, and sent blue flashes of magic darting between the ruins.

After a minute or so of watching the storm, Ridley leaned
down the side of the bed and slid her hand into her backpack.
She removed the picture frame and placed it on her lap on
top of the covers. Mindful of what Dad had said earlier about
keeping light to a minimum, she made sure not to create any
while her curtain was open. But there were so many flashes
of lightning and magic outside that it wasn't too hard to make
out the picture in the frame. She looked at Mom and Dad with
their dark hair and bright smiles, at her own young face and
pigtails, her hair so light it was almost white. After brushing
her fingers over the faces beneath the glass, she carefully returned the frame to her bag.

"Ridley?"

She turned swiftly at the sound of Archer's voice, her
pounding heart ridiculously happy to see him leaning around
her partially open doorway. He'd also looked through the
shop Callie had located downstairs, and he was now wearing
the shorts and T-shirt he'd found there.

"Yes?" Ridley asked, hating the way she sounded just a
little bit breathless. "Is everything okay?"

He smiled. "Don't worry, everything's fine. I just ..." He
stepped into the room and rubbed one hand along the back of

his neck. "I missed you."

A shiver that had nothing to do with the ambient temperature raced across Ridley's arms. She let out a quiet laugh. "You saw me ten minutes ago."

"Yes, but ... we didn't get a chance earlier to properly talk about ... this." He gestured to the space between them.

She pressed her lips together, trying to hide her smile. "So you're here to *talk*?"

"Well, I mean ..." He lifted his shoulders in an exaggerated shrug. "There's a chance I might accidentally kiss you while we're talking." She laughed again, and he pushed one hand through his hair. "Look, I could try to play this cool. Pretend I have all the time in the world to figure out if you're really interested in me while I act as though I may or may not be interested in you. But I don't want to do that. I'd rather just tell you how much I like you and that I don't want to waste any moment I could be spending right next to you."

A blush heated Ridley's face, then quickly spread out across her entire body. Was that possible? For her whole body to blush? And why couldn't she think of a single thing to say? Why couldn't she even *look* at him?

Stop being so silly and shy, she told herself, forcing her eyes back up to meet his. *This is just Archer.*

She exhaled slowly before shifting over on the bed to make space for him beside her. He closed her door, then crossed the room and sat, facing her, on top of the duvet. She was grateful he didn't get beneath the covers. Her heart was pounding fast enough just inviting him closer. Having him climb *into* bed with her would have been crossing another line she wasn't ready for yet.

"You're good, you know that?" she said quietly.

He lifted one hand and gently brushed her hair away from her face and behind her ear. "This isn't an act. That's what I'm trying to say. Life is so brief. There isn't time for games. If I feel something for you, then I should tell you. So this is me telling you. You know," he added as his lips curled up on one side, "in case it wasn't obvious from all the kissing earlier."

"Good thing you cleared that up," she said. "Here I was thinking you kiss all your friends like that."

He grinned. "Do you kiss *your* friends like that?"

Waving goodbye to the shy version of herself, she gripped the front of his T-shirt and pulled him closer. "Can I show you how I *don't* kiss my friends?"

Their lips met as Archer pushed his fingers through her damp hair. She felt his hand curl into a fist at the nape of her neck, tugging her hair just the tiniest bit as he pulled her closer. Her hand let go of his T-shirt and slid up and around his neck. She tasted toothpaste as his tongue trailed over hers, and as the kiss deepened, a new heat grew inside her. His lips moved to the side of her mouth and along her jaw, and his five o'clock shadow lightly grazed her cheek. "I thought you only wanted to *talk*," he whispered as his lips reached her ear.

Ridley let out a breath of laughter. "I changed my mind. This is so much better." She turned her head to find his lips again, breathing in the scent of whatever ten-year-old hotel shampoo he'd used. She might be biased and not exactly thinking straight, but in her opinion, it smelled incredible. She wrapped her arms tighter around him, pressing so close that she thought it might be possible she could feel both her heartbeat and his thudding against her chest.

She wasn't sure exactly how or when it happened, but somehow they were both lying down side by side, legs entangled, Archer's hands pressing into her back and hers trailing through his hair. Her thoughts were a tangled, intoxicated blur, and nothing mattered outside of this moment. A moment she could lose herself in forever. It was only when Archer's hands brushed the skin beneath the edge of her pajama top and traced their way up her spine that a hint of alarm broke through her drunken state.

"Just so you know," she said breathlessly before he could get any ideas about removing articles of her clothing, "this is as far as things are going tonight."

He paused, his eyes opening as he pulled his head back slightly. "Oh, of course, I know. I wasn't expecting—I mean, that's not why I came to your room." In the dim, flickering light provided by the magic and lightning outside her window, Ridley could make out the flush rising in his cheeks.

"Archer Davenport," she said with a wicked grin. "Did I actually manage to make you blush?"

"Ridley Kayne," he answered. He softly kissed her lips before saying, "Did I actually manage to make you lose control of your magic?"

"What?" Her heart skipped a beat as she moved her gaze to her hands and arms, but they appeared normal. There was no glow rising from her skin. She smacked his arm. "You did not."

"Your eyes are magic blue."

"My eyes are always blue."

"No, I mean they're glowing."

She looked down immediately, hoping her eyelids would hide most of the glow. Did this really have to happen *now*? Why couldn't she just enjoy kissing Archer without part of her body lighting up like a magic-mutated animal freak from the wastelands?

"And your lips," Archer said quietly, raising his forefinger and brushing it gently along her lower lip in a way that made goosebumps rush across her skin and butterflies come to life in her stomach. "And your cheeks, which I'm going to take to mean that you're blushing too."

She groaned and covered her face with both hands. "I'm sorry."

"Why?" He pulled her hands away and laid one gentle kiss on each of her eyelids. "I told you before that your magic is beautiful. Didn't you believe me?"

"No, of course not. It's looks so weird when—"

"It does not look weird."

She tried to pull away from him, but he shifted his position so he was partly on top of her, pinning her down in a way that made the butterflies go crazy in her stomach again. "I have no idea why you think being made of magic makes you ugly. You have no idea how exotically—" he kissed her jaw "—entrancingly—" a kiss on her nose "—captivatingly—" and a kiss on her lips "—beautiful it is."

She shook her head and tried not to roll her eyes. "Well, how can I not believe you when you use so many adjectives?"

"Exactly. I must be telling the truth."

Okay, so maybe she believed that he thought it was beautiful, but that didn't mean she wanted to become a glowing beacon for anyone who happened to be out in the storm to see through her window. She let out a long, steadying breath and asked, "Is it gone? The glowing?"

Archer turned his lips down in disappointment. "Yes, it's gone."

"Okay, look," she said with a teasing smile, "if the only reason you want me is because of my magic, then—"

He took her face between his hands and pressed a lingering kiss against her mouth. "I definitely want more than just your magic," he whispered against her lips.

Heat curled low in her belly, and her mind filled with the kinds of thoughts that made her face burn. She bit her lip and pushed him away before she could do anything crazy. "Okay, time to slow down."

He chuckled as he rolled onto his back. "Hey, I just came in here to talk. You're the one who decided to show me how you *don't* kiss your—"

"Oh, whatever," she protested with a laugh. "I was not fooled by your *talking* excuse." She shifted closer, crossed her arms on his chest, and leaned her chin on her hands. Her eyes traveled his face as she gave her heart time to calm down. While her body may have wanted more, the sensible part of her brain that remembered just how inexperienced she was compared to Archer—and that her father was two rooms away, for goodness' sake—was relieved that nothing more was happening. For now, she was content to lie here and listen to the rain and stare into Archer's captivating dark eyes while he traced lazy patterns up and down her back.

Her heart couldn't possibly return to a normal pace though. Not with him looking at her like that, his eyes brushing over every inch of her face, making her feel as if she were the only thing in his world. But even as the thought warmed her insides, a tiny, insecure voice reminded her of his reputation and the number of girls she'd seen him with over the years. If he had a habit of moving on quickly, then wasn't it likely he would move on quickly from her too? But he *had* changed. He wasn't the same person he'd been at school. Did that mean he'd changed in all areas of his life, or were there some things that would always be the same for a person like Archer Davenport?

"I thought about you a lot while I was away," he said softly, almost as if he could hear her uncertain thoughts and wanted to reassure her.

"Liar," she snorted. She raised her head from his chest. "I bet you didn't think of me at all until you suddenly needed a birthday present for your mom last week and decided, for some reason, to go antique shopping."

"And what do you think that reason was?"

"Uh … because your mom already owns everything that was made within the last century?"

"Because I wanted to see *you*, silly girl."

She laughed quietly. "I'm sorry, but I don't believe that."

"It's the truth," he said, and there was no teasing in his gaze. "Before I got lost on the side of a mountain and found an elemental community, you were the only one I knew of. After I saw what they could do, the way magic came from their own bodies instead of just the environment, I kept thinking back to you. To that moment so many years ago when you accidentally used your own magic while you were in our home." He brushed a strand of hair off her forehead. "I wondered if you knew what you were. I wondered if you could do the things those other elementals could do, turning yourself to fire or air with just a thought. So ... I don't know. By the time I got back, I was curious, and I wanted to see you. It was stupid, of course. I already had that agreement with your father that I wouldn't get you involved in any way, so it's not like I was planning to actually talk to you about elementals and your magic. But ... yeah. I just couldn't stay away."

Ridley tilted her head to the side. "So you were honestly thinking about me while you were away? There wasn't some other exotic elemental woman who captured your attention?"

He opened his mouth, paused, then said, "Okay, I'll be honest: there was someone."

Ridley nodded and tried to keep her smile in place, but it scared her to realize how much it hurt when he spoke about someone else.

"But it wasn't like that for very long," Archer added quickly. "I was in this weird space. I wanted to change, but I was still the old me—the one who didn't think he was worth anything if he didn't have at least three girls pining after him. She was kind to me, and pretty, so I sort of directed all my attention toward her from the start. But she was already in a committed relationship, and she made it clear that there would never be anything between us. She was still friendly though. Still happy to explain things to me. We soon became good friends, and I realized I was happy to just be me, on my own, without basking in the attention of girls who probably only wanted to be with me because I'm a Davenport. So, in the end, whenever I cast my mind back toward Lumina City, along with my parents and Lilah, you were always somewhere there in my thoughts. My only other point of reference when it came to elementals."

"Okay," Ridley said softly. "You know, I like this side of you. When you open up and share personal things that remind me you're not always the super confident, invulnerable person you appear to be."

A silent moment passed in which Archer's lips lifted in a slow smile. Then his hands tightened around her waist, and he flipped her over onto her back. He pressed kisses against her neck and whispered, "I like all sides of you."

She laughed and tried to squirm away from him. "You idiot, I was trying to say something serious."

"I know. It made me want to kiss you."

For a few moments, she let herself drown in his dark, depthless gaze. Then she placed her fingers over his lips. "No more kissing, or I won't be able to control myself."

"I don't mind the sound of that."

"Yeah, until my dad hears something and walks in. Then I would die of complete mortification, and this whole escape-into-the-wastelands adventure would be over for me."

"Yeah, okay, that's no fun."

"Exactly." She snuggled closer and rested her head just below his shoulder and her palm on his chest. His arms tightened around her. "My face isn't glowing again, is it?" she asked. He shifted his head, probably to look down at her.

"Nope, don't worry, you're all good. The magic glow is under control."

"Okay. Good. It's just … Now I wonder how close I've come before to giving my secret away. As far as I know, it's never happened with any other guy, but what if it had? I could have landed myself in prison. Got the death penalty just for kissing someone."

"I don't know. Maybe it's a subconscious thing."

"Meaning?"

"You feel safe with me because I already know your secret, so it's completely okay if you don't pay attention to keeping your magic hidden."

Ridley chewed on her lip while she thought about that. "Maybe. But still. I doubt I'll ever relax again while kissing someone who isn't supposed to know about my super secret elemental heritage."

"Or you could just *not* kiss anyone else except me, and you'll be totally fine."

She smiled. "That could work." She was quiet for another few moments before something occurred to her. "Hey, I didn't get a headache earlier. I mean, I felt super crappy from the arxium, but after that wore off, and after I became air so I could find you and then bring you back, I don't remember noticing anything."

"Fantastic. Clearly it helps to let go properly."

"Yes. I guess you and Grandpa really did know what you were talking about."

Archer trailed his hand up and down her arm. She could hear the smile in his voice when he said, "I'll try not to say 'I told you so.'"

She shook her head against his chest, then let out a sigh. "It's okay. I'm happy for you to be right about that."

They lay in silence for a long time, and Ridley's eyes grew heavier as the storm rumbled outside and Archer's heart beat steadily beneath her ear. Eventually, he said, "I should go. Your dad would probably use some horribly painful conjuration on me if he discovered me in bed with you."

"Mmm, maybe," Ridley said sleepily. "He doesn't usually come into my room during the night though, so you're probably safe. You can stay if you want."

"He may not come into your room, but he'll be going into mine about halfway through the night to wake me so I can keep watch."

"Oh." She peeled her eyes open and shifted her head to look at him. "I didn't know the two of you were doing that."

"Probably not necessary, but it's best to be careful."

"Then we should all take turns instead of just the two of

you staying awake."

Archer shook his head. "We figured we'd let you elementals get some rest. It can't have been good for you, breathing in all that arxium today. Plus whatever arxium they drugged you with last night."

"But—"

"Don't feel bad." He kissed the top of her head. "You'll be doing all your elemental tricks tomorrow to get us back into the city, so your dad and I may as well do our part tonight."

"Okay." She tucked her head down again and let her eyes slide shut.

"But I can stay here until you fall asleep," he said quietly, brushing his fingers through her hair.

"Mmm, okay."

Another minute or two passed before Archer's voice reached through her drowsy haze again. "I want to tell you everything. Why I left in the first place, and all about my complicated family, and all the things that changed me while I was away."

Ridley smiled. "Okay," she murmured, though she was almost too sleepy now to form words. "I want to hear ... everything ... soon."

CHAPTER 20

AN ODD NOISE WOKE Ridley. By the time her eyes were open and she'd figured out where she was—not at home, and not in the bunker—she wondered if she'd simply dreamed the sound. She rolled onto her side and pushed herself up, listening carefully. The storm was gone, dull light filtered through the cracked window, and whatever she thought she'd heard—a thump? Callie moving around in the room next door?—didn't repeat itself.

Her mind replayed everything from the night before in a quick rush, and her body filled with a surge of warmth. But the strangeness of the sound she may or may not have dreamed nudged at the back of her mind, and she climbed out of bed to investigate. Her bare feet made no noise against the carpet as she padded to the half-open door, her awareness going to her magic. She might have to use it at a second's notice. She slowly pulled the door open and peeked around it. There was nothing suspicious in the passageway directly outside her door. She stepped out—

And there was Dad. On the floor. His eyes closed. A woman leaning over him.

"Christa?" Ridley said. For a moment, she was too shocked to move. It was a moment too long.

Christa grabbed a cylinder-shaped something and sprayed the contents directly into Ridley's face. Ridley backed up against the wall, coughing and gasping as her throat began to close. The passage tilted and slid away at the edge of her vision. "You should have hidden yourselves better," Christa said, spraying the arxium at Ridley's face again. "I'm sorry," she added as the edges of everything began to darken. "I really ammm sssorrreee ..."

Ridley rode an endless wave of dizziness from the depths of a dark dream all the way to consciousness. Memories of the past few days seeped into her brain one at a time, ending with the most recent horrible truth: Christa. She was the one who'd betrayed them.

Ridley finally managed to force her eyes open. She was lying on a hard surface, with a plain gray ceiling above, plain gray walls, and a single light. It was so similar to the room she and Archer had been locked in when she first visited the bunker that she wondered if that's where they were now. Back in the bunker.

She sat up, realizing she was barefoot and still in her pajamas. But someone—Christa, presumably—had decided to put her jacket on over her pajama top. *How kind*, Ridley thought, her internal voice laden with sarcasm. *Christa's happy to let me die at the hands of the Shadow Society, but she doesn't want me to be cold while it happens.*

She twisted around and saw Malachi and Callie stirring on the floor behind her. No Dad. No Archer. Fear twisted her insides as Malachi asked, "You guys okay?"

"I'm tired of waking up confused and dizzy and nauseous," Callie moaned as she sat up.

"I think this is only the second time," Malachi reminded her, "but yeah. That's two times too many, in my opinion."

"Can either of you use your own magic?" Ridley asked. She tried to let hers go, and though she could do it without winding up unconscious, the crazy spinning of the room made her stop before she was ill. "I can force it out," she said breathlessly, "but it's not pleasant."

"Yeah, same," Malachi said. "But I doubt there's any point. I assume every surface in here is reinforced with arxium, so we'd never get out, even if we could transform into one of the elements. Well, except perhaps for that." He pointed past Ridley. She turned and saw what she hadn't noticed while lying down: one of the walls was partially covered by a large mirror. Probably one-way glass. No doubt someone was watching them right now.

Sure enough, the reflective quality of the mirror vanished as light appeared on the other side, revealing a small observation room. A lamp stood on a desk, and a young man with wavy blond hair and a tan that couldn't possibly be natural waved at them. Scooting forward on what must have been a wheeled chair, he grinned. "Hey there."

Ridley raised an eyebrow while Malachi muttered, "Creep."

Climbing to her feet, Ridley asked, "Do you feel safe on the other side of that mirror?" She ignored her shaky legs, walked right up to the mirror, and pressed her palms against the glass. "You might have made it difficult for us to use our own magic, but we'll recover soon. And until then, we can still pull magic from the air in here. I'm sure we could easily smash right through this thing."

The man's grin stretched wider. "Go ahead and try," he told her, his tinny voice reaching her from a speaker somewhere in the ceiling. "I'd love to see what happens when the magic rebounds and slams into you."

Great, so now people had figured out how to mix arxium into glass as well. She supposed that made sense. They would never put a gigantic mirror in here if it wasn't elemental-proof. She pushed away from the mirror and turned her back to the guy sitting on the other side.

"So, who wants to talk first?" he asked.

"About what?" Malachi grunted.

"Where you're headed, how many other elementals you know, the locations of other communities around the world, that sort of thing. Obviously. What else would we want to know from you?"

Ridley forced out a laugh and turned to face him again. "Too bad we don't know anything useful."

"Well, unless you want to die a slow and painful death, I'd

come up with something useful quickly. The chairman will be here soon, and whoever volunteers to go and talk to him first can choose a swift and painless death instead of the alternative."

"What chairman?" Malachi asked.

Blond Guy sighed. "Why does that make a difference?"

"It's part of the Shadow Society structure," Ridley said, remembering what Grandpa had told her. "Each chapter has its own chairperson. A director oversees the whole society."

"Correct," Blond Guy said. "Though how that helps you decide to share your useful information or not, I have no idea."

Ridley folded her arms. "Where are the other two men who were traveling with us?"

Blond Guy's eyebrows inched up. "Two? You mean there was a fifth person?"

Crap. She should have kept her stupid mouth shut.

"Who's the fifth person?" he pushed, but Ridley refused to answer. She'd seen her father unconscious on the floor, so it must have been Archer who got away. He was supposed to be keeping watch, wasn't he? Why hadn't he warned them? Or had Christa got into the hotel without him knowing?

"If you hurt him—the other man you took—I will not tell you or your chairman a single thing," Ridley said. "And unlike these two—" she nodded to Callie and Malachi "—I actually know a few things." Hopefully that came across as believable, especially since it was actually the truth. She knew a few other elemental names. She wasn't planning to share any of them, but that didn't change the fact that she did know them.

"Why did Christa give us up?" Callie asked. "Is she part of the Shadow Society?"

"Christa?" Blond Guy asked.

"The woman who caught us in the hotel."

"Oh, her. Sorry, I don't know anything about her," Blond Guy said with a shrug. "I was told where to pick you guys up. I got to the hotel with a few other society members, and she was there, making sure you were all still unconscious. I don't know her name. I don't think she's in the society; I've never seen her at any of the meetings. All I know is that she has some kind of agreement with the director. She delivers elementals when she discovers them. As for *why*?" He shrugged again. "No clue."

"Hey, Eric!" An older man shoved open the door into the observation room and poked his head inside. "What are you doing? Shut the hell up."

"What's the problem?" Eric shouted back as the newcomer pulled his head back out and slammed the door. "Who cares what they know?" he shouted at the closed door. "They'll be dead in a few hours."

A twinge of panic tightened Ridley's chest, but she refused to entertain it. There had to be a way out of here. Someone would eventually have to come into the room to give them more arxium, if nothing else. They could fight back then. Or, if they could keep themselves alive long enough ... She turned to the Callie and Malachi. "Remember what Archer told us," she said in a low tone. "The voice message he sent when he came looking for us."

"Yes." Malachi paused, and Ridley could see his mind working. "But we have no idea how long it could be until … you know."

"If you're talking about someone coming to rescue you," Eric said loudly, "don't get too excited. We're outside Lumina City. *Far* outside. Even if someone's already coming for you, there's no way they'll find this place."

Ridley looked at him. "I think you're lying."

He laughed. "You can believe whatever you want. But it makes sense, don't you think? It's easier for us to get certain things done out here where we don't have to worry about any laws or police or government red tape. We can experiment with arxium … experiment with elementals … It's fun, you know?"

Hot fury burned through Ridley's veins, seeming to clear some of the effects of the arxium. *Experiment with elementals?* Was he serious?

The door swung open again, slower this time. "Ah, looks like your time is up," Eric said, rising from the chair. "Good morning, sir."

The chairman stood in the doorway, just beyond the circle of light cast by the lamp. Ridley saw a suit jacket over a shirt, and the upper half of a pair of tailored black suit pants. Finally, he stepped forward into the lamplight.

Ridley heard a sharp intake of breath from both Callie and Malachi, but she wasn't exactly surprised to see Mayor Madson. She had guessed he was part of the Shadow Society, and she knew he liked to be in charge. It made sense that he was the chairman of the Lumina City chapter. With pale skin and blond hair, he was a slightly more rotund version of his son Lawrence. Though she hated him and whatever he'd done to try to eliminate her kind, there was a part of her that felt sorry for him. He'd just lost his son, after all. The past week must have been rough for him.

"Thank you for waiting for me," he said, moving toward the mirror. His voice was cold as he stared straight at Ridley and said, "I want to be able to look into her eyes as the life fades from them."

Ridley swallowed as a chill crept over her skin. Clearly Mayor Madson knew that she was the girl someone had reported seeing at the scene of his son's death. Apparently he didn't need to know whether she'd actually pulled the trigger. She was guilty by virtue of being present.

"Um ... what?" Eric asked. Ridley tore her gaze from the mayor's, and her eyes landed on Eric's confused face. "I thought you were coming to question these people."

"Then you were misinformed," the mayor said. "I don't have time to question people who don't know anything. My contact overheard them when they were making plans to leave. They don't know where they're going. One of them didn't even *want* to join any other elementals. No, the only thing we're doing with these people is killing them, and *that* one—" he pointed at Ridley "—is the one I most want to see die."

"Wait, hang on," Eric protested. "That one said she knows something."

"Well then she was lying." He folded his arms across his chest. "Turn the gas on, and make sure it's the strongest we've got."

The gas? Ridley looked up and noticed two air vents in the ceiling, one on either side of the mirror. She couldn't see any other way to pump gas into the room, so that must be where it came from. "I think we're actually about to die," Callie said faintly. Without answering, Ridley reached for Callie's hand and held onto it tightly. Her eyes continued to dart back and forth from one side of the ceiling to the other. Two silly air vents. Was that really how she was going to die?

"Well, what are you waiting for?" the mayor asked Eric. "I gave you an instruction."

"Um ..."

"Maybe we can keep it out," Ridley said in a low voice. "Like we did with the hole in the door at the shoe shop." She was already tugging her jacket off. "I think I'm almost able to use my magic. Or we can just pull from the air."

"Good idea," Malachi said, reaching over his head for the back of his T-shirt. "A simple conjuration should do it."

"Yes." Before the Cataclysm, people had used magic to move objects around all the time. It wouldn't be too complicated to send their clothing up to the ceiling and press it against the vents.

"Then you'll have to come in here to stop us," Malachi said, and Ridley saw he was speaking directly to the mayor now, his eyes narrowed as he balled the T-shirt in his hands. "No more hiding on that side of the—"

"Do it now!" the mayor said sharply to Eric. "Or are you planning to just stand there and let them hatch their own plans?"

"I—okay—sorry." Eric reached toward the wall just below the mirror, and his hand moved out of sight. But from the motion of his arm, it appeared he was turning a dial.

"All of them, you idiot," the mayor snapped. He leaned past Eric and turned his hand at three different spots. A hissing sound reached Ridley's ears as she pulled magic hastily from the air. Though she felt as though she could probably use her own magic now without sending her body into a dizzy, stomach-emptying state, she figured it was safer not to try.

"Quickly, quickly, quickly," Callie muttered, wringing her hands and bobbing up and down. "I think it's starting to come through."

With precise movements of their fingers and hands, Ridley and Malachi performed the basic conjuration within seconds. Ridley pushed the resulting magic toward her jacket, which she'd dropped onto the floor a few moments before. The magic wrapped around it and lifted it straight up, while Ridley's hand swayed this way and that to direct the jacket toward the vent on her side. Within moments, she'd managed to completely cover the parallel slits of the vent. Glancing to the other side of the ceiling, Malachi had done the same with his bunched-up T-shirt. "Some of it's probably getting through the fabric," he said to Ridley, "but it's better than breathing in a full blast of it."

The mayor moved to the wall beside the door and pressed

a button on what appeared to be an intercom. He leaned toward it and barked, "Tell them to increase the pressure on those canisters linked to cell eight. Immediately."

He dropped his hand, and turned back toward Ridley. She met his gaze as his eyes pierced into hers. "I will watch you die," he said, softly enough that she could barely hear his voice through the speakers. She gritted her teeth and refused to look away. The magic she'd conjured still held her jacket in place, but with her hands raised toward it, she could sense the growing force behind the jacket as the pressure on the other side of the air vent grew. The mayor's thin lips curved upward. "It's only a matter of time," he said. And yet ... was it Ridley's imagination, or was the pressure decreasing now?

"Wait!" a woman's voice screeched. She rushed into the observation room and grabbed the doorframe to pull herself to a stop. "Waitwaitwait! Don't do that. We're supposed to—"

"Get the hell out of here!" the mayor snapped at her.

"But he said to stop!"

"I DON'T CARE!" Mayor Madson bellowed. "My word is law in this base. That girl was involved in the death of my son, and *I WANT HER DEAD*!"

An older man, breathless and flustered, appeared beside the woman. "Nat's closed the vents," he said. "We received orders to—"

"Shut up!" the mayor hissed, then cursed beneath his breath. "Sometimes," he muttered, "if you want a job done, you have to do it yourself." He tugged at something out of sight below the mirror, and when he stepped back, there was a small, black object in his hand. A gun, Ridley realized with sinking dread. The mayor shoved aside the two newcomers and stepped past them.

"Wait, are you *crazy*?" Eric shouted. "You can't go in there!"

"Nonono," Callie moaned.

"This is our chance," Ridley said, blood pumping wildly through her veins.

"Ridley," Malachi said sharply. "I can do what your father did outside the wall yesterday."

Ridley hesitated, her brain taking a second to figure out what he was talking about. "Okay," she answered as the memory flashed across her mind, knowing there was no time to ask how Malachi knew that conjuration.

"What are you talking about?" Eric shouted through the glass at them.

"Distract him when he comes in." Malachi was pulling swiftly at the air now, and the sound of numbers being punched into a keypad came from the other side of the door. "Just get the gun away from him!" Malachi added in a rush of breath as a loud beep reached Ridley's ears. She dove forward, thinking of air and hoping she didn't land flat on her face in a nauseous heap.

She vanished before hitting the floor. The use of her own magic made her want to gag, but she could *just* maintain her hold on it. As the door swung open, she spun as fast as she could, whirling herself into a small tornado, then rushing past the mayor. But she was so dizzy, and she couldn't see if she'd knocked him aside, and Eric was yelling something, and the magic was too much to hold on to. She dropped out of the air and landed heavily on her feet.

The gun was on the floor in front of her.

The mayor was struggling to his feet out in the passageway.

She could get to the gun. She could grab it before he did. She could—

"Get back!" Malachi yelled, and at the last second, Ridley launched away from the gun instead of toward it. A sparking flash of magic flared past her, separating almost instantly into three blue fireballs. It might have been catastrophic if they'd landed on a surface somewhere within the arxium-lined cell, but Malachi had aimed for the passageway, and that was precisely where the magic struck.

CHAPTER 21

THE SHOCK WAVE THREW Ridley backward, but her instinctive reaction—*air*—saved her before she hit the wall. Callie wasn't so lucky. As Ridley rose toward the ceiling to get her bearings in the aftermath of the explosion, she saw Callie slumped on the floor against the wall. In the passageway, which now had three small craters in the floor and cracks zigzagging in every direction, the mayor was in a worse state. Blood smeared the wall he'd been thrown against, and his large figure lay motionless on the floor. Malachi had vanished, so he must have concealed himself with air as well. Knowing he could take care of himself, Ridley turned to Callie.

She swooped down, wrapped her invisible self around Callie, and sped through the door and over the mayor. The man and woman who'd tried to stop him from administering the arxium gas leaned over him, while Eric shouted into the intercom in the observation room. Ridley didn't stop to listen to any of them. She needed to find Dad, and she needed to get out of here.

The other doors off this passageway were all open, and

the rooms they led to were empty. Ridley reached the end of the passage and realized there were probably rooms on the other side of the one she'd escaped. So she darted back around and glided through the air as fast as she could, past Eric and the man and woman trying to resuscitate Mayor Madson. But the other two rooms at the far end of the passage were just as empty, and after that, there was only a dead end.

She swooped back, dragging a gust of wind past the four people on the floor as she raced by. She was probably giving herself away, but who cared? She was invisible, already flying around the corner, long gone before anyone could run after her. But she was still stuck inside this stupid building, and she hadn't seen a single window to the outside world yet.

Into the next corridor, and then another, and another. Finally, she came to a closed door, which meant she'd have to use actual hands to open it. She let herself become visible, then staggered to the side as Callie's weight almost dragged her to the floor. The unconscious woman slipped from Ridley's one-armed grasp around her waist and slumped to the floor.

"Crap," Ridley muttered. After glancing behind her—why did it feel like someone was there?—she crouched down and pressed two fingers to Callie's neck, just to be certain. There hadn't been time to check when she fled the cell they'd been locked in. A steady pulse beat beneath her fingers, and she let out a relieved breath. She straightened, stepped over Callie's arm, and reached forward to open the door. Then she pushed her magic outward again, ready to conceal them both as air.

"Let me help you."

Ridley's heart almost jumped clear of her chest until she realized the voice behind her belonged to Malachi. "Holy-freakincrap," she breathed, her shoulders sagging.

"Sorry." Malachi bent to pick Callie up.

"How did you manage to follow me if I was invisible?" Ridley asked.

"I don't know. I just sort of ... sensed you."

"Oh. Weird." She frowned, remembering the feeling of someone behind her a minute ago. "I think I noticed something like that too. Anyway, let me just check ..." She darted ahead to look into the next room. It was windowless, and through the open doorway on the other side was another bare corridor. "Oh *come on*. How big is this place? I wish they at least had some signs up. I don't know where they keep other prisoners, or where the exit is, or—"

A deep boom shuddered through the building, rattling the door on its hinges. "What was that?" Malachi asked, whipping around to look behind him.

"Maybe we should go that way," Ridley said, taking a step past him.

"You want to go *toward* the source of the bang?"

"If it's the kind of explosion that broke through a wall, then maybe we can get out that way." And once she was out, she could get a better sense of the building's layout. Then she could come back inside and find Dad.

"What if it's the kind of explosion that turns into a great big fire and kills people?"

"We're elementals, Malachi. Fire doesn't kill us."

Malachi adjusted his grip beneath Callie's knees. "Okay, you have a point."

"But it might kill my dad, if he's anywhere near it." Ridley's stomach churned at the thought. "So I'm heading that way."

Malachi sighed. "Fine, let's go toward the bang."

Within the next heartbeat, they'd both vanished. Ridley rushed along another empty corridor with Malachi just behind her. Not that she could see him, but she sensed there was someone there, occupying the space.

She wondered at the fact that they hadn't come across a single person since leaving the corridor with the unconscious mayor. Perhaps Eric hadn't been lying when he said this building was far out in the wastelands. It would make sense, then, that there weren't too many people here.

She swerved around a corner—and finally found something that wasn't a plain room or passageway. She slowed and glided past three rooms, each with a large, clear window through which one could observe whatever happened inside. There were still no people anywhere, but the contents of the rooms were enough to send a shiver through Ridley's invisible body: Tables with operating equipment. Beds with leathers straps and buckles—*restraints*—hanging from the sides.

She felt the floor beneath her feet and realized, with only a vague sense of concern, that she'd completely lost hold of her focus and was now visible. She stepped slowly past the third room and saw that the next one—with a glass door and a glass wall providing a complete view of the interior—was a laboratory. Was this where they made their arxium gas and spray? So they could experiment with immobilizing and killing elementals? It made her heart hammer against her ribcage and her blood burn like—

Infernos that cleanse lands.

Unbidden, Grandpa's words rose to her mind. *I could be the kind of fire that consumes this place*, she thought. It was a wild and terrifying thought. She'd always avoided fire because of how volatile it could be. She'd reminded Malachi that it couldn't kill them, and yet she'd always been afraid of it.

"Ridley, come on!" She flinched, her head jerking toward the voice. Malachi was visible too, still holding Callie in his arms. Perhaps he'd sensed Ridley was no longer behind him and had come back.

"How can you stand to look at this?" She jabbed her hand toward the laboratory while somewhere nearby, another boom resounded. "This is where they concoct evil substances meant to harm and kill us. And did you see those beds back there? They *experiment* on people here."

"I *can't* stand to look at it," Malachi said, "which is why I'm trying to find a way out of here. Do you want me to leave you behind? Or do you want to find your dad and get out of this place?"

"Let's get out of here," Ridley muttered. She moved toward him, becoming air in an instant. Together, they rushed away from the horrors behind them and swooped down a set of stairs. The sounds of fighting—shouts, gunshots, explosions—grew louder.

And then right there, at the bottom of the stairs, they found the source of all the commotion. Ahead of them was an enclosed courtyard covered by a glass ceiling. At least, Ridley assumed it had been enclosed before something blasted a hole through one of the walls and smashed through part of the ceiling. Broken pot plants and scattered soil littered the mosaic tiled floor, while flashes of magic darted across the courtyard. She counted five people: a man lying prone on the floor, two women with guns, and two—

Archer! And Dad! She almost shouted their names before remembering she was concealed by air. She darted around the edge of the courtyard, her eyes glued to both of them. They were using magic—Archer included—their hands and arms sweeping through the air and moving in rapid patterns before shoving the magic away. Fireballs, sharpened stones, a thick, flat piece of metal that deflected bullets. They performed conjuration after conjuration that Ridley had never seen before. Half the courtyard was destroyed, and yet the two women with guns had managed to survive so far.

In a rush of wind, Ridley spun away from the wall. She twirled faster and faster, almost letting go completely, and yet not quite trusting the elemental magic around her. If it whipped up a sudden hurricane, would Dad and Archer survive? So she spun herself into a small tornado and plunged past the two women. Everything became a confusing blur. By the time she'd slowed enough to figure out what was going on, the two women were down, and Archer was tying something around the one's hands while Malachi raced toward the other.

"Dad!" Ridley called out in a breathless gasp as she landed and staggered forward a few steps before regaining her balance. Her father's arms caught her and pulled her tightly against him. "How did you get away from them?" she asked.

"Archer found me. What happened to you guys? Is Callie okay?"

Ridley's eyes darted about behind Dad until she spotted Callie, lying on the floor beside an overturned fern. "There was an explosion, and I think she hit her head against a wall. I hope she's okay. It was that conjuration you did yesterday with the fireballs. Malachi knew how to do it."

"Oh, yes, I taught him last night after the rest of you went to bed."

"Ridley!"

Ridley stepped out of her father's embrace as Archer called her name. She'd barely taken a step before he was right in front of her. "I'm so, so sorry I left you," he said as he swept her into his arms. "I was on the wrong side of the hotel, keeping watch, and by the time I got back, it was too late."

"It's okay," she answered as her arms wrapped tightly around him. She let her eyes slide shut as she breathed him in for a moment—dust and sweat and hotel shampoo. Then she stepped back and saw smeared blood behind his ear and down the side of his neck, along with a nasty gash. "You made quite a mess with your AI2," she said with raised eyebrows.

"Yeah, well, I was desperate. I had to get the damn thing out and there was no time to be neat and tidy." He looked back over his shoulder at Malachi, who'd just finished tying the second woman's wrists with shoelaces. "After I got in, I found your father quite quickly." He faced Ridley again. "We were looking for you, and even though there don't seem to be many people around, those three found us and chased us back this way."

"We've seen a few others," Malachi said, walking toward Callie. "Including the mayor. We should get out of here quickly."

"Yes," Dad said. "Then we can take a closer look at Callie."

They hurried across the courtyard, and as they climbed through the hole in the wall, Ridley looked at Archer and asked, "Did you do this?"

"Yes. I couldn't find a way in, and I got impatient. I removed my AI2 and decided to just blast my way in. I wasn't exactly concerned about being covert if it meant I might be too late to get you guys out."

Ridley looked forward as she stepped beyond the boundary of the Shadow Society's base. Eric had told the truth about it being out in the wastelands, but it wasn't as far from Lumina City as Ridley expected. Beyond the crumbling overgrown ruins, she could see tall buildings in the distance, glittering in the few rays of morning sun that peeked through the clouds. A shadow shifted over her, and she glanced up quickly, her heart beating faster. But it wasn't a threat. It was a large metallic panel, one of several floating a short distance above the building. Presumably these panels were the same as the arxium ones that hovered high above Lumina City. *Makes sense,*

Ridley thought. The mayor would want to keep himself and his base safe from the unpredictable magic out here.

"Okay, I'm doing the air thing," Malachi called back to Ridley. "We need to get far away from here."

"Yes, okay," Ridley said, but something drew her gaze back toward the building. She thought of the laboratory, and those rooms with the operating equipment. Images of people tied up on beds flashed through her mind. "I have to go back," she murmured.

"What was that?" Archer asked.

"Get far away from the building, okay? I'll be back in a few minutes."

"Wait, what are you—"

"We can't leave this place standing, Archer."

"Ridley—" His hand flashed out to grab her arm, but she'd already moved beyond his reach.

"I won't be long!" she shouted as she took off. She ran, ignoring Archer's voice, Dad's voice. She breathed as evenly as possible, telling herself to relax. *It'll be okay. I don't have to be in control. I don't* want *to be in control. I want to be a racing wildfire. A raging inferno. I want to bring the entire place down.*

She dove forward, and by the time she hit the ground, she was fire. She sensed the heat, and yet she didn't burn. She became the flames, licking, leaping, racing across the courtyard. *Let go, let go*, she told herself. And then, just like with the air, she felt herself drifting away, spreading out, until she was in every part of every flame that raced through the Shadow Society's base. She sensed concrete, glass, chemicals, arxium—

which she instinctively recoiled from—and people. Shadow Society members. Those who were convinced they needed to eradicate her kind from the world. She blazed further and further until sensing she'd reached the limits of the building. The flames grew, the heat intensified, and Ridley felt the crack and shudder of the structure as it began to come apart.

She became aware then of a whisper of fear. What would happen if she didn't get out? Would she be consumed along with everything else inside this building? The fear grew, and all of a sudden she felt her consciousness snap back into its limited, contained form.

She was trapped somewhere inside, leaping from flame to flame, trying to figure out where she was. *Don't panic*, she told herself repeatedly. *Keep your fire form and you'll be fine.* She raced through the blaze, but like before, she couldn't find exterior windows.

Then she heard creaking and groaning from somewhere above her. She braced herself—her mind, if not her body— even though she knew, logically, that nothing could hurt her in this form. Pieces of brick and concrete began to fall.

And then light streamed through an opening! Ridley shifted immediately into air and soared upward. She flew away from the inferno, into the clean, rushing wind, and up between the arxium panels. She whirled higher and higher before finally spinning around and looking down. As the wind tossed her about, she managed to make out tiny figures— people the size of ants—escaping one side of the blazing building. A blazing building that couldn't possibly be saved from the kind of fire she'd sent racing through it.

She let the wind take her then, relaxing completely until she felt herself begin to fragment. Her magic mingled with the magic in the air, and she had the strangest feeling that it was pleased with her. *You're welcome*, she replied. At least, that's what she *felt*.

Now she needed to find the rest of her companions. *Where are they?* she asked. She soared over the ruins and rubble of what used to be the suburbs of Lumina City, becoming aware of the area she needed to aim for. The wind was already taking her there, so she made no effort to direct herself. Only when she saw Dad and the others standing in the overgrown remains of a park did she feel herself snap back together.

She steered herself down the final distance, dropping amid the tall grass on bare feet and almost landing on her backside. Her hands and legs shook, and she was breathing heavily even though her body technically hadn't done anything since the moment before she became fire. There was no headache pounding behind her eyes though, which was amazing.

"Ridley!" Dad called the moment he saw her. He rushed toward her, but her knees had already given in, depositing her on the grass.

"Oh, man," she gasped. "Anyone else feeling insanely hungry and exhausted?"

CHAPTER 22

"SO YOU'RE SAYING I shouldn't have done it?" Ridley asked several minutes later when Dad had finished shouting about how stupid and dangerous it was for her to go back inside the base. "You'd prefer it if I'd left that building intact so the Shadow Society could continue to experiment with new ways to torture and kill elementals?"

Dad exhaled loudly. "No, Ridley, obviously that's not what I would prefer. I just wish you'd stop putting yourself in danger."

"Dad, you have to—" Her eyes moved to the others standing behind him. All three—including Callie, who was now awake—looked awkward, as if they'd rather not be listening to this argument. "Dad, I appreciate everything you've ever done for me," Ridley continued in a low voice, attempting to keep their conversation a little more private. "But you can't protect me forever. I can't stay inside a bubble and not do something—the *right* thing—just because it's dangerous." She didn't add that the magic out here had seemed pleased with what she'd done. Dad might think she was crazy. She felt a little crazy herself, just thinking about it.

Dad rubbed the bridge of his nose with his thumb and forefinger. Lowering his hand, he said, "Sometimes I wish you were still a little girl who had no choice but to do whatever I said."

One side of Ridley's mouth curved up. "Who says I always did what you told me to do back then?"

"I suppose that's true," Dad answered with a laugh.

"So, are you guys done?" Malachi asked loudly. "Because we need to decide what to do now."

Ridley walked around Dad to where Callie was sitting on a weatherworn bench surrounded by grass that reached above her knees. "Hey, are you okay?" she asked

"I think so," Callie said. "Just feeling really weak. It's been a long time since I had a proper meal."

"Yeah," Ridley said. "I'm not feeling great either." She looked over at Dad. "Do you think ... should we go back to the hotel to get our bags?"

"Absolutely not," Dad said. "Someone could be watching the hotel. That's a risk we don't need to take."

Ridley nodded, a dull ache taking form in her chest as she thought of the picture frame in her backpack. But Dad was right. It would be silly to risk going back there when someone with arxium spray or gas might be lying in wait for them. "I wonder what happened to Ember," she said quietly.

"The cat will be fine," Dad told her. "She's probably spent most of her life in the wastelands."

"Okay, so we don't really have any choice but to go back

to the city, right?" Callie asked. "We don't want to starve out here."

Archer was about to answer when the air gusted unnaturally fast through the park, rustling the tall grass and whipping Ridley's hair across her face. Her chest tightened and magic rose immediately to her hands. On either side of her, Archer and Dad pulled hastily at the air.

And then five, six—no, *seven*—people materialized in front of them. Four women and three men. One of the men, dark haired and maybe a little younger than Dad, took a step forward. Archer and Dad immediately raised their hands higher, while Ridley got ready to grab both of them and vanish.

"Hey, it's okay, we're friends," the man said. "You saw us shift out of air right?" Then, without pause, his form became water. The water fell, splashed onto the ground, then leaped up again and returned to the shape of a man. "See?" he said as he reappeared. "Elemental. Anyway, someone called for help?"

Ridley blinked. "But ... wow, that was really fast."

She looked at Archer, who said, "Yeah, I left a message yesterday afternoon. I thought you guys were days away."

"We can move quickly when we need to," the elemental man said. "And since the world out here is already ruined, we don't have to worry about damaging anything with supernaturally fast wind."

"And you knew to come right here," Ridley said, "because of ... the elements?"

He smiled at her. "Yes. All it took was a little listening. I'm

Nathan, by the way."

"Nathan, please tell me you guys brought food," Callie said, "because some of us might pass out from hunger before we've all finished introducing ourselves."

Nathan laughed and reached for a strap on his shoulder. He removed a backpack and said, "Food, medical supplies, some clothes, a few camping bits and pieces." He looked around at his six companions. "We weren't sure what to expect, so we threw in whatever we could think of as quickly as possible. There might even be some soap in Lara's bag."

Callie let out a sound that was part sigh, part moan. "I love you all already," she said.

Nathan moved forward with a chuckle and placed his bag on the bench while everyone began introducing themselves. As Callie hovered near the bench and Nathan removed containers of food, Archer spoke with another one of the men and one of the women asked Ridley if she wanted to change out of her pajamas. "Definitely," Ridley said with a laugh. She looked around for the nearest wall that would provide enough privacy for her to change behind, and instead caught Archer's eye. He smiled at her, and suddenly all she wanted to do was wrap her arms around him and fall asleep. *Later*, she thought as she returned the smile.

"So, are you planning for us to get back to your community in less than a day?" Callie asked. Her voice sounded a little odd, and when Ridley looked at her, she realized Callie had half a sandwich in her mouth. Ridley almost started drooling.

"No, we can't go that fast with those who aren't elementals," Nathan said. "Traveling so quickly requires giving our-selves over fully to the magic of the elements. Fragmenting ourselves, essentially. Those who don't have magic within their own bodies can't do that."

"Oh, well that's a relief," Callie said as Ridley decided to investigate the food first and *then* change out of her pajamas. She didn't say anything, but she was just as relieved as Callie. She had no idea now whether to expect any more headaches. "I'm still very new to this elemental magic thing," Callie add-ed. "Until a day or two ago, I'd never used it the way these two use it." She gestured to Ridley and Malachi. "So I'm glad we can't go too fast."

"No problem," Nathan said. "We'll go as slow as you need to go. The point is, you're safe now. We'll be home soon."

CHAPTER 23

THEY REACHED THEIR NEW home on the evening of their
third day of travel. Inside what used to be a national park before the Cataclysm, the settlement was situated beside a lake
at the foot of a mountain. Ridley couldn't have imagined a
more beautiful home if she'd tried. The sun had just dipped
behind the mountain as they approached the collection of log
cabins, and Ridley rubbed her hands up and down her arms to
ward off the chill. It was definitely colder here than in Lumina
City. A large bonfire had been lit a short distance away from
the cabins, and several people were already gathered around
it, sitting on blankets.

As Ridley and the others she'd traveled with drew nearer,
two women stood and walked toward them. Nathan shouted a
greeting to them, and they smiled and waved. Then the older
woman came to an abrupt stop. "Maverick?" she called. Startled to hear the familiar name in this unfamiliar place, both
Ridley and Dad stopped. A smile returned to the woman's
face, even wider than before. "Oh my—I can't believe—how
are you alive?" As she ran the final distance toward them,

Ridley thought she saw fear flash across Dad's face. But it must have been shock, because a moment later his expression morphed into an amazed smile. The woman—middle-aged with shoulder-length auburn hair and skin so pale it was even lighter than Ridley's—threw her arms around Dad.

He returned the hug with a laugh, saying, "This is amazing."

"It's incredible," she answered, stepping back, her eyes shining with unshed tears. "I always thought you and Claudia didn't make it." She pulled back and smiled at Ridley. Blinking repeatedly and wiping away a stray tear that managed to escape, she asked, "And this is?"

Dad turned to Ridley. The emotions warring in his eyes hinted at some internal struggle Ridley couldn't identify. "This ... this is Ridley."

"Ridley?" the woman repeated, staring at her. "Baby Ridley? You survived too?"

Ridley waited for one of them to say who the woman was, but the silence grew to the point at which it became awkward. "Dad?" she asked eventually, and the woman's eyes shot toward him. "Are you, uh, going to introduce us properly?"

"Right, of course." Dad cleared his throat and smile. "Ridley, this is Saoirse. We were good friends years ago before ... well, there was that attack and we fled." He looked at Saoirse again, his expression more serious now. "Is there anyone else? From our previous community? I never knew who survived."

"Just the three of us," she said. "Cam and Bria and me. Well, there might have been a few others who got away, but if so, I never heard from them again." She looked around, pointed to the younger woman she'd been walking with—currently introducing herself to Archer, Callie and Malachi—and said to Ridley, "That's Bria, my daughter."

"Hey, you guys know each other?" Nathan said, walking up to Ridley, Dad and Saoirse. "That's amazing."

"Isn't it?" Saoirse answered, beaming at him.

"How about we show our newbies around," Nathan said, "and then you can catch up."

He led them to one of the larger log cabins where he gave Ridley and Callie a room to share and directed Dad upstairs to a loft area that had been partitioned into smaller private spaces. After finding a room with a small bathtub, Ridley had a quick bath—using her own magic to fill it and a heating conjuration to warm the water—before dressing in some clean clothes from the pile someone had left on her bed. The jeans were a bit long, as were the sleeves of the hoodie, but she was happy to be wrapped in something clean and warm.

After pulling on a pair of fluffy slippers, Ridley walked outside, hoping to find Archer. Traveling in a group of twelve had given them barely any time alone over the past few days. There'd been so many people to get to know, and so many questions to ask and answer, that she and Archer had decided to wait until they reached their new home before telling Dad they were together. She remembered the way her heart had skipped a few beats at the sound of the word 'together.' Such a trivial thing compared to the life-and-death situations they'd found themselves in recently, and yet it made her ridiculously happy.

Music reached her ears as she neared the bonfire. Someone was beating a drum with his hands, while someone else played a percussion instrument Ridley couldn't remember the name of. A keyboard-shaped thing with a set of wooden bars. She took in the scene and almost laughed out loud. Wasn't this what holiday camps of the good old pre-Cataclysm days used to be like? Sitting around campfires playing musical instruments? But the music was so enticing, so hypnotic, that she found herself moving her head in time to the beat instead of laughing.

She walked closer, aware of the magic all around her. Even after several days, it was still strange to see so much of it out in the open. The blue wisps glowing here and there as people made use of basic, everyday conjurations. A smile curved Ridley's lips as she thought of Anika, Meera's younger sister. She was always so curious about the way things were before the Cataclysm. She would be in awe out here.

But Ridley's smile faded as the hollow ache that always accompanied thoughts of Meera filled her chest. She couldn't get over the guilt of not having explained things to her best friend. Of not being able to say goodbye. Thoughts of Meera then led to thoughts of Shen, and Ridley wondered yet again where he'd ended up. She'd thought he might be here, but when she'd finally worked up the courage to ask Nathan while they were traveling, he said he didn't know of any Shen.

Walking around the side of the bonfire, Ridley finally

saw Archer. He was sitting on the ground talking to Nathan, but when she waved, he rose and walked toward her. "Isn't this all so amazing?" she asked as he stopped in front of her and reached for her hand. "It's so beautiful, and there's magic everywhere, and no scanner drones to worry about, and no arxium smothering everything."

He nodded, smiling, as his fingers wove between hers. Then he leaned forward and kissed her. The soft pressure of his lips made butterflies come alive in her chest again. They beat their tiny imaginary wings, refusing to calm down even when Archer pulled back a few inches. "I'm sorry," he said. "I know this isn't exactly a private spot, but I couldn't wait any longer."

Ridley smiled as she leaned her brow against his. "I have zero problem with you kissing me right now. It's possible I might have been dreaming about it since that night in the hotel."

"Oh really?" Archer looped his arms around her waist, pulling her a little closer and giving her a roguish smile. "Want to tell me more about those dreams?"

She laughed. "Nope. That's not happening." Her arms snaked up around his neck, and she rested her cheek against his chest. And for some time, she simply stood like that, appreciating his arms around her, and the dancing light of the fire, and the drumbeat resonating through her chest and sinking into her bones.

"Well, isn't this interesting."

Ridley started at the sound of Dad's voice behind her. She

spun to face him, heat blooming in her cheeks. "Oh, Dad, hi. Um ..." Though she'd been hoping to tell him about Archer as soon as possible, she suddenly couldn't remember any of the words she'd planned to say.

With an amused expression, Dad looked down and began quietly counting something on his fingers. "Um, what are you doing?" Ridley asked.

"Just counting the days since you told me, with great fervor, that 'it's really not like that' with Archer." His smile stretched wider, and his eyes twinkled in the firelight. "I think it's been less than a week?"

Ridley bit her lip as Archer moved to her side and placed an arm around her. "It's not like that, huh?"

"Okay, so maybe it was a tiny bit like that?" she said as the heat in her face intensified.

Dad laughed. "I had kind of figured that out."

"So you're, uh, okay with this?" Archer asked Dad, and Ridley wondered for the first time if he'd actually been worried about getting her father's approval.

"Yes," Dad said. "I know you're not who the world thinks you are. Just ... don't hurt her, or I'll be forced to bring out some conjurations you've never even heard of."

"Dad," Ridley groaned.

He laughed again. "Sorry, Riddles. As your overprotective father, I'm supposed to say things like that, right? Oh, there's someone I haven't greeted yet," he added before Ridley could answer. He leaned sideways to look behind her. "Saoirse's husband, Cam."

"Thank goodness for that," Ridley muttered.

"You two be good now," Dad said as he walked past them.

Ridley covered her face with her hands and let out another groan. Archer's hand rubbed up and down her arm. With a chuckle, he said, "You know he only said that to make you feel awkward."

"I know. It worked."

"Do you want to sit by the fire for a bit?"

Ridley lowered her hands and looked around. "Yeah. Maybe a little further back from everyone else. I want you to myself for just a bit longer." She pointed and added, "That tree over there?"

They walked toward it, Archer's arm sliding away from her back and moving down to take her hand. "Any headaches yet?" he asked.

She smiled. "No. Well, a little bit of discomfort here and there, but nothing major. With all the flying we did to get here, I should have passed out from the pain by now. But I mostly did it the way Grandpa told me to. Letting go properly and kind of being *everywhere* in the wind instead of directing it myself."

They sat on the ground, Archer with his back against the tree, and Ridley between his legs. He wrapped his arms around her, and she leaned back against his chest. The sun had set completely now, and stars blazed overhead, brighter than Ridley had seen them in years. In the trees around them, the chirp and buzz of insects filled the air. As the beat of the drum reverberated through her body, she rested her head back into the gap between Archer's neck and shoulder. "This moment is perfect. I kind of wish I could stay in it forever."

He kissed the top of her head, then asked, "Does this perfect moment include me?"

"Oh, crap, sorry. What I meant to say was that everything else *except* the handsome idiot I'm currently snuggling against is perfect." She tilted her head back to look up at him. "Of course it includes you."

He laughed, a low sound that vibrated through her back and into her chest. "You don't even know my whole sordid history yet."

She shook her head as she tilted it forward again. "I think the net tabloids and social feeds told me more than enough. Besides, as you keep pointing out—and as you've repeatedly proven—you're not the same person. Your sordid history is exactly that—a *history*. It isn't who you are now."

He tightened his arms around her. "It isn't," he said, his voice quiet beside her ear. "I promise it isn't."

They sat in comfortable silence for a while until Nathan walked over and joined them. Archer loosened his grip on Ridley, and she sat forward a little. "What do you think?" Nathan asked as he took a seat on the ground beside them. "Could you call this place home?"

Ridley shrugged and said, "I guess it's got a few things going for it."

"Just a few?"

She laughed. "It's amazing. I still can't believe everyone uses magic whenever they want. I'm still telling myself I don't have to look over my shoulder and hide it."

"Yeah." Nathan looked around. "I take it for granted, but every time someone new joins us, I see all of this—and the way we live—through fresh eyes."

"It's the way we were always meant to live," Archer said quietly.

Nathan nodded. After a moment of quiet, he looked at Ridley and asked, "How would you feel if it was like this everywhere? In all cities in the world. Elemental and non-elemental living side by side, everyone using magic."

Ridley felt her brow pulling down. "Well, that would be great if it wasn't illegal and impossible."

"What if it's not impossible?"

Ridley's heart pattered a little faster. This had to be a joke, and yet Nathan seemed entirely serious. "What do you mean?" she asked.

"I mean we have a plan, Ridley. A plan to bring down the walls, bring down the shields, break up the Shadow Society." Firelight sparkled in his eyes as his smile stretched wider. "We're going to return magic to society."

Acknowledgments

Thank you ...

To God for helping me find the calm headspace required to complete this book amid the chaos of finishing building a house!

To Kimberly Belden and other early readers for your story feedback and editing notes.

To Jess Will for proofreading, and my advance review readers for letting me know about the typos you spotted.

To every book reviewer, book lover, bookstagrammer and more who helped spread the word about the Ridley Kayne Chronicles.

To Kyle for supporting every new literary adventure I find myself on.

And to you for continuing Ridley's journey!

Rachel Morgan spent a good deal of her childhood living in a fantasy land of her own making, crafting endless stories of make-believe and occasionally writing some of them down. After completing a degree in genetics and discovering she still wasn't grown-up enough for a 'real' job, she decided to return to those story worlds still spinning around her imagination. These days she spends much of her time immersed in fantasy land once more, writing fiction for young adults and those young at heart.

www.rachel-morgan.com

26197326R00199

Printed in Great Britain
by Amazon